AS
the
SPARKS FLY
UPWARD

AS
the
SPARKS FLY
UPWARD
A WINSLOW BREED NOVEL

GILBERT MORRIS

HOWARD BOOKS
A DIVISION OF SIMON & SCHUSTER, INC.

NEW YORK   NASHVILLE   LONDON   TORONTO   SYDNEY   NEW DELHI

Howard Books
A Division of Simon & Schuster, Inc.
1230 Avenue of the Americas
New York, NY 10020

First Howard Books trade paperback edition November 2011

HOWARD and colophon are trademarks of Simon & Schuster, Inc.

For information about special discounts for bulk purchases, please contact Simon & Schuster Special Sales at 1-866-506-1949 or business@simonandschuster.com.

The Simon & Schuster Speakers Bureau can bring authors to your live event. For more information or to book an event contact the Simon & Schuster Speakers Bureau at 1-866-248-3049 or visit our website at www.simonspeakers.com.

Manufactured in the United States of America

10 9 8 7 6 5 4 3 2 1

Library of Congress Cataloging-in-Publication Data

Morris, Gilbert.
  As the sparks fly upward / Gilbert Morris.
    p. cm.
  I. Title.
  PS3563.O8742A92 2011
  813'.54—dc22   2011003067

ISBN 978-1-4165-8748-4
ISBN 978-1-4391-8274-1 (ebook)

To Mikki Thrieme

One of my favorite lines in the Old Testament:
Many daughters have done well, but thou excellest them all.

I pray that this verse will fit your life, Mikki!

WINSLOW FAMILY GENEALOGY

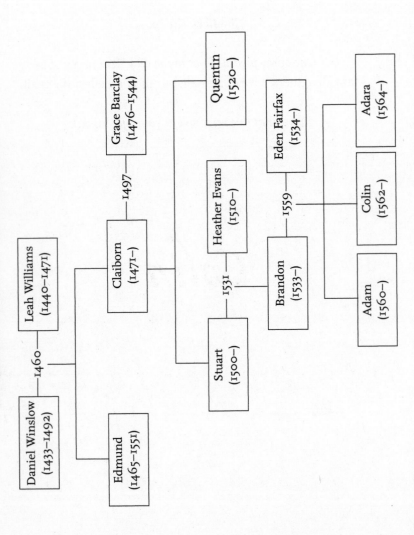

PART ONE

Colin

(1568–1579)

1

June 10, 1568

Early dawn had always been a favorite time for Eden Winslow, and now, standing in the midst of her garden, she savored the sight of the hills that made a thin, irregular line in the north. Pale sunlight ran fresh and fine, flashing against the steeple of the small village church and cutting long, sharp shadows from the houses that made up the village. Overhead the stars were still visible, cold and brilliant in the sky, and light from the east had begun to dilute the darkness of the earth. She moved among the flowers, bending over to touch the green buds of the roses, and suddenly a sound from overhead caught her attention. Glancing up at the sky she thought, *The birds have come back.* She stood still, savoring their morning twitter and clatter, their shrill cries and whistle notes. A harsh, distant noise sounded, and glancing upward she saw the familiar V-formation of geese as they made their way across the sky. "I wonder how they decide which one will be the leader?" she murmured, then laughed at herself. "Talking to myself! Next thing I'll wind up in Bedlam!"

Eden moved through the garden, noting that the crabapple trees had displayed their pink and white blossoms. The hawthorns had put on white buds, and as she passed by them they gave off a sweet scent that blew in the wind. The new flowers were her delight, but something troubled her. Though she tried to ignore the thought, it refused to go away. *It was our tenth anniversary yesterday and Brandon didn't even mention it.* The thought brought a frown to her face, but she realized how foolish it was to be disturbed over that. *Brandon has been such a good husband. No woman could ask for better. He is a bit forgetful at times, but I must not mind that. He's so good to me and the children in every other way.*

She shook her head and quickly returned to the house. She was tall, and at the age of thirty-four had the figure of a much younger woman. Her hair was light brown with just a touch of red, and her heart-shaped face was accented by a small cleft in her chin. Nearing the front door of the castle that had been her home now for a decade, she spoke to one of the maids who was scrubbing the floor, then made her way to the stone stairs that led to the second floor. She turned to her left and entered the bedroom that she shared with Brandon. Glancing around at the familiar room, she once again had to put aside the thought that he had forgotten their anniversary. Restless, she began moving about and wondered where Brandon had gotten off to. He had disappeared at noon the previous day. She entertained a faint hope that he had gone to buy her an anniversary gift, but he had been gone all night. Standing at the window, she gazed out at the village and the fields that surrounded the castle, taking in the sheep and cattle and listening to the faint cries of the shepherds and the men who had gone out to plow as they called to their oxen.

She was a thoughtful woman, the Right Honorable Lady Stoneybrook, and able, at times, to put everything aside and live in her thoughts. She did this now, thinking of her children and her hopes for them and, of course, her husband, Lord Stoneybrook. Then suddenly, without warning, a pair of arms surrounded her, and she gasped as she was lifted off the floor.

Twisting around, she saw her husband's smiling face. "You put me down, Brandon!"

"I won't do it, woman! I can't afford to let you go!" But he did put her down and turned her around to face him. She put aside the thought that he had forgotten what was so important to her, asking, "Where have you—?" She never completed the sentence, for he closed her mouth with a kiss.

Finally she pulled away from him and demanded, "Where in the world have you been?"

Ignoring her, Brandon said, "Woman, you are due for a good loving. See me tonight."

Eden struck at him, but he warded off her blow and whispered, "Wear that silk gown I paid far too much for."

Eden's eyes sparkled as she pushed him away. He had the uncanny ability to lift her out of her moods. "All you think of is getting me into a bed."

"No!" Brandon said quickly, and his eyes sparkled. "Sometimes I think of getting you in a soft patch of moss out in the woods."

Eden, as always, could not resist him. "You are a fool, my lord!" she laughed. She studied him for a moment. He was a tall man, almost six feet, and in the prime of his life. He had auburn hair with golden glints in it, light blue eyes, and a tapered face that was very expressive.

"I've always been a fool for you, sweetheart." He kissed her, then let her go but still held her hands. "You're all worn out getting ready for that blasted progress of the queen's. I hate the very idea of that thing! Senseless and completely out of keeping with good taste."

The "progress," as it was called, was something most of the nobility dreaded. It consisted of a visit from the reigning monarch, who brought a large entourage, sometimes as many as fifty people. They also brought enormous appetites, and the host was expected to feed them royally—and expensively. No one spoke against it for fear that the queen would hear of the complaint, but many felt it was unjust and hated the very thought of it.

"Well, it's our turn," Eden sighed. "I suppose we can get through it."

"Yes, we've survived worse. I had better go make sure we have enough food on hand." Brandon kissed her on the cheek and turned to go. At the door, he suddenly stopped and turned back, snapping his fingers. "I *knew* I came in here for a reason." He turned his back to her, reached into his pocket, and pulled out a small leather bag. "I thought you might like this."

Eden reached for the bag, pulled at the drawstring, and lifted out the most beautiful necklace she had ever seen. At the end of a dainty gold chain was an enormous ruby mounted in gold. Giving a cry of delight, she reached up and pulled Brandon's head down to kiss him. "You didn't forget!"

"Forget? Well, bless me, no. How could I forget ten years of the best life a man has ever had?"

"It is so beautiful, Brandon!"

"Payment for ten happy years, my sweet." He took her in his arms and said, "You have made my life sweet, dear one."

Eden blinked the tears away and reached up to put her hand on his neck. "You're the best husband in the whole world."

"And the handsomest, don't forget that."

"Yes, that too." Eden put the necklace on, giving him a mischievous look. "I will have your present tonight."

Brandon laughed. "Well, now, I wonder what that could be?"

After Brandon left, Eden sat before the mirror for some time. The mirror was made of highly polished metal and did not give a true picture, but it was the best available. She could see well enough to admire her necklace.

"Lady Stoneybrook, are you up?"

Eden turned and saw her maid, Dorcas Loring, standing in the doorway.

"Yes, come in, Dorcas."

The young woman came to stand beside Eden. "My! That's a new necklace, isn't it?"

"Yes, my husband just gave it to me."

"It's beautiful, ma'am."

"It is, isn't it? It's for our tenth wedding anniversary."

"Well, I hope my husband, when I get one, will be as thoughtful as yours."

"You'd better be sure he's thoughtful *before* you marry him. Women don't usually reform their husbands a great deal."

"Oh, I'll be careful. But I been wondering about how it is between you and the master."

"What do you mean, Dorcas?"

"Well, most men don't pay much attention to their wives, but Lord Stoneybrook still holds your hand—and in public, too. And I've heard him talking to you, saying such sweet things."

"You're right. I don't think he has missed a day in our married life telling me how much he loves me, except when he is gone from Stoneybrook."

"Was he like that before you married him, my lady?"

"I had a strange upbringing, and my husband and I had a strange courtship."

Dorcas moved behind Eden and began combing her hair carefully. "How did you two meet? You never told me."

Old memories flooded into Eden, and she hesitated for a moment. "I had an odd childhood, Dorcas. I was kidnapped by a Spanish pirate when I was just a child. I was brought up in Spain. I didn't know my real parents and I was very unhappy. Then one day a man came and I was impressed with him."

"And that was your husband, Lord Stoneybrook?"

"Well, he wasn't Lord Stoneybrook then, but yes, it was."

"And did you fall in love with him at first sight?"

Eden laughed. "No, not right away. You see, I didn't know it, but my real parents had just found out I was alive. They thought I had been lost at sea all that time. When they discovered the truth, they sent Brandon to get me away from my kidnapper, who was about to make me marry a man I didn't love."

"And then what happened, my lady?"

"Brandon promised to get me away, and he did. He stole me right out of captivity, and brought me on a ship to England and returned me to my parents."

"And you fell in love with him."

Eden smiled. "It was a stormy affair. I felt he had made me fall in love with him just so he could collect the reward my father had offered for my safe return. So it took some doing, but we found each other and have been together ever since."

"Oh, my, it sounds like one of the love stories the actors sing about!"

Eden started to speak, but a knock drew her attention. "Come in," she said. She smiled as a man entered, and said, "Hello, Quentin."

"Hello, Eden." Quentin Winslow was Brandon's uncle and a favorite of the whole family. He had the Winslow look about him, except that his auburn hair was turning silver. As Eden rose to greet him, he took her hands. "Well, you're looking beautiful as usual, my dear."

"You always say the nicest things."

"I understand the queen's progress is coming. What do you think of that?"

"I dread it, and so does Brandon. Why does she do it? It costs so much!"

Quentin shrugged. "She is selfish to the bone, my dear, like all kings and all queens. Queen Elizabeth is a fine queen and brilliant in many ways, but she will do as she pleases. I think she goes on these progresses to save money in the royal treasury."

"These progresses have bankrupted two noblemen that I know of."

"I'm not surprised. Anyway, how are the children? I brought them some gifts."

"They're down at the brook. You'll be staying for the progress, won't you?"

"Oh, yes. First I have to see my little friends. I will see you later, Eden." He turned and left the room.

Dorcas said, "All the Winslow men are fine looking, aren't they, my lady?"

"Yes, they are, and Quentin dearly loves the children."

"I've never seen a preacher as handsome as him. Is he married?"

"No, he never married, although he's had plenty of chances. Now that's enough with my hair. I have to go help Brandon get ready for this awful progress!"

Adam Winslow, at the age of eight, was two years older than his brother, Colin, and four years older than his sister, Adara. The three of them had been playing in the cool water of the brook for some time. Adam and Adara were shouting and splashing, but Colin had moved downstream and had paused to look at something on the edge of the water. Adam was irritated and shouted, "Come back here, Colin, we're going to build a dam!" Colin did not move, and Adam became angry. "Look at him, Adara! He pays no attention to me!"

"Make him come!"

"I will!" Adam waded out of the stream toward where his younger brother was crouched. Adam was a strongly built lad with golden hair and hazel eyes, unlike the blue eyes that most Winslow men had. He was a stubborn boy and, since he was the eldest, always wanted to have his own way with Adara and Colin. He moved to where Colin was staring at something. "Didn't you hear me? I said we're going to build a dam!"

"I don't want to build a dam." Colin had chestnut hair and light blue-gray eyes. He had always been dominated by Adam and was accustomed to being yelled at. "Look, it's a turtle."

"Who cares about a stupid old turtle?"

"But I've never seen one like this, Adam. I want to take him home."

Adam reached down and pulled Colin to his feet. "Come on. We are going to build a dam."

"No. I want to watch this turtle."

"You are always looking at snakes or bugs. Come on."

"I don't want to! Let me go, Adam."

As always, Adam grew angry when he was crossed. He shoved Colin aside and kicked at the turtle.

"Don't hurt him, Adam!" Colin tried to pull his brother away, but Adam hit him in the chest. The blow knocked the boy face forward into the stream, and Adam shouted, "There, that's what you get if you don't mind me! You have to do what I say because I'm the eldest, Colin! And remember, one day I'll be Adam Winslow, Baron of Stoneybrook, and you'll still be nothing but plain old Colin Winslow!"

Brandon had joined Quentin, and together they went to the creek where the children were playing. They arrived just in time to see Adam knock Colin into the stream. As soon as Brandon saw Adam strike Colin, he ran forward, with Quentin following him. Brandon seized Adam by the arm and shook him. "What do you mean, hitting your brother like that, you rascal?"

Adam stared up at his father, showing no signs of remorse. "I wanted him to help us build a dam, but he just wanted to watch an old turtle! That's all he ever does, Father! He cares more about a dirty old turtle than he does for me!"

"He has manners enough not to hit his own kin!" Brandon said angrily. He waded out and pulled Colin to his feet. There was a small cut on his forehead where he had hit his head on a rock. "Are you all right, Colin?"

"Yes, Father."

Brandon gently touched the cut. To Adam he said sternly, "Your uncle has come and brought you all some gifts, but you don't deserve one, Adam."

Quickly, Colin said, "He didn't hurt me, Father. Let Uncle Quentin give him a present."

Brandon hesitated, but Quentin came forward and put his hand on Colin's shoulder, saying, "I'll tell you what, Brandon. Let me give Adam his gift, and you can discipline him some other way."

Brandon nodded reluctantly, and Quentin picked up Adara and kissed her. "How is my favorite lady friend today?"

"What did you bring me, Uncle Quentin?" Adara demanded. She had striking red hair, bright green eyes, and a heart-shaped face that showed early signs of great beauty. She also showed early signs of being spoiled to the bone. Quentin particularly indulged her.

"How about some nice juicy snails?"

"Give them to Colin!"

"I don't give presents to dirty children. All of you go up to the house and get cleaned up, and if you're all good until after dinner, I will give you your presents."

"Good enough," Brandon said quickly. "Go along now." As they left, Brandon shook his head and groaned, "I have never seen three children so different."

"But they're fine children," Quentin said with a smile.

"Adam is stubborn as a mule!"

"I think we both know where he got that from—and it wasn't your dear wife!"

Brandon laughed. "You're right. I was exactly like Adam

when I was his age and long afterward. I hope he learns a little humility soon. Come, let's go to the house."

As they walked back toward the castle, Brandon said, "Eden and I are worried about Colin."

"He is not sick, is he?" Quentin asked quickly.

"No, he's healthy, but he's so different from Adam—and, for that matter, all the male Winslows."

"You mean physically?"

"Well, that way too. He's smaller and not built as strongly as most of us. You were always strong. So was I, and so was Father. But Colin looks almost frail when he stands beside Adam. Still, it's not so much that Colin is different physically—he's strange in his ways."

"Why, he's bright enough."

"Yes, I give you that. But remember, he didn't start talking until he was almost three. Eden and I were afraid he wasn't normal."

"But he talked well enough once he got started, didn't he?" Quentin said with a chuckle.

"Yes," Brandon smiled. "As a matter of a fact, he started talking in complete sentences. It came as quite a shock to us. We waited and prayed for him to talk. Then one day he just up and said to Eden, 'I want a drink of water.' Eden nearly fainted! It was the same way with reading. He taught himself, more or less, when he was only four."

They reached the house, and Quentin said finally, "I remember the day he was born, Brandon. You and I were so nervous waiting for the birth. When we went in, Eden was so proud. She said, 'I've given this child to God.' At that point we all agreed that God would touch Colin's life, and I believe He will."

Brandon sighed deeply, then said, "He's just so—odd!"

"That may be because God needs different things from different people. Colin, Adam, and Adara are unique, and they all face a hard and dangerous world." He put his hand on Brandon's shoulder and added, "Have faith in God and believe that he will protect and use all three of them."

Brandon smiled and looked relieved. "You sound like Eden. She is the one with faith. But with all the faith I have, I'll pray for my children."

2

June 14, 1568

"You know, Eden," Brandon said sourly, "all this reminds me of one of the plagues that the Bible speaks of."

Eden looked up at her husband, surprised. The two were standing at the gate of Stoneybrook with their children, waiting for the arrival of the royal party. "What are you talking about, Brandon? What plague was that?"

"You remember when God sent Moses to deliver the Israelites from the Egyptians? He had to send plagues to force Pharaoh to listen. One of them was an enormous cloud of locusts. The Bible says they swarmed over the whole land, ate everything green, and stripped the land."

"Why does this remind you of that?"

Brandon put his arm around her waist and drew her close. "Because these progresses do about the same thing."

Adam had been listening carefully. He asked curiously, "Are you angry because the queen is coming, Father? I thought it was an honor."

Glancing down at Adam, Brandon shrugged slightly. "It's just that the queen and her court and all these hangers-on are going to cost a fortune to feed and house. We'll be fortunate if we have a farthing left after this is over."

Indeed, the progress had become a tradition with the Tudor monarchs. It involved a complicated process: a route was decided on, and the officials were sent out to ensure the queen's safety and to inform the unfortunate dukes, barons, and earls that they were about to be blessed with a visit from the court of Queen Elizabeth.

For Elizabeth this was a way of showing herself to her people. She generally traveled by horseback, but occasionally by litter. Sometimes she journeyed in an open coach so that the people could get a good view of her. The progress was as ostentatious as her ministers could possibly make it.

As soon as news was received of the queen's intended arrival in a town, the mayor and his officials set to work removing dung hills, pillories, and stocks. To prepare the town they bought fireworks, and there were Latin notations to rehearse. Stages were erected, and canvas forts and wooden castles were built for mock battles and military pageants.

The houses or castles in which the queen stayed belonged to the wealthy members of the nobility. All of them contemplated her arrival with alarm, and most owners were aware that when the queen's choice fell upon a house, the cost could run as high as a thousand pounds a day. Once, when the queen stayed for five days with Sir Nicholas Bacon, the Lord Keeper, he was forced to employ several London cooks and obliged to purchase sixty sheep, thirty-four lambs, twenty-six pigs, eighteen calves, eight oxen, and ten kids. He had to provide dozens of birds: over 350 chickens, more than two hundred pigeons, twelve dozen ducklings and herons, ten dozen geese, sixteen dozen quails, and much more.

In addition to the food and the drink, there were musicians to employ and deer to round up for hunting. Some noblemen were forced to enlarge their houses to care for the queen and her court, for Elizabeth once said to a baron bluntly: "You have made your house too small."

"How long do you think she will stay, dear?" Eden asked anxiously. Her eyes were scanning the road, looking for a cloud of dust that would announce the arrival of the queen.

"There's no way of telling. Once she stayed for a month with the Duke of Norfolk."

"Look, Father, they are coming!" Adam cried out.

"You are right, Son," Brandon said glumly. His eyes swept the town that bordered the castle, and it seemed that every soul in the village had left his home. A babble of voices filled the air, and everyone was peering to the west down the narrow road that led to London. As the horsemen drew near, Brandon whispered, "For what we are about to receive, dear wife, may we be duly grateful."

"I wish they would never come," Eden murmured.

"Try to look happy, dear," Brandon whispered. "Every nobleman becomes a hypocrite when he is chosen for one of Her Majesty's progresses. Every one of us hates it, but we can never do anything but pretend that it is nothing but the greatest blessing from our sovereign."

The procession filed by until finally the litter bearing the queen halted right in front of where the family stood. Noblemen in full attire were waiting to open the door. One of them gave Elizabeth his hand, and she stepped out of the litter.

Brandon bowed and Eden curtsied and the children did as they were taught. Brandon smiled and said, "We welcome you to Stoneybrook, Your Majesty. It is good to see you again."

"I hope we will not be too great an inconvenience, Lord and Lady Stoneybrook."

"Not at all, Your Majesty. It is our pleasure." Brandon was noting the man who stood closest to Elizabeth, Lord Burghley, the secretary of state. He was the individual Elizabeth trusted most in the world and made most of the decisions that affected the realm. Slightly farther back stood Sir Francis Walsingham, dressed entirely in black. He was the head of what amounted to

Elizabeth's secret service. He was a dangerous man but totally loyal to his queen. These two remained slightly back, and the queen leaned on the arm of her favorite, Robert Dudley. He was rarely far from Elizabeth, who had named him the Earl of Leicester. Leicester, a good friend of Brandon, was a handsome man attired in the best clothes that money could buy. He stepped forward and said, "My dear Lord Stoneybrook, I fear that we impose on your hospitality."

Brandon quickly gave the expected response. "It is never an imposition to have you, Lord Leicester, and Her Majesty brightens any home that she chooses to grace."

Elizabeth nodded with approval, then turned to speak with Eden. The two women had known each other for some time, and Eden was one of Elizabeth's favorites among the noblewomen. "How are you, my dear?"

"Very well, Your Majesty, and you are looking most splendid."

"Thank you, but I fear the sun is making toast out of my skin. I must tell you we will be going to your parents' home later in the progress."

"I'm sure they will be happy to welcome you, Your Majesty."

Elizabeth smiled slightly, knowing that there was little truth in this but that it was the expected form of reply. Studying the children, she exclaimed, "What beautiful children!" Lifting Adam's chin gently, she asked, "Who is this?"

Brandon answered, "This is our eight-year-old, Adam, our eldest."

"You look much like your father," Elizabeth said. "And are you a good boy?"

"Oh yes, Your Majesty! Very good!"

Elizabeth laughed heartily. "I asked your father that once when he was very young, and do you know what he said?"

"No, Your Majesty."

"He said, 'No, I'm not good,' and when I asked him why not, he said, 'I was born in sin and in sin did my mother conceive me.'"

Great laughter followed this, and Leicester clapped Brandon on the shoulder. "An honest boy you were, Stoneybrook."

Brandon flushed and muttered, "I was hoping you would have forgotten that, Your Majesty."

"I never forget what a man says. And who is this?"

"This is Colin. He is six." Elizabeth bent over and in a stage whisper asked, "And are you a good boy, Colin?"

Colin looked up and his face was serious. "Not always, but when I am naughty Father paddles me. So I try to be good as much as I can."

Elizabeth found this amusing and put her hand on Colin's head. "He looks like you, Lady Stoneybrook. I hope he has all your good qualities." Then she turned to Adara, smiling. "And who is this little one?"

Eden responded, "This is Adara, Your Majesty. She is four."

"Aren't you a beauty!" Elizabeth exclaimed.

And Adara said, "Yes, I am!"

Elizabeth was momentarily surprised by the reply but laughed. "She is honest; I like that very much indeed."

Brandon said, "Come and have some light refreshments, Your Majesty. Tonight we will have something more substantial and dancing. I claim a dance with you."

"You shall have one, my lord."

Brandon led the party to the great hall and Eden joined him, seeing to it that food and drink were available.

The great hall was filled and the number of voices speaking made it almost impossible to hear conversation. The smell of cooked meat was in the air. A minstrel was singing, and the dogs from time to time would fight over scraps that fell to the rushes that lined the floor.

Brandon stayed busy, but at one point he looked up and saw the queen gesture toward him. He went to her at once. She asked, "Is there a room where we can talk?"

"Of course, Your Majesty. Please follow me." He led her

through the crowd and into a small room off to one side. It contained merely a table and several books and two chairs. "I call this my misery room." He smiled as Elizabeth was seated. "When my wife hurts my feelings I come here and wallow in my misery until she forgives me."

"I somehow doubt that, Stoneybrook. You are not one to be sullen, and your wife is not a woman to mistreat a good man like you."

"Can I bring you something to drink?"

"No, sit down and talk with me." Elizabeth waited until Brandon was seated, then she smiled. "I thought you were an honest man, sir. Your father, Stuart, was completely honest. I'm saddened and grieved to see that you have not inherited his good qualities."

Brandon blinked with surprise. "Indeed I am not the man he was, Majesty, and I never was. But where have I been dishonest?"

"You didn't tell the truth when you greeted me. You said you were glad to welcome me."

"Why—" Brandon stopped and his face turned red. "You think I am not glad to see you?"

"Me, perhaps, but what man in his right mind would welcome this mob? I have some idea of what this progress will cost you." She smiled when she saw the guilty look on his face. "Never mind, Brandon. I will tell you a secret. You must never let anyone hear of this." She leaned closer. "On a progress, I always stay longer with people I dislike and people who have not pleased me." She laughed then. A deep laugh, and her eyes gleamed with pleasure. "Why, we stayed a full month with the Duke of Norfolk. It must have cost him a hundred thousand pounds to feed the lot of us. All the time he was smiling and bowing, but I knew he hated everyone there."

"I am shocked, Your Majesty."

"Oh, I am a devious woman! But your father was a favorite of mine. I love you for his sake, because you're his blood. I have a surprise for you."

"A surprise, my queen?"

"We will stay the night, but we will leave early in the morning." She waited for his reply and blinked with shock when he said, "Good! I will be glad to see the backs of the whole—except, of course, you, my queen."

Elizabeth laughed again. She smiled as she reached out and touched his cheek and said, "I have dozens of men who load me with compliments. I know well they give them to get something out of me. But there are a few like you, Lord Stoneybrook, men I admire. Now I promised you a dance. Do you think your wife will be jealous?"

"Oh, yes indeed, Your Majesty, very jealous."

"Then we will make her more so. Let us show these bumpkins what a dance should be!"

Brandon stood as far back to the wall as he could get, for the small room was crowded with the queen and the men who ran the nation of England. Elizabeth had asked for a conference room; then, to his surprise, she asked him to remain.

Brandon studied the faces of the men. To the queen's right was Lord Burghley, who was always close to her. To her left was Robert Dudley in all his glory, and across the table was Sir Francis Walsingham. Brandon realized this was, in effect, a meeting of her counsel, for these were the men she most trusted, who acted on her will and directed the affairs of England. The meeting went on for some time. Brandon was shocked to see Elizabeth, more than once, flare up with anger. There was another man in the room whom Brandon had heard of by reputation, Sir Francis Drake, by all reports the premier seaman in all the world. The Spanish called him a pirate because he raided their ships and ports regularly. He sat back smiling from time to time, a man of below-average size with small, brilliant dark eyes and a pointed beard. He said very little, but Brandon knew that Elizabeth trusted him completely in matters concerning the navy.

The meeting was interrupted when Eden stepped inside. "Pardon me, Your Majesty, but there is a gentleman to see Sir Francis Walsingham. He is very insistent."

"Did you get his name?" Walsingham demanded.

"Mr. Collins, he said."

Instantly, Walsingham rose and, without another word, left the room. "That man frightens me sometimes," Leicester said.

"We need men like that, Robin," Elizabeth said. This was her pet name for Leicester.

"I know we need a network of spies, Your Majesty, but he is a rather daunting individual."

"I know Sir Francis can be quite ruthless."

"I would hate to have him as an enemy," Burghley said sourly.

"He is invaluable," Elizabeth shrugged. "Now, about the need for more ships. I'm not satisfied that we need more. They are very expensive."

At once Burghley said, "We live on an island, ma'am. The sea protects us from our enemies. France and Spain would love to rule over this country, and they well know the only way they can do it is to come by sea."

"Yes, and Spanish galleons are being built that are not made for commerce," said Sir Francis Drake. He had a pleasant voice and did not look like the ruthless pirate that the Spanish dubbed him. "They are war ships," Drake said. "We must be able to meet the challenge, Your Majesty, and it will come by sea. As for the expense, what would it cost if Spain took over our country?"

Elizabeth questioned Drake for some time, then the door opened and Walsingham returned, his face glowing with anger.

"What is it, Walsingham?" Elizabeth demanded.

"Evil tidings, Your Majesty." Walsingham paused and narrowed his eyes. "Mary, Queen of Scots, has fled Scotland and landed on our coast."

"Impossible!" Elizabeth cried. "That cannot be!"

"I fear it's true, Your Majesty. Collins has seen her with his own eyes."

Leicester said at once, "She must not be allowed to remain! She will bring terrible disorder to us. You must send her away at once, Your Majesty."

Elizabeth looked down at her hands, heavily bejeweled with rings, for some time, and everyone waited for her response. "Why did she leave Scotland, Walsingham? She is a queen. No one can lift his hand against the Lord's anointed."

Every man in the room knew that Elizabeth was a firm believer in the divine right of kings. She believed, as her sister and her father had, that God put the ruler in place. And to strike at the monarch was to strike at God himself!

Walsingham answered at once, his voice hard. "She may be a queen, ma'am, but she is a dangerous one. You know her history. She married the French dauphin when she was sixteen. Then in 1561 she returned to Scotland and married her cousin Lord Henry Darnley. Then she fell in love with her secretary, who was killed by Darnley and his friends."

Instantly, Elizabeth said, "That was Darnley's crime, not Mary's! She cannot be held responsible for what her husband did."

"We all know, ma'am," Walsingham said, "that she murdered her husband." His eyes burned with anger and he spit out the words, "It was never proven, but it is common knowledge that she was behind Darnley's death. He died in an explosion, and then immediately Mary married an outlaw, the Earl of Bothwell. The Scots put up with her ways for a long time, but now they have had enough."

"But why did she come to England? There's nothing here for her," Leicester said.

"There is a crown for her," Walsingham said sternly, and his eyes went to the queen.

Elizabeth stared at Walsingham. "She could not have such a thought!"

"Your Majesty, you know better than any of us how Spain tried to gain your crown. Your sister married King Philip of Spain, and we all know it was not for love. Philip wanted to wear the crown of England, and Mary well knows this. My agents have brought me many reports on this business." Walsingham gestured sharply with his long-fingered hand. His lips made a hard line as he said, "You have many enemies, Your Majesty. They want a Catholic on the throne of England, and Mary of Scots is a Catholic. There are groups all over Europe that would join together to pull you down and put Mary on your throne."

Walsingham's words echoed in the stillness of the room, and finally Elizabeth said, "I do not believe it!"

"You refuse to believe it because you have a high regard for royalty, but Mary is unscrupulous. If you allow her to remain in England, she will draw every hot-headed Catholic to her cause. Danger lies not only on the continent but in all of England."

"I fear Walsingham is right, my queen," Burghley said heavily. "We cannot take the risk of allowing Mary to stay in England."

The eyes of every man in the room went to Elizabeth, and as she arose her face was flushed with anger. "I cannot harm a fellow monarch!" She whirled and left the room. As soon as the door closed behind her, Walsingham struck the table with his fist. "The queen of Scots must not be allowed to stay in this country! She will stop at nothing to get the crown!"

"You are right, Walsingham," Burghley nodded. "But Elizabeth is a stubborn woman and has an exalted idea about her fellow rulers. I fear it may not be possible to persuade her to cut her ties with Mary." He turned to Leicester. "You have more influence with her than any of us. You must persuade her to send Mary away."

Leicester said, "I think we all know what she will say. She will say that no harm can come to her from another queen. However, I will do my best." He dropped his head and muttered, "God help us if that female wolf is permitted to live among us!"

3

April 4, 1574

"I'm twelve years old today—and yesterday I was eleven."

Colin Winslow disturbed his parents and others as well by talking to himself. Perhaps it was because he was a lonely boy who did not fit into any of the family niches. He thought of how displeased his father had been to hear him talking to animals as if they were people. It had disturbed him so greatly that Colin had concealed his habit of conversing with animals and snakes and bugs and practically anything in nature. He still did this, but not while people were present.

"Yesterday I was eleven, but today I am twelve years old." Colin mulled over the sentence as he made his way through the thickness of the forest. It was an environment he knew very well, for he spent as much time there as he could. Even now, as he moved quickly down a path that wavered to the east and terminated at the small river that irrigated much of the Winslows' farm, his eyes moved from side to side, missing nothing. He noticed a female hedgehog and her small offspring. Colin stopped and remained absolutely still. He had learned by experience that if one wants to get to know the creatures of the forest, he must turn himself into something else. He always pretended he was a tree standing in a windless spot. Though he did not move his head, his eyes tracked the progress of the hedgehog and her off-spring as she came toward him. She bumped into the toe of his shoe, then backed up and tried to push it aside. Finally deciding it was useless, she made a detour around his feet. Turning his head slowly, Colin watched the pair as they disappeared into the thickness of the ground cover.

It was late in the afternoon, and Colin had finished his chores in time to come out for a special errand. Glancing up, he saw dark clouds moving swiftly in from the west. "That cloud looks like a dragon." He smiled. He had an ability to create a world inside his head and to see things others could not see, at least in the dark woods. Turning quickly, he made his way through the thickets. Tim Hemley, the chief hunter for the Winslow family, had taught Colin many useful facts about the animals that lived their lives out around the woods of the castle. Hemley had become a fountain of knowledge for Colin, and even now the boy could hear the man's voice in his head. *You always watch now when you're in the wood, Master Colin. Never stop lookin'. Look up and down; always keep your head a-swivelin'. You hear me now? If you don't, you'll miss it all.*

Indeed, Colin missed little as he made his way to Diamond River. The name seemed odd to Colin, who had looked for diamonds in the water but had never found one.

Reaching the edge of the stream, he was still thinking how strange it was that even though he was only a year older than he was yesterday, he felt no different. *I wonder if I'll feel different when I'm thirteen?* He sat down at the edge of the river and watched carefully. The surface of the water at times did sparkle like diamonds, but right now it was cloudy. He heard the sound of the current as it broke over the rocks at his feet. The song of a bird caught his attention. He watched as the bird, which had a snowy white breast and a brown ladder back, sailed overhead and made a whistling noise. Colin made up his mind to ask Tim Henley what kind of bird it was.

Finally he opened up a small canvas bag he had fastened to his waist and removed a cord and a hook. He tied the hook carefully at one end and fished through the bag until he found a chunk of meat and impaled it on the hook. Then, pulling the cord to its full length and holding on to the free end, he threw it out as hard as he could. A weight of lead he had tied to it sank it at once, and Colin sat back and remained perfectly still. He saw a heron pausing almost out of sight around the bend of the river. He watched as the heron's bill went down like a sword and came out with a silver fish. The bird tossed the fish in the air and caught it headfirst. Colin could see it go down the bird's throat, and the sight pleased him. A school of silvery minnows darted by. He was interested in their movements because they moved as one creature. When they turned, every one of them turned. "I wonder how they all know how to turn at the same time, since they can't talk and they can't smell."

Time passed, and he thought back to the time when Adam had shoved him in this very stream. He remembered it clearly. Colin not only remembered things vividly, he never seemed to forget a thing. Then, Colin thought of how greatly he had disappointed his parents, and the thought troubled him. He had never had any interest in fighting, weapons, or hunting, and those were the things that pleased his father. Adam loved them all, and at the age of fourteen, he was almost the equal of grown men with weapons that his father had tutored him in. "I must be doing something wrong." Colin's voice broke the silence of the forest. "I want to please Father and Mother but I just don't seem to know how"—hearing, a sound he turned and saw John Nixon, a neighboring farmer, approach, dragging a sack tied to a rope.

"Hello, John. What's in your sack?"

"Biggest turtle I ever seen," John exclaimed. "I caught him, but I don't want him. Thought I'd take him home and find somebody who likes to eat turtles."

"My parents love turtle soup," Colin said at once.

"Why, you just take him, Master Colin."

Instantly, Colin ran and took the rope, saying, "Thank you, John. I'll tell my parents it's your gift."

"Well, hope they likes 'im." John turned and moved quickly down the path, and Colin at once began to drag the heavy sack. It was so heavy he had to stop and rest several times. He decided not to follow the faint trail in the wood, for the awkward carcass would catch in the roots and the saplings. Instead he set out on the worn path that followed the river. The woods were thick even along the path. He released the line from where he had tied it to his belt. Finally he came to a well-worn passageway that ran east. He hesitated, then glanced down a path that ran behind a gnarled yew tree. He looked at the small dwelling that occupied the center of a cleared space. Carefully he approached, moving from tree to tree until he was within twenty feet of the house.

A harsh voice broke the stillness of the day. "Who are you? Come forward if ye have business." Colin started and whirled to see a woman standing beside the cabin, almost hidden by a small hedge. He was not a fearful boy, but he had to resist the impulse to turn and run away. He had a strong streak of pride that would not let him do such a thing. "I'm—I'm Colin Winslow."

"Do you know who I be?"

"Yes, you're Meg Caradoc."

The woman had dark eyes deeply set in the midst of a face tanned by the sun, causing it to have almost the texture of leather. Her whole face was sharp and she was not old, as Colin had heard. People called her an old woman, but her worn clothing revealed a body that was still strong.

"You're a Winslow, are you? Well, come here, boy." When he hesitated, she laughed harshly. "You think I'm going to turn you into a frog?"

Actually, Colin had considered something of that nature. As

he stood in front of her, he remembered that many had warned about this woman being dangerous. Still, her features were not cruel as he had imagined. Her hair was dark, with a single silver streak.

"What are you doin' here, boy?"

"I—I'm on my way home," he stammered.

"What were you doing in these woods?"

"I've been to the river."

"Did you catch anything?"

"I didn't, but a friend of mine caught the biggest turtle I ever saw." His eyes were sparkling as he said this.

"Where is it, then?"

"Back there on the trail."

"Well, go get it," she said quickly.

Colin moved quickly and grabbed the string and pulled it until the turtle was in front of Meg Caradoc. "It is the biggest one I ever saw," he said again.

"It *is* a big one. I expect you better leave it here with me."

"No, I'm taking it home. My parents like turtle soup."

Meg Caradoc suddenly frowned. "Do you think I'm a witch?"

"Well, I don't know—"

"Maybe I'm not the only witch in these parts. I cut things open, you know."

"That's what I've heard." Colin was not sure this was the right thing to say.

"Well, I'm not the only one in these woods who does that, am I?"

Colin suddenly felt a chill, as if an icicle had gone down his spine. "What is that supposed to mean?"

"There's only two of us here."

"How do you know that?"

"Maybe I'm a witch."

"No, I don't believe that."

Meg suddenly laughed. "I like you, boy. Most people are

afraid of me. They only come to see me when they are sick and they want my medicine."

Colin blurted out, "I wish I could do that—give medicine to sick people."

"Maybe you can."

"No, I can't. I don't know how."

"Tell you what, you give me the turtle, and I will teach you a few things."

Colin was torn with doubt, but he said, "Our bird keeper Dooley has got an awful cough. It sounds like it will tear him in two."

"Well, what about this, young Winslow? I give you the medicine for your bird keeper, and you let me keep the turtle."

"All right."

Meg turned quickly and disappeared into the cottage, returning almost at once holding two bottles. "This one is a mixture of horehound and comfrey. Have him take it in the day. The second one should be taken at night. I can't promise a cure, but it can't be of any harm to him."

"What's in the second one?"

"Diacodium. Don't tell anyone you got it from me. We'd both be in trouble."

"You won't be in trouble. My father wouldn't let anyone hurt you. He is Lord of Stoneybrook."

"Why, harm can come to any of us, boy." Her bright eyes sparkled and she straightened up. A thought lit up her eyes and she said, "Good thing I never had wealth. The rich find it hard to leave this life. To the poor it doesn't matter so much. But for most people, money and things of that sort are the savor of life."

"I'm sure I don't understand you, Miss Meg."

"Why, the sweet taste of life! When you're young, all sensations have savor; all the fruits are good. But when you're old, they lose their relish. That's why I'm glad things were never sweet to me. I won't have to grieve over them when it's time to go."

Colin studied the woman, then asked, "Have you ever been married?"

"Never."

"Or have a sweetheart?"

"I once did, but he loved another."

"I'm sorry."

Meg moved her shoulders restlessly and laughed. "Well, there is no doubt that he would've beaten me and sent me to an early grave. Now you can help me cut this turtle up."

"How did you know I cut things up?"

"Why, I'm a witch."

"No, you're not."

"I know you cut things up, but you have never cut up a turtle this big."

"I like to do it, but my father and mother don't like it when I do it."

"Well, I will keep that secret." Meg laughed and winked. "Parents don't have to know everything a lad does."

Adam's face was tense and his mouth was drawn into a thin line. He circled around his father, seeking a break in his guard. Each time he attempted to close, his father simply parried the stroke. Finally he said with disgust, "I can't do it, Father!"

"You're fourteen years old, Adam, and you're very good. You're the equal of many full-grown men."

"Will I ever be as good as you?"

"You will be better, Son," Brandon said with a warm smile.

The remark pleased Adam and he said, "I hope so; I do like swords. Tell me some more about the battles you've been in."

"Later. Let's go back to the house."

As the two started on their way, Adam said, "Do you know that Colin's been visiting a witch?"

"What do you mean?" Brandon asked quickly.

"Why, old Meg Caradoc. He goes to her house all the time."

"He has no business going over there."

"I'll tell you why he goes. I talked to him about it. He is interested in her herbs—and to be truthful, some of the things she gives sick folks work. It healed Dooley of his cough, whatever it was that Colin brought back. But you know, Father, everyone is saying Colin is crazy. He cuts up birds and animals and snakes—and he stays by himself. He doesn't care about swords or weapons or horses."

"He's still young. Now, you go take a ride on Thunder."

Brandon watched as the boy ran away, and when he entered the castle he found Adara pestering her mother. "What does she want now, Eden?"

"She wants to use cosmetics," Eden said impatiently.

"I'm old enough," Adara said quickly.

"You are *not* old enough," Eden said. "You don't need them anyway; you have a beautiful complexion."

"Mary Harten uses cosmetics. Queen Elizabeth does, too."

"Well, Queen Elizabeth needs them, but you don't."

"She does wear a lot of makeup and fancy clothes."

"She is the queen, Adara. She can do whatever she wants to."

Brandon picked up Adara and began to swing her around. "When you are forty, darling, you can put all the mess you want on your face."

"Please, Father, let me put some on."

"You heard your mother. No makeup." He put Adara down and she said, "You are so mean to me!" then stomped off with her nose in the air.

"She is so headstrong, Brandon!"

"Well, she's able to get what she wants out of people."

"She was able to get that opal ring out of you."

"That's completely different!"

Eden laughed at him. Then he changed the subject. "I'm worried about Colin."

"Why?"

"He's so strange. He talks to animals out loud, and he's been spending a lot of time with Meg Caradoc."

"I know, he told me. She's teaching him about plants."

"Well, he can't make a living pulling weeds from the ground! What will he do for a profession, Eden? He's not strong enough to be a soldier. I'd hate for him to become a lawyer."

"Maybe he will go into the church."

"No, he doesn't seem to be turning that way."

The two continued their talk, each realizing the other was worried. Finally, Brandon said, "When he's old enough, we'll send him to Oxford. They'll make something out of him."

"I doubt it. He's a good boy, but he has a stubborn streak." She changed the subject quickly. "Do you still plan to go to court?"

"Yes, the queen wants to see me."

"Do you know what about?"

Brandon moved closer and put his arm around Eden's waist, then leaned forward and whispered in her ear. "She likes handsome young men."

Eden hit him in the chest, exclaiming, "The very idea! You are absolutely filled with pride!"

"I don't really want to go," Brandon sighed.

"You have to go, Brandon. And why don't you take Colin with you?"

"Why would I do that?"

"Because he needs you, and I think it would be good for him to get away for a few days."

Brandon knew Eden had deeper insight into people than he had. Then he suddenly laughed aloud. "We could take the queen a field mouse he has pulled apart and opened up. That would be a different gift!" The thought amused him, and he held her tighter and kissed her. "You are even prettier than a mouse that has been pulled apart."

"Thank you, Husband. You always say the nicest things!"

Elizabeth looked up as Helen Tallon, one of her maids, entered and said, "Your Majesty, Lord Stoneybrook and his son are here to see you."

"Show them in at once." She was sitting at the clavichord and playing, and did not look up as the two entered. When she finished her piece, she rose and went to Brandon, holding out her hand. "Well, Lord Stoneybrook, you are here."

Brandon took her hand, bowed, and kissed it. "Yes, Your Majesty. I'm glad to see you again."

"Remind me who this is."

"My son Colin, Your Majesty."

Elizabeth moved over and stood in front of Colin. She stared into his face and knew that her intense scrutiny made him uncomfortable. Finally, she demanded, "Are you still trying to be a good boy, like you told me the last time we met?"

"Yes, I am, Your Majesty."

Elizabeth was delighted at the boy's instant response. "And how do you do that?"

"I love my family and obey my parents and don't tell lies."

Elizabeth ceased to smile, and a somber look came over her face. She did not speak for a moment, then she turned and asked, "Is this a dwarf you have here, Brandon?"

"Sometimes I think so, Your Majesty. But he tells the simple truth."

"That should make him a novelty at court!" She called out, "Helen, take this young man out while I speak with his father, and see he gets something good to eat."

"Yes, Your Majesty."

After Colin left, Elizabeth shook her head and said, "I don't know what to make of him. So young, but he talks like an adult."

"I know. He did not say a word until he was almost three years old. Then he started talking in complete sentences."

"He is too smart to be only twelve. You might keep an eye on that one." Elizabeth leaned forward and said, "Now, come with me and walk in the garden."

"Yes, Your Majesty." Brandon followed Elizabeth outside and when they were amongst the flowers, she said, "I need a very special favor from you."

"You have only to ask, Your Majesty."

Elizabeth laughed. "You promised too quickly. Don't you know that women can get you into trouble that way?"

"Maybe some women, but you wouldn't, Majesty."

"All right then, I want you to visit Mary, Queen of Scots."

Brandon stared at her, and he looked as if he regretted his promise. "Why would you want me to do that?"

"I think you know. All of my counsel tells me that Mary is plotting to take my throne."

"But I am no spy, Your Majesty."

"No, you're not, and that is what makes this perfect. Mary would know at once if you were, for she's clever. I'm asking you to become a friend to her. It will not be hard for you. You are a good man. She will see that, and it will appeal to her. Take Colin with you, and then take your wife. Mary is clever, but you are a smart man, Brandon. Try to find out what she's doing."

Elizabeth spoke for some time and then dismissed him, saying, "I will not forget this. Please let me know when you find out what her plans are. I can't believe she is as evil as my counselors tell me. Now bring that son of yours back, and leave us alone. I want to know him better."

Brandon bowed as she left and then went to find Colin. "The queen wants to visit with you, Son. When she dismisses you, we'll be on our way."

Brandon waited for Colin to return, and finally Colin came

out of the queen's chamber. As they walked back to their horses, Brandon asked, "What did she talk to you about, Son?"

"She asked me questions."

"About what?"

"She asked if I thought she was beautiful."

"And what did you say?"

"I said no."

Brandon was shocked. Elizabeth kept a full court of men to tell her she was beautiful. "Did she get angry?"

"No, she laughed and said that I was about the only honest man in her kingdom."

The two mounted their horses and Colin asked, "Where are we going, Father?"

"To see another queen, Son."

4

April 19, 1574

"Is this where the queen lives, Father?"

Brandon and Colin had just ridden up to the barbed gates of Tutbury Castle, which rested on a slight hill. "Yes," he nodded, "this is where she lives. She's under house arrest—sort of like a prison. But I'm not sure you should call Mary 'the queen.'"

Colin looked up at his father with a puzzled expression. "But some people call her that, don't they?"

"Well, Son, there's a great deal of confusion about Mary. She was a queen in France at one time, and then she went back to Scotland, where she was also a queen. Then she left there and came here, where half of the English people, the Catholics, think she is still a queen. The rest of us acknowledge Queen Elizabeth."

"What should I call her, then?"

"Just call her 'Your Majesty.' Come along now."

Ten minutes later the two had been admitted into the presence of the Earl of Shrewsbury, a short, fat man with small eyes and a tight mouth. "Well, Lord Stoneybrook, I'm surprised to see you here," he said.

"Queen Elizabeth asked me to come and visit her dear

cousin, Mary," Brandon said. "Will there be any problem with that?"

"Not in the least! As a matter of a fact, I'm glad you've come. Queen Mary grows lonely at times, being cut off from all she has known. She's a lovely woman, you know. I can't see why people dislike her so."

Brandon tried not to smile, for his father had told him that stronger men than the Earl of Shrewsbury had fallen under the spell of Mary, Queen of Scots!

"I'm sure she is a charming woman," Brandon said agreeably.

"She will be most happy to receive you. Allow me to lead the way."

Colin had said nothing but was missing nothing. Tutbury Castle was smaller than his father's castle, but richly arrayed with furniture and wall hangings that gave a bright and cheery aspect to the halls. He walked quickly to keep up with his father and listened as the earl expanded on the many graces of Queen Mary. Sneaking a glance at his father's face, he saw displeasure there. He tucked that away in his memory. *Father doesn't share the earl's admiration of Mary.*

"If you will wait right here, my lord, I will see if the queen will receive you."

The earl slipped through a door guarded by two soldiers. He was back almost at once with a smile wreathing his face. "The queen is delighted! Come right in, sir."

Colin stayed close to his father as he entered the room, and he was impressed with the opulence of it. The furniture was rich and gleaming walnut. The walls were covered with colorful hangings, and silver and gold ornaments were on the tables that flanked the walls. His eyes, however, were immediately drawn to the woman who rose to greet them. Colin had an almost photographic memory for people as well as for words in a book. He knew at that moment he would never forget this gracious woman. She was tall and graceful and very good-looking, and there was something about her that most women did not have. Colin was not sure what it was, but he would study her until he found out.

"It's a kindness of you to see us, Your Majesty." Brandon stepped forward, took the hand that Mary extended, bowed, and kissed it. "Please allow me to introduce myself. I am Baron Winslow of Stoneybrook, and this is my son Colin Winslow."

"You are welcome indeed, Lord Stoneybrook." Mary turned a full smile upon Brandon. Colin, even as young as he was, noticed his father was drawn to the woman. Somehow it came to him that she was able to charm men. Colin found himself looking up at Mary, and when she extended her hand, he took it, bowed, and kissed her hand, saying, "I am pleased to meet you, Your Majesty."

"What fine manners you have! I am completely taken captive by you Winslow men."

Colin liked being called a man. He smiled at the queen and replied, "Thank you, Your Majesty."

"We will have refreshments brought in." She clapped her hands together, and at once a tall man appeared. "Yes, Your Majesty?"

"We need something good to eat, Benjamin. Bring us the best you can find."

"Of course, Your Majesty."

"Now sit down, and let us get acquainted. I want to know more about you. How did you happen to come and visit?"

"We were at court, and Queen Elizabeth asked us if we would come and meet you. She's very concerned with your well-being. If you have any message for her, I will be most happy to take it back."

"That is very kind of my sister queen. But now you must tell me what is going on in the outside world. I'm so cut off from everything in this prison."

Colin looked around and saw that there were at least half a dozen servants in the room, including three rather attractive young women. There were also three older women. Including the others outside, he quickly calculated that there must be at least thirty servants. *She doesn't seem cut off, not with all these servants!* He listened as his father and the queen talked. She asked his father questions about the royal court, and then about the English army, the navy, and the ships. She put her questions in a very subtle way, and as young as he was, Colin sensed that Queen Mary was a woman who knew how to manipulate men.

Finally the food came, and it was a feast indeed. It consisted of mutton, chicken, fish, and several exotic dishes that Colin could not identify. The wine was served with the food, and Queen Mary asked, "Are you old enough to drink wine, Colin?"

"Perhaps a little, Your Majesty."

"You will like this, I believe."

Colin had tasted wine only a few times, but the queen poured him a full flagon, and he took a small sip. "Very good, Your Majesty."

"I am glad you like it."

The meal lasted for some time, but finally after it was over, Queen Mary said prettily, "You must come back often to see me. Will you do that, Colin?" She came forward and extended her hand, and he took it. Colin saw that her eyes were quite penetrating, and for one moment he felt as if she were looking at his very soul.

"Yes, ma'am," he gulped, "if my father will allow me."

"I am sure he will. You must bring your wife, Lord Stoneybrook, and your other children. I would love to meet them all."

"It would be a pleasure, Your Majesty." Brandon bowed deeply and Colin did the same, then followed his father out the door. As soon as they were outside, Brandon turned and asked, "Colin, what did you think of her?"

Colin could not answer for a moment. He was afraid to speak his utmost thoughts, but finally he asked, "Is she a witch, Father?"

"A witch? No. Why do you ask that?"

"She scares me. She knew what I was thinking. She looked right down into me!"

"She has been called worse than a witch. But don't be afraid of her, Colin." He put his hand on his son's shoulder. "Don't be afraid of anyone, Son!"

Brandon and Eden entered Colin's room, stopped, and looked around almost in despair. It had been four months since Brandon and Colin had visited Queen Mary. Eden had been taken along with Adam and Adara to meet Mary. She had been somewhat intimidated by the queen, and when they were alone, she had warned her husband about Mary. "Brandon, you must be careful of that woman."

"Careful? What do you mean?"

"She devours men."

"Well, she won't devour me, sweetheart," Brandon had said instantly. "But I know what you mean. I'll be very careful."

While surveying Colin's room, Brandon remarked, "Will you look at this? What a mess!"

Eden nodded. "It is, rather."

Indeed, the room was packed to overflowing with live specimens—frogs, mice, snakes, and several small birds in cages. There were also stuffed specimens of animals, which, while not done expertly, at least pleased Colin. *He loves every living thing,* Eden thought.

The two continued to discuss the room but turned when Colin entered. He halted abruptly, then said nervously, "I didn't know you were in here."

Brandon said sharply, "Son, this room is a disaster!"

Eden saw that Colin was embarrassed and said quickly, "It does need some work." She looked at a table that contained the body of a bird that had been laid open. "What are you doing to this bird?"

"Oh, I'm seeing what the inside of this thrush looks like."

Eden sighed deeply, then asked, "Why do you do such things as this, Colin?"

"Why, the bird was dead, Mother. I didn't kill it, but I wanted to see her organs and muscles."

"Why would you want to know about that?" Eden asked curiously.

"I don't know." Colin thought deeply for a moment. He was tall for twelve and stood almost as high as his mother. Adam had nearly the bulk of a grown man at the age of fourteen, but Colin did not have the strength of his father the way Adam did.

Eden waited patiently. While most young men would say right away what was on their minds, Colin often paused to arrange his thoughts before he spoke. "If I knew how animals and birds work inside, maybe I could find out the way people work."

"And what would you do if you found that out, Son?"

"I don't know. Maybe I could help people."

Eden searched for something to say. Finally she said, "Son, I think you need to spend more time with your family and with friends and less time with animals and birds."

"I feel more at home with them than I do with people, Mother."

"Son, you shouldn't say that! These creatures don't love you as we do."

Colin dropped his head, and Eden saw she had hurt him. He was the most sensitive of all her children, and quickly she put her arm around his shoulders. She saw his eyes were troubled, so she said quickly, "Don't worry about it."

"I—I promise to spend more time with you and the others."

"That's a good boy, Son." Eden kissed his cheek and stepped back, but said, "I think you're spending too much time with Meg Caradoc."

"No, Mother, she's a good woman."

"You know what people say about her, that she's a witch."

"Oh no, she's not! She's nothing like a witch! She knows every plant and which ones help the sick. You remember how Dooley our coachman got sick, and I brought the medicine from Meg and it cured him?"

"Yes, I remember that. I'm sure she's helpful."

"She gets lonely, Mother, and I like to spend time with her. She's teaching me all about herbs and how to use them for remedies."

"All right. I know you are her friend, and I don't want to come between you and a friend. Hurry now, we're going to have supper soon."

Colin nodded and didn't speak, and as soon as the door shut he looked down at the thrush and said, "Now look what you have done! You've made my mother sad." He picked up his quill, dipped the tip into the ink bottle, and began to draw some of the muscles of the bird. He had struggled to transfer what he saw to paper. For a while he worked on his drawing, then finally he took a deep breath and expelled it, saying, "You're a little miracle, you are! Just as all living creatures are miracles!"

A few days after this meeting with his mother, Colin was sitting with Meg inside her shack. It was smoky and dark, but he felt comfortable there. "I brought you this, Meg." He handed her a small package, and when she opened it she exclaimed, "Why, that is *pepper*! A very expensive spice, indeed!"

"I know it, but we'll never miss it. I brought you a wild turkey, too, but I left it outside."

"How did you catch it?"

"One of the dogs caught him and was killing him. He was dead when I got there, but they didn't tear him much."

"What a good boy you are!"

"What are you working on, Meg?"

"I am going to pull a frog apart so you can see how it works."

Indeed, that is what Meg did for the next hour. She had careful and sure hands, but finally she let Colin take over part of the work. Colin eagerly plunged into the process, and soon the frog was all spread out, ready to be drawn.

"Do people ever tell you to stay away from me, Colin?"

Colin bit his lip and finally said, "Some people do."

"They may be right. I'm not a safe woman."

"Why, you would never hurt me, Meg."

"No, I wouldn't, but others might."

"I don't understand what you are saying, Meg."

"You are so innocent, Colin! The world is full of evil beasts, and you walk around as if there is no danger. You'll get hurt sooner or later. If I were ever hanged for being a witch, they would want to hang my friends, too."

"They won't do that!"

Meg put her hands on his shoulders, and when Colin looked up he saw concern in her eyes. "You will be hurt, Colin, and I wish I could stop it. But all of us get hurt. As the Bible says, 'Man is born unto trouble, as the sparks fly upward.'"

Meg's words made Colin feel uncomfortable, and he changed the subject, saying, "Let's cook the turkey."

"Right you are, boy! Go bring that turkey in, and we'll have a feast!"

Colin had eaten enough of the turkey to make him somewhat overfull, then he left, knowing his parents would worry if he were late. He was almost home when he saw two boys. They were standing around something, and when he got closer, he saw they were tormenting a bird that was apparently wounded.

Without thinking, Colin moved forward. He did not know the boys, but they looked rough. He said quickly, "Please don't hurt that bird."

The taller of the two had a blunt, cruel face. "Where do you get off telling us what to do? You get out of here or I'll break your face!"

Colin was afraid of the two, but when he saw the injured bird, something turned over in his heart. "Don't hurt it anymore."

"What will you give us?" demanded the smaller of the two, a thin boy with a fox face.

"I've got some money. You can have that."

"All right, let's have the coin," the taller boy said.

Colin handed over the coins, and the larger of the two took them, then laughed. "Now we have the money, and we'll do with the bird as we want." He turned around and poked the bird again with a stick. Suddenly anger filled Colin, and he threw himself at the larger boy. He had no experience with fighting, and immediately something struck him in the back of the head and he felt blows landing all over his body. He kicked and tried to defend himself, but he didn't cry out.

Finally the blows stopped, and he heard the larger boy say, "Now, you mind your own business!" He laughed and said, "Come on, Sid. Leave the bird lover alone."

Slowly, Colin got to his feet. His face was bleeding, and he was sore from the punches he had taken. He ignored the pain, reached down, and picked up the bird. He started for home, talking to the bird, saying, "You'll be okay. Don't you worry . . ."

Adam Winslow was not only large and strong, but he had a persuasive manner about him. Somehow he had wrangled permission from his parents to allow him to go on a voyage with Sir Francis Drake. Now he stood before his parents and Sir Francis, his face alight with excitement. "I'm so thankful to you, Sir Francis, for allowing me to go with you."

"Why, lad, I'm not sure I'm doing you a favor."

"Oh yes, sir! It's what I want more that anything in the world!"

Sir Francis turned to Adam's parents and said, "Stoneybook, you know the dangers, as do you, ma'am. I'll take care of the boy as best I can, but I can't guarantee his safety."

"I'm sure you'll do your best, Sir Francis," Brandon said.

"I'll be all right, Father, and Mother, you must not worry about me. No stranger can get the better of Sir Francis Drake! He is a Seahawk, you know!"

"Yes, I know," Brandon said. He bit his lip and turned to study the visitor. Drake was not a very large man, but there was something in his eyes that was almost magical. They glowed with excitement. Brandon had kept up with Drake's exploits, as had practically everyone in England. Drake had taken small ships on raids and stolen riches from the Spanish treasure ships in the coastal towns in Spain. The Spanish king was incensed with rage and vowed that Drake would never do it again.

"You have made the king of Spain very unhappy, Sir Francis. Won't that make it more dangerous?" Brandon asked.

"I trust the good Lord to keep me safe, sir, but the voyage will be dangerous."

"I'm not afraid, Sir Francis!" Adam said pridefully.

"Well, it's up to your parents. You may be gone for as long as a year."

"What does the queen say to this?" Brandon asked.

"She is trying to stay friendly with Spain in case France wants to declare war." Drake smiled, and his entire face lit up. "She is a crafty one, our queen is! She wants no trouble with

Spain, but when I raid them she doesn't turn down her share of the treasure." His face suddenly grew solemn, and he shook his head. "One of these days we are going to have to fight Spain. I want to help train men who will drive them from the seas." He moved forward and put his hand on Adam's shoulder. "You will have a hard time, my boy. We all did, growing up at sea, but you'll become a wonderful sailor."

"I want that more than anything!" Adam said.

Brandon and Eden were troubled. They had given Adam permission, but now they were reluctant to face the absence of their son. As Drake was speaking of his plans, Colin came in. Eden was shocked to see that his face was bloody, and he was holding something in his arms. "What in the world happened to you?"

"Nothing, Mother."

"Don't be foolish," Brandon snapped. "You've been beaten."

"I'm all right, sir, but this bird is hurt with a broken wing. I think I can cure it."

Eden said quickly, "That is kind of you, to try to save the bird."

Adam asked, "How did you get beaten up?"

"Well, two boys were poking the bird. I tried to stop them, but I wasn't able to do much."

Adam was disgusted. "You can't take care of yourself, Colin. You need to learn how to fight."

"I don't want to."

Eden stepped in and stopped the argument. "Tell your brother what you are going to do, Adam."

"I'm going to sea with Sir Francis Drake!"

Eden watched Colin, for she could tell something was not right.

He said nothing, just studied the bird he carried.

"Come along, Son, and I'll get you cleaned up." They left at once and went to a room where the medicine was kept. While Eden was dressing his wounds, she asked, "What's wrong? You look sad, Colin. I think it was a fine thing you did. I'm proud that you have compassion for weak and helpless things."

"I wish I were more like Adam and Father."

"God made you different, Colin, and you must strive to become what God wants you to be, whatever that is!"

5

November 2, 1578

"**I** hate London!"

Colin had spoken unthinkingly, and now he turned to see a smile on his father's face. "Do you like London, Father?"

"No, I don't, Son, but we have to come here from time to time to take care of things. We just have to put up with the noise and the stench and the hordes of people. It's a big city."

As they made their way down a cobblestone street, Brandon saw to it that they walked as close to the shops as possible. Overhead, almost all of the shops had apartments for the owners of the businesses. Many of the shop owners had the nasty habit of throwing garbage and night soil out the window. The safest thing was to walk under the overhanging structure, but of course that meant you met people coming from the opposite way. This caused a constant struggle and sometimes resulted in cursing, accompanied by pushing and shoving.

The streets were punctuated by narrow alleys that could barely fit two pedestrians along them. Sign boards for almost every business hung almost nine feet off the ground. In theory, this would allow a man on horse to pass under. Colin kept his eyes on one of the signs that had paintings of Cupid and a torch.

"What does that mean, Father?"

"That's the sign of a glazier, Son. That one there with the cradle? That means a basket maker. And see that one with the elephant? That's where ivory and other things can be bought."

As the two moved among the throngs, Colin wanted to put his hands over his ears. The heavy vehicles clattered loudly on the street, which was barely fourteen feet wide. At times it became narrower, and then a shouting match proceeded. Iron wheels crashed and screeched over the uneven cobblestones. Horses were whinnying, dogs barking, and the geese driven down to market were making their honk-honk noise. Cats howled, singing birds chirped, and pigeons cooed on the roof. Street vendors yelled their advertising slogans, and from the windows came the sounds of loud conversations. "It is so *noisy*, Father!"

"It is, after the quiet of Stoneybrook. All big cities have such clamor. It's true, Son, there's not much to like about London, but it's the only place to go for some things."

Colin did not answer. He himself liked the woods and forest—and especially the towering oaks and yew trees that sur-rounded Stoneybrook.

Brandon suddenly gave Colin an affectionate glance, saying, "Well, Son, you're sixteen years old today. Do you feel like an old man?"

"I don't feel any different today than I did yesterday. I've always thought a fellow should feel some difference when he be-comes a year older overnight, but I never do."

"When you're a young fellow the years seem to drag by. But when you grow old, they fly by faster than a falcon." Brandon stopped and gestured toward a small shop. "Here's where we'll get your new clothes."

"I don't need any new clothes."

"Of course you do! You've been wearing Adam's hand-me-downs for too long, and they never did fit you." Adam had been bigger and broader in almost every aspect, so his castaway clothing made Colin look slightly ridiculous. "The tailor will fit you just right. Come now, don't sulk!"

"Let me have a look at you." Brandon examined Colin carefully, then smiled with approval. "You look like a prince, Colin. And you've grown a lot in the two years since we visited the queen."

Colin squirmed uneasily. He was wearing the new clothing the tailor had made, which included a padded doublet with full sleeves. The shirt beneath the doublet was pure white, and the britches were in the full Venetian style. Many men padded these garments to make them look full, but Colin had stubbornly resisted this, so now the britches simply fell, lying flat against the lower part of his body. He wore light blue stockings with gaiters just below the knee. The new leather shoes with pointed toes hurt his feet, and he muttered, "I feel like a fool!"

"You'll fit right in at court. You're growing up fine, Colin."

"I'll never be as big as you or Adam."

"Maybe not, but size isn't the best measure of a man. You're just right for a young fellow of sixteen." Indeed, Colin was trim and slender, whereas Adam was bulky with heavy muscles. Colin's lighter weight had made a fine runner out of him. The one thing he could beat Adam at was foot racing; indeed, he had beaten all the boys of the village and some of the grown men. His hair was chestnut in color, crisp and tending to curl, which annoyed him. He was wearing a soft crowned bonnet with a narrow brim. Now he tugged at it, muttering, "Who needs a fancy hat like this?"

"No more complaining now, Colin." The two made their way to the palace where Queen Elizabeth was holding court. As soon as they arrived, Brandon sent his name in and the servant came back after a considerable wait, saying, "It will take a little time, my lord, but the queen will see you."

"Thank you." Brandon turned and said, "Colin, I have to go see a man who owns some property that adjoins ours. I want to lease it. You wait right here."

"What will I do if he comes to take me to the queen?"

"You go right with him, and keep the queen entertained until I get back." Brandon smiled. "You can just charm her with your fine manners and handsome clothing."

Colin shook his head stubbornly. "I don't think I could charm a queen."

"You never know until you try. Besides, you've charmed Queen Mary, so you've got the hang of the thing."

Colin shrugged and watched as Brandon left. He felt ill at ease in the palace. For a time he paced nervously. Then his eyes fell on two young women, no doubt ladies in Elizabeth's court. He had seen some like them on his previous visits. Now he saw that they were whispering to each other and giggling. The two offered a contrast, for one was tall and blond with a thin figure, while the other was short and chubby. They approached him and said, "Good morrow, sir."

"Good morrow, ladies," Colin said and bowed stiffly.

"You are waiting to see the queen?"

"Yes, I am."

"Well, you can tell us about yourself, then. My name is Cora." The speaker was the tall blonde, who had an inviting look in her blue eyes. The shorter woman had dark hair and a mark on her cheek. "And I'm Caroline," she smiled. "Are you coming to stay at court and serve the queen?"

"No, I'm here on a visit with my father."

The two girls moved closer to him and Colin felt hemmed

in. He had no experience with ladies of nobility, and the two began to tease him.

"Tell us about your love life," Caroline said.

"I—I don't have any."

Both women laughed and Cora moved closer. "That will have to change. You need a woman to teach you about courtship."

The two were obviously experienced and Colin wished desperately that they would go away. The talk went on for some time, but then Colin saw Caroline wince and touch her arm. "Is something wrong, lady?"

"I spilled some hot grease on my arm and the burn still hurts!"

"Let me see." Colin looked at the forearm when she pulled her sleeve up. "I have something that will ease the pain, if you'll just wait right here." He turned quickly and left, walking to where the horses were tied. He rummaged through his saddlebag until he found a soft leather pouch. He hurried back inside and found the two girls still waiting. "I think this will help," he said and removed from the pouch what looked like a tiny twig with thick leaves. "Let me put this on your burns." The young woman tentatively put her arm out. Colin squeezed the plant, and when a few drops came out he moved the leaf over the burn.

"Oh, that is wonderful! It stopped the pain!" Caroline exclaimed. "Are you a physician, sir?"

"No, it is magic." Cora smiled.

"Are you a magician, then?"

"Oh, not at all!"

"Well, it works wonders!"

She moved closer to Colin and whispered, "Surely I must find some way to show my gratitude." Colin tried to think of an excuse that did not sound childish or impolite, but only managed to sputter a meaningless phrase or two. He was relieved to see his father appear and smile at him.

"Well, Colin, are you making friends at court?"

"This—this young lady had a burn and I wanted to help her."

"He did, sir," Caroline gushed. "He must be a physician."

Brandon laughed as the two women stood flirting with Colin. Then the uniformed servant appeared and said, "The queen will see you now."

"You must come and look after my injury," Caroline smiled. "I'll be watching for you." Colin did not answer, but as soon as they were out of earshot, Brandon said, "You'd better be careful of these women at court. They're not good company for a proper young man. Remember what Proverbs says about women who trap men?"

"Yes, sir, I remember. It's in the fifth chapter. 'For the lips of the adulterous woman drip honey, and her speech is smoother than oil; but in the end she is bitter as gall, sharp as a double-edged sword. Her feet go down to death; her steps lead straight to the grave.'" Colin proceeded to recite the entire chapter from the Bible dealing with the adulterous woman.

Brandon, as always, was amazed at the prodigious memory of his son. "You might do well to become a lawyer, Colin. You have such a memory you could quote cases going back to William the Conqueror."

"Oh, no, sir! I would rather not be a lawyer."

"You have to do something. You must have some profession."

Colin looked at his father and smiled. "Well, maybe God will show me what to do."

"Good boy! I trust that he will." Brandon started to say more, but they were approached by a tall man who had an air of authority. His dark eyes seemed to see everything.

"Lord Stoneybrook, the queen wishes to see you alone." He smiled and added, "I will keep your son company until you are finished."

"Thank you. Son, this is Sir Francis Walsingham, one of the

queen's closest advisors. This is my younger son, Colin, Sir Francis."

Colin bowed and said, "I am happy to meet you, sir."

Walsingham said, "Come with me, Mister Winslow, and we'll have something to drink. Do you like wine?"

"Yes, my lord, I do."

Colin followed Walsingham to a room, and Walsingham picked up a flagon, filled two silver cups, and smiled. "I hope you like it."

Colin took a sip. "It's very good, sir."

"I know your brother, Adam. Sir Francis Drake informs me that he is becoming an exceptional sailor."

"Yes, sir, he's always been good at things like that. I-I'll never be the man that he is, and certainly not the man my father is. I'm not much good with a sword, and I never could handle a lance as Adam does."

"England is in need of such men—but many men can handle a sword. What our country needs most is men with brains." Colin saw that the man's deep-set eyes were fixed on him with a dark intensity. It made him uncomfortable, and he felt much as he did when he was in Queen Mary's presence— that he was being examined not only outwardly, but inwardly as well.

"Do you know what I do, Colin?" Walsingham asked abruptly.

"Not really, sir."

Walsingham laughed, "Everyone else seems to know. I protect the queen."

"But you don't even have a sword!"

"No, I depend on weapons that are stronger than a sword. I surround the queen with men who are excellent soldiers. They all have swords, but there are other dangers."

"I don't understand, Sir Francis."

"In this country, Colin, there are men who would harm our

queen. If they are not stopped, they will send assassins to murder Her Majesty. My job is to find out who these men are and arrest them before they can attack her. For this, Master Colin, I must have men who are intelligent, who know how to listen and watch for things. You, for example, might be a young man who could serve the queen in this fashion."

Colin was shocked "Me, sir? I would not be good at a thing like that!"

"You go with your father to visit Mary, Queen of Scots?"

"Yes, sir, I do."

"You could watch and listen. Many would like to see Elizabeth removed so Mary could assume her throne. I can't be there to watch Mary in person. She would know at once that I am suspicious of her. But she would not be on her guard against a young man like yourself. You have visited her quite a few times, have you not?"

"My father has taken me four times. He has taken the rest of my family to visit her too."

"Does the queen seem friendly?"

"Yes, sir. I believe she is lonely."

Walsingham laughed. "She's not lonely, Mister Winslow. She is surrounded by her own servants and loyal friends. Now it might be that you would hear something or see something that would help me protect our queen."

"But—I would not know what to look for."

"Perhaps not, but if I told you what to look for, you would understand, wouldn't you?"

Colin felt the intensity of Walsingham's gaze and protested, "But sir, I can't betray a queen!"

"Not even to save your true queen?" Walsingham had a persuasive manner. He continued to speak of how important it was that traitors be found before they attacked the queen. Despite himself, Colin was deeply fascinated by this powerful man, but he still felt relieved when his father returned and said, "The queen would like to see you, Colin, but she has many more important meetings."

"This is a fine son you have, Lord Stoneybrook," Walsingham smiled. "I've been explaining how our service to the queen works. Perhaps you would speak to him on how he might help protect Queen Elizabeth."

Brandon shifted uneasily, and Walsingham observed this shrewdly. "I know it is not a thing to your liking. You would rather fight with a sword. But what I desire is to see the queen protected *before* an attack. Think about it, both of you." He bowed and left without another word.

"We must go, Colin." As soon as they were out of the palace, Brandon asked, "What did you two talk about?"

"He wants me to spy on Queen Mary."

"That's what I have been doing for some time now."

"Why do you do that, Father?"

"Because Elizabeth has asked me to, and though I don't like it, I agreed."

"Do you want me to spy on Queen Mary?"

Brandon hesitated and then, with a touch of sadness, said, "We must do all we can to protect our sovereign. Think about it, Colin. It won't be difficult. All you have to do is to watch what goes on, who comes and goes—and keep your ears tuned to any talk about treason."

"I will, sir!"

For three days Colin thought of little else other than his conversation with Sir Francis Walsingham. Finally, in despair, he went to Meg's house. He found her cooking lamb in a stewpot. She grinned at him, saying, "You must have quite a nose, boy. You always come when I am cooking."

"You're a fine cook, Meg." Colin sat down on a bench and watched her, and the two talked for some time. Finally, Colin said, "Meg, you remember I told you that one of our maids was very sick?"

"So you told me. Alice, you said her name was. What was wrong with her?"

"A pain in her stomach. It kept getting worse and worse. Three days after she got sick she died. Nothing the doctors gave her made her better."

"Some things can't be cured by herbs, boy. A broken leg, for example. No medicine will cure that."

Colin was quiet for some time and then said, "I wonder what was wrong with Alice."

Meg looked over at him and, without saying anything else, scooped the meat into two carved wooden platters and motioned for Colin to eat. Colin took a large spoonful of the stew, then said abruptly, "But there must have been *some* way to find out what was wrong with her."

"There *is* a way. You have to look inside and see what looks bad."

Colin was shocked. "Why, you can't look inside a person!"

"Why not? You look inside birds and animals all the time"

"But—that's different!"

"Really not so different. Last month Giles Henderson sent for me to treat his sick cow. He didn't know what was wrong with her, of course. I reached in through her elimination tract and found a growth. I told him about it and offered to cut it out. The foolish fellow wouldn't hear of it, so the cow died."

"You mean if someone had cut Alice open they might have found a growth like that?"

"It is possible."

Colin thought, *Maybe Meg is a witch! Only a witch would think of such a thing.* The very thought of cutting open a human being brought a chill to him. He had grown accustomed to opening animals, snakes, and birds, but this was completely different. He asked thoughtfully, "Have you ever done such a thing? Cut into someone?"

Meg's eyes gleamed and then she laughed, a high-pitched

cackle. "It's against the law, boy. If I said yes, you could have me hanged!"

Colin ate his stew, knowing that he would find out more about cutting into people from Meg, but he changed the subject. "Meg, there is a man of the court, a servant of the queen; his name is Walsingham."

"Yes. Everybody knows him. He's a clever man, he is, and the queen trusts him as she trusts no other—except for Lord Burghley."

"He wants me to spy on Queen Mary and report to him."

"And that's something you don't fancy?"

"I don't want to be a spy."

"We all have to do things we don't like sometimes. Here, have some more meat."

"No, I've had plenty." Colin set his bowl down on the table, and reaching into his inner pocket, came out with a small pouch. "I got a present for you when I was in London."

"A present?" Meg stared at the leather bag. "For old Meg?"

"You are not old, Meg. Yes, it's for you."

Meg put her bowl down, took the small leather pouch, and opened the drawstring. She turned the pouch upside down and then stood staring at the pearl earrings that glowed with a life of their own. "You bought these for me? Why, they're too fine for me, boy!"

"No, they're not."

Meg looked up and Colin saw tears in her eyes. She whispered, "Thank you, Colin, and believe this, when I'm buried, I'll be wearin' these!"

November passed quickly, but not a day went by that Colin did not think of two things: Francis Walsingham's offer and Meg's hint that opening up a body was not an impossible thing. Two weeks before Christmas, Colin was in his room dissecting a mouse. He heard his name called, and stepping outside he saw his father looking up the stairs. "Come downstairs, Colin. There is someone I want you to meet."

Colin went downstairs and Brandon led him to his study, where his mother and a gentleman were waiting. The man was small, with delicate mild features. He was smooth shaven and had a pair of close-set brown eyes. "This is Mister John Chadburn, Colin. He's the master at Oxford. Mr. Chadburn, this is our son Colin."

"I'm most pleased to meet you, Master Winslow, and to give you an early welcome to Oxford."

Brandon saw the expression change on Colin's face and said quickly, "Your mother and I have decided to send you there to study."

Colin felt his heart go cold. "But I don't want to go, sir!"

"You can't stay here the rest of your life. Mr. Chadburn will help you."

As soon as Colin left the room, Chadburn said, "The boy's not happy, Lord Stoneybrook."

"No, he is apprehensive."

"How does he do with his studies?"

"Outstanding! He is brilliant and has a memory such as you have never seen. But he is somewhat difficult. He can't seem to find his place."

Eden had said little during the interview, but now she came over and took Brandon's arm. "I know it is necessary, Brandon, but it breaks my heart. Colin's not like Adam. He is a gentle young man."

Chadburn tried to make them feel better. "I will watch out for him as best I can. But you should know, scholars there can be hard on new boys."

"It's that way in the army and everywhere else," Brandon said heavily. "He must learn to be strong—to stand on his own two feet." Brandon gripped Eden's hand and said, "I know you don't like this, dear, but I think it is essential now."

Eden did not answer. She dropped her eyes and quietly murmured, "I know. We'll miss him, but he needs to learn where his life is going to take him."

"Oxford is a place for young men who haven't found their calling," Chadburn said. "I'm certain that your son will find his way."

6

January 15, 1579

The sun was shining with a sidereal brilliance over the spires of Oxford, but the beauty of the university meant nothing to young Colin Winslow. He stood uncertainly in his student garb, watching as his father rode away and finally disappeared into the distance. Colin fought down a desperate longing to run after him. *It wouldn't do any good—I've begged them for weeks not to send me to this place.* He didn't know a soul there, and when he glanced at the throngs of students laughing and talking loudly, a sense of loneliness and fear paralyzed him.

"Well, now, you must be new."

Colin turned quickly and found himself facing a tall, husky young man wearing the black gown that marked him as a student. Locks of tawny hair escaped the black mortarboard that he wore tilted at a sharp angle.

"Yes, sir, this is my first day. I'm Colin Winslow."

"I'm Knox Traverson. Welcome to Oxford. I suppose you're glad to be here?"

"Not really, sir."

Traverson blinked with surprised. "I'm surprised to hear that, Winslow—and you don't have to call me 'sir.' You know, most of us couldn't wait to get out from under the rule of our parents."

"I liked it at home."

"Well, you'll like it here after you get settled in. Are you headed for a class?"

"Yes. Latin."

Knox smiled. "The first form, I take it? We'll go together. I've failed the blasted course twice already. Come along, we're already a little late."

Colin had to hurry to keep up with Traverson's long paces and when they turned to enter one of the ivy-covered buildings, he asked, "Is the master hard?"

"A demon! He assumes every one of his students is an idiot—and in some cases, he's not far off. Step lively, now!"

The two entered a large room illuminated by beams of light from high windows. Colin's glance took in the dozen or so students, then focused on the master. He felt his arm grasped firmly as Traverson pulled him up to the bulky man, who stared at him with a pair of gimlet eyes. "Professor Biddle, this is a new scholar for you. His name is Colin Winslow."

"Ah, Winslow, is it?" Biddle had deep growl of a voice and examined Colin for a long moment before demanding, "You're the son of Baron Winslow of Stoneybrook?"

"Yes, sir."

"Well, I've found that the sons of earls and dukes and barons are just as empty-headed as the sons of butchers. Your father's title won't get you any credit with me!"

Colin was speechless. Then, feeling Knox's grip pulling him away, he went at once to a place at one of the long tables. One of the scholars was a hulking fellow with muddy brown eyes. He leaned over to whisper, "The Honorable Mr. Winslow, is it? We'll have some fun with this one, Simon!"

"He looks like a plucked chicken, don't he, Ives?" The speaker was a thin individual with hazel eyes and a smirk on his narrow lips. He glared at Colin, saying, "You know what I'm thinking? I'm thinking you won't make it here."

Knox said shortly, "Ives, put a lid on it—and you too, Simon."

"You have much to say, Mr. Traverson," Biddle's voice cut into the silence. "Suppose you amaze us by translating this line: *'Emas, non quod opus est, sed quod necesse est: quod non opus est, asse carum est.'*"

Colin glanced at Knox and saw that he was at a total loss.

"I—I think it's something about—about a dog," Knox stammered.

"You are as ignorant as ever, Traverson!" Biddle snapped. "But I am sure Mr. Lofton can enlighten us."

Lofton, Colin saw, was the hulking fellow to his right—and his face was a blank.

"No? Why does that not surprise me? What about you, Mr. Simon Matthews? No? I thought not! You are three dunces! You will each translate fifty lines to be handed in tomorrow!"

Biddle glared around the room and informed his pupils that they were as ignorant a crew as ever drew breath. Finally his eyes fell on Colin and he snarled, "Well, Winslow, I don't have any hope that you are any different from your fellow clowns. Can you translate just one word of the quotation which your fellows cannot?"

Colin rose and said, "Yes, sir, I think I can."

Biddle stared at Colin in disbelief, then snapped, "I suppose I must give you the lines again?"

"No, sir, I remember them," Colin said. " 'Buy not what you can use, but what you cannot do without. What you do not need is dear at any price.'"

Biddle stared at Colin as if the young man had fallen from the moon into his classroom. He cleared his throat and asked, "And do you happen to know who is the author of the lines?"

"I believe it was Cato, sir." Colin felt a touch on his leg and looked over to see a frown on Traverson's face, and when he nodded slightly, Colin turned to see that both Ives Lofton and

Simon Matthews were glaring at him with hatred in their eyes. *I shouldn't have answered the professor! But—it's too late to take it back.*

"Well, now, Winslow. How old are you?"

"Sixteen, sir."

"Now how does it happen that you are a Latin scholar?"

"My father loves Latin, sir, and he taught me."

"Hmmm. Well, evidently Lord Stoneybrook is a fine teacher. You don't belong in this form, but in a much higher one. However, I will keep you here, young man. You will give me some relief from the abysmal ignorance in this class. You will assist the duller fellows—especially my three pets, Mr. Traverson, Mr. Ives, and Mr. Matthews."

"But, sir, I don't feel—"

Biddle cut off Colin's protest with a chop of his meaty hand. "You will do as I say, Mr. Winslow! In the church and elsewhere you will obey God, but in this class you will obey *me!*"

The remainder of the time in the classroom was torture for Colin. Professor Biddle used him as a weapon to humiliate any student who faltered, and by the time Biddle dismissed the class, Colin had no hope that he would ever have a friend in Latin One.

Simon Matthews stood and glared at Colin. "You'll be sorry you made the rest of us look bad." He turned and left, and Colin turned to Traverson. "I guess I made a mistake, didn't I?"

"Yes, but it's too late to try to look dumb. Just stay away from Simon and Ives as best you can."

"I hate that fellow! He's been here two months, and he's made us look like clods!" Ives Lofton shot a glance of hatred at Colin Winslow, who was walking across the commons with Knox Traverson. "I'd like to slit his bloody throat!"

"We can't do that, Lofton," Simon Matthews said. He had been leaning against one of the columns that supported a walkway, but he straightened up, and his eyes followed the pair as they entered a two-story building covered with ivy. "The fellow isn't worth hanging for, but I've had enough of him. Thinks he's somebody special! He's got all the faculty fooled, even Master Chadburn. The old fool is so proud of Winslow, always pointing him out as just what an Oxford man ought to be."

"I say we catch him out after dark, Matthews, and beat him so bad he won't be able to walk." Lofton's eyes gleamed as he took pleasure in describing ways to hurt young Winslow. "We can wear masks, and nobody will know it was us who did it."

"No, it's too risky. Everybody knows we hate him. We'd be the first ones they'd look for." A sly smile crossed Matthews's face. "I've been thinking about a way to get at him, and I think I've got it."

Lofton grinned, "You always were one for planning, Simon. What's the scheme?"

"It'll take a little acting on our part, Ives, but if we play it right, we'll fix Winslow good! Now, here's what we do . . ."

Colin had been at Oxford for two months, and the early misery had faded to some extent. He had been shocked to discover how easy the studies were—at least for him. His phenomenal memory served him well, and he excelled in all his classes. But he missed being in the woods, and next to his family he missed Meg Caradoc most. He had not realized how fond of Meg he had become, and he determined to see her as soon as vacation came.

The first month had been the hardest, for some of the older students could not forgive him for earning good marks so easily. But his quiet ways and lack of pride made a difference, and he made a point of helping those who were struggling. Some of the older students had made life hard for Colin, but he expected this. Lofton and Matthews had been the worst of his tormentors, but it seemed that lately even they had mitigated their efforts to hurt him. Knox Traverson was his best friend, and the two of them spent much time together.

He knew that he would never love Oxford, and he had no clue as to what he would do with his life. He had no preference for any of the professions that a young man should choose. He hated the idea of the law and had no inclination for the church. Some young men went into the army, but Colin knew himself unfit for that life.

The choice of a profession pressed on Colin greatly, and one afternoon he made his way to the large fountains that threw up a beautiful spray, the drops glittering like jewels as they caught the gleams of the sun. He sat down on a stone bench and watched the huge crimson carp as they swam lazily in the green water. He suddenly wished that he could catch one and dissect it, but he knew that for him that time had passed.

"Well, Winslow, what's happening with you?"

Startled, Colin looked up to see Simon Matthews standing close by. "Why, nothing much. Just thinking." Colin spoke nervously, for it was possible that Simon might push him into the fishpond.

"Mind if I join you?"

"Why, no, not at all."

Simon sat down and stared at the fish. "Those are the biggest carp I've ever seen. Do you have fish like that on your grounds at home?"

"We do have a large pond, but the fish aren't as large as these." Colin kept his eyes on Matthews, but it seemed for once he was in a good humor.

"Winslow, I've got a confession to make. I'm not very good at admitting I've been wrong, but I've been wrong about you."

Colin stared at him and asked, "What do you mean?"

"Well, I've been too hard on you. Most new boys go through a certain amount of initiation, but Lofton and I have gone too far. The truth is, a lot of us are jealous of you. Most of us work ourselves into the ground just to get by, and you manage all the studies so easily! I've been wrong, and I hope you won't hold it against me."

"Of course not."

"Well, we are going to make it up to you, me and Lofton. We are going to take you out to watch a play. There is a traveling one that I thought you might like."

"I really don't—"

"No protest, now! Lofton and I have talked about it. The play is a good one, and we'd like to go tonight. It's going on at the old theater just north of the university. You have yourself ready, put on some good clothes. Who knows, we may find ourselves some good female company!"

Colin desperately tried to think of a way to refuse the invitation, but he knew he could not. "All right. I'll be ready."

All that day Colin worried about going anywhere with Matthews and Lofton. He mentioned this to Traverson, who said, "I wouldn't go if I were you, Winslow. They are always getting into trouble. They'll drag you down with them."

"I guess I'll have to go."

"Well, don't let them get you drunk. That's all I can say."

Staying sober was Colin's plan, but when they left the campus and headed toward the theater at the edge of Oxford, Matthews said, "We're too early. Let's get something to eat, and maybe some good ale."

Colin protested, but Lofton and Matthews laughed and took him to a tavern called The Blue Elephant. They were greeted by a barmaid they introduced as Dolly Bly. Matthews said, "This is a fine new scholar at the university, Dolly. I want you to be especially nice to him."

Dolly Bly was an overblown young woman wearing too much makeup. Her dress was cut lower than any Colin had ever seen. "Why, of course I'll make him welcome, Mr. Matthews, you can be sure of that!"

"Fine! Now bring us something to drink."

That was the beginning, and although Colin tried his best to avoid getting drunk, he was forced to drink a great deal. He was not accustomed to it, and soon he felt his legs were going dead and his lips were so numb he couldn't speak clearly. Finally they went to the play, but he remembered little about it. By the time it was over, he could scarcely walk.

"We will have a little more ale," Matthews said, "and then we will go back."

"I don't think I can have another drink . . . ," Colin protested. His protests were in vain. He was led back to the tavern, where he drank until he passed out.

While Colin was slumped in a chair at the tavern, Matthews moved to the bar and grinned at the barmaid. "Dolly, we're going to play a little joke on Winslow—and you have to help us. We want to put him in your bed, and then you undress and get into the bed with him."

"He is a nice enough young chap. Why would I do that?"

"Because I say so, and because I am paying you."

"Paying me? Well, now, that's business!" Dolly grinned. "Just playing a joke, is it? I've always liked jokes. Bring 'im up."

The charade went off very well. Lofton and Matthews carried Colin upstairs, took his clothes off, and threw him into bed. Dolly stripped down to her shift, but suddenly demanded, "What's the joke? I don't see one."

"There'll be a man coming, and when he sees his prize scholar in this condition, he'll have a fit!"

"And what will 'appen to this poor lad?"

"Oh, nothing serious. He's a friend of ours, Dolly. We wouldn't do him any real harm."

Leaving Dolly's room, Matthews went downstairs and found Lofton talking with a blunt-featured man. "All right, Madison, do you have it straight?" he demanded.

"No problem. You got the cash?"

"Here's two sovereigns. Two more after you've done the job. Tell me again what you're to do."

"Go to the master, John Chadburn, and tell him one of his prize scholars is about to ruin a young woman. Then I brings him back 'ere, and I takes 'im to Dolly's room."

"See you do it, then!"

Colin awakened with a horrible headache and a man yelling at him. He opened his eyes to see the master, Mr. John Chadburn, standing over him. "I am shocked, Mr. Winslow! Shocked! Such behavior! And I am sure your parents will be as well!"

Colin stared around wildly and couldn't understand what happened to him. He tried to speak, but his lips seemed to be frozen.

"You want us to take him back to the university, Mr. Chadburn?" The voice came from Colin's left. He turned to see Simon Matthews there, a grin plastered on his face. "I hated to inform on you, Winslow, but we were afraid you would get into trouble with the law. Making threats the way you were and trying to attack Miss Dolly here."

"That's right, sir," Dolly piped up. She had pulled the sheet up to cover herself, and seemed to be overplaying her role. "I almost lost my innocence, sir!"

John Chadburn stared at the barmaid and knew something was terribly wrong here. But the evidence was insurmountable. "I will take him back myself, Mr. Matthews. Get dressed, Winslow."

Somehow, Colin was able to scramble into his clothes and left The Blue Elephant. He was placed in a carriage, sitting next to Mr. Chadburn. When Chadburn demanded, "How do you account for your behavior, Winslow?" Colin could only mumble, "I don't know, sir." Colin did know, but he was aware that he would never convince the master that he had been tricked.

"You are on the strictest probation, Winslow, with all privileges revoked—and your parents will be informed. You are a shame and a disgrace to them and to this university!"

Colin looked out of the carriage window, and the night was no darker than his soul at that moment.

January had come and gone, bringing snow, then February brought even colder weather. Colin had endured the harsh rebukes of his father and the taunts of his fellow students. He had borne the restrictions of his probation without protest. Traverson had stuck close to him through it all, saying, "Let them have their fun, Colin; it'll all be forgotten."

"I won't forget it!"

"You might as well. We all have things that we have to forget."

Colin threw himself into his work. He had no trouble with his studies; indeed, he continued to thrive academically. Finally he was taken off probation, and the first thing he did was dress warmly and leave the halls of Oxford. He walked until he reached some woods a good two miles away. As he entered them, a peace seemed to enter his soul. When the sun dipped down in the west, he reluctantly turned his steps back toward Oxford. Just as he reached the border of the forest, he found a squirrel that had evidently died of natural causes. Memories of how he had dissected many animals when he was home came to him. An impulse took him, and he pulled out his knife and began cutting it open. He did not know what he was looking for, but it was something he had done for a long time. He was shocked when a voice came from right behind him: "What are you doing, boy?"

Colin whirled and saw a tall man somewhat bowed with age, who looked somewhat like a crane. His silver hair was wild, looking as if it had never been brushed, and his beard was scraggly. He had piercing hazel eyes, a beak of a nose, and bushy eyebrows. "What are you doing to that animal?"

"Why—nothing, sir."

"You're cutting up that squirrel!"

"It was already dead, sir. I just wanted to—"

"Wanted to what?"

"I wanted to see what he was like on the inside."

"What's your name, boy?"

"Colin Winslow, sir."

"An Oxford student, are you? I've heard of you. You are the one who got drunk and debauched a young barmaid." He cackled in a strange high pitch. "I did not think that was possible— to debauch a barmaid! Most of them are debauched from the beginning."

Colin had nothing to say. He had heard enough about it. "May I ask your name, sir?"

"I am Doctor Phineas Teague."

Suddenly a fragment of a conversation concerning this man, a teacher at Oxford, came to mind. *He's a physician and he's crazy. Why, he told a group of doctors that Galen doesn't have a clue about medicine!*

"You are a physician, sir?"

"I am a little bit of that and a little bit of something else."

The old man moved forward and began to point out the various inner parts of the squirrel. Taking the knife away from Colin, he opened the animal further and explained its inner workings to the young student with what seemed like pure joy. When he finished, he said, "You like to cut up beasts, do you, Winslow?"

"Yes, sir, I've always done it."

"Why do you think you do it?"

Colin could not think of a proper answer. "Because I want to understand how things live and how they work."

"So do I, Winslow, so do I! Do you like life at Oxford?"

"No, not very much, Dr. Teague."

"What do you intend to make of yourself—a lawyer?"

"No, sir, not that. I don't have any idea what I can do. I think my parents sent me here to find myself, but I'm as lost as ever! Sometimes I feel like a man who's in the middle of a bridge, and I've forgotten both ends of it. I'm just standing there, looking down at the river and not knowing which way to go."

Teague stared at Colin silently, then said, "I've heard some of the professors talking about you. They say you never forget anything."

"Oh, I'm sure I forget some things."

Teague frowned, and Colin expected him to walk away. He was shocked when Teague said, "Winslow, I would like you to study with me. I will arrange it with Mr. Chadburn."

Immediately, Colin brightened. "Could you teach me about things like this?" He motioned to the squirrel.

"I can teach you if you want to learn. Come along, we'll walk back together and I'll talk to Chadburn when we get there."

Colin's chance encounter with Dr. Teague transformed his life. He had doubted whether Teague could persuade Mr. Chadburn to allow him to study under him, for all the talk he had heard about Teague was negative. Some of the professors laughed at Teague, but he was so brilliant that they could not afford to let him go. Teague was demanding and did not suffer a fool gladly, but he soon discovered that Colin was an apt student. They did dissections every day after Colin's scholarly work was finished. Teague was pleased to learn the gossip was right: Colin never forgot anything!

Teague had a house on the outskirts of the woods where Colin had first met him, and despite rules to the contrary, the old man often kept Colin overnight. He sometimes shouted at Colin when he made a mistake, but Colin didn't mind, for he was learning about something he loved. He was shocked on one of his overnight visits when he was awakened from a sound sleep. He sat up, and a hand was placed over his mouth. "Winslow, you are coming with me. Put your clothes on, and be quiet about it."

"Where are we going?"

"Get dressed!"

Colin scrambled into his clothes and followed the tall, angular professor outside. A bright moon shone overhead and the snow that had fallen two days earlier was gone. The air was still thick, and Teague said, "Bring that cart, and be quiet about it!" He move away quickly, and Colin seized the two-wheeled cart and struggled to keep up with the old man.

Teague did not speak. Finally they arrived at what appeared to be a small cemetery across from a church. Teague stopped abruptly and pulled a lantern from the cart. When it was burning with a clear yellow flame, he pointed at a fresh grave. "Dig up that corpse, Winslow."

Colin stared at the old man, and by the silvery light of the moon he could see his features clearly—and suddenly a fear touched him. *He looks like a ravenous bird!* "You want me to dig up a body, Doctor? Isn't that against the law?"

"Of course it is! Now do what I tell you. Here, take this shovel."

Colin had wondered why the professor had brought a shovel, and as he began to dig he discovered he was excited.

Teague walked around, looking up from time to time, sometimes examining Colin's progress.

To Colin's surprise, the earth was soft and not frozen. He commented on this and Professor Teague said, "They just buried him yesterday. He'll be a nice, fresh corpse."

When the coffin was uncovered, Phineas Teague came forward and held up a lantern. "Take the lid off."

The coffin was made of pine boards and held together loosely. As soon as the cover was off, Teague held the lantern over it. "Now, that's a fine, juicy corpse!" he grinned, smacking his lips with satisfaction. "Just what we needed. Put him on the cart, Winslow."

Colin looked down at the body and noted that the man in it was middle-aged. He also noted that one eye was open and one closed—and that the lips were set in a fixed smile. With some effort he pulled the body of the man out of the coffin, and Teague helped him pull the body out of the grave and dump it into the cart. "Now put that coffin back, and cover it up just like we found it."

Colin did this quickly and fixed the grave so that it looked as it had before. Finally he whispered, "Dr. Teague, isn't this against the law?"

"Certainly!" Teague nodded. "Now we are going to take this fine, fresh corpse to my house and dissect it. I am going to show you the miracle of God's greatest creation. Yes, you are a criminal now, Winslow, as am I."

Colin abruptly laughed. He knew they were in danger of being caught and sent to prison, but he said with wonder in his voice, "This is what I want to do, Professor!"

"Ay, I saw it in you. A mighty good physician you will make when I am finished with you."

Colin forgot his problems and was filled with an inexplicable joy. *I've found my place!* He said, "You know, Dr. Teague, sometimes a fellow bends over to pick up something, and when he straightens up the whole world has changed! That's what I feel like now. I've never known what I wanted to do with my life. Now, I *know* what I want to do. I want to be a physician!"

"Well, boy, if we don't get this body hidden, you will be confined to a life sentence in prison. Let's get this gentleman to my house. I have a room there I keep under lock and key. This won't be the first body I have pulled apart." He stared at Colin, and his laugh was a cackle. "You're a resurrection man, Winslow."

"A what?" Colin asked in a startled voice.

"That's what they call fellows like us who dig up bodies and cut them open. They say we're giving the corpses an early resurrection."

Colin looked up at the sky and saw that it was filled with what seemed to be millions of gleaming diamonds. He said nothing, but his heart suddenly was full. *I want to be a physician; Dr. Teague will help me!*

They reached the doctor's cottage. The two of them moved the body into a locked room, where there was a table exactly the right height for working on a corpse. Colin eagerly asked, "Can we start tonight, Dr. Teague?"

Phineas Teague laughed and clapped Colin on the shoulder. "That we can, boy! We will start tonight. You will get your first look in God's greatest wonder—a human being! I can't show you this man's soul, but I can show you the miraculous work that God Almighty has created for the soul to occupy!"

PART TWO

Resurrection Man

(1581–1585)

7

May 3, 1581

Phineas Teague glanced upward at the azure sky and saw a host of white, puffy clouds heading toward the sun. Without breaking stride, he watched as they curtained the sun and brought a shade down over the earth. Phineas glanced at his companion and said, "Don't walk so fast, Mr. Winslow! I'm not nineteen years old like you." The two had gone on a walk looking for herbs, something they often did.

"You're as able as you ever were, Dr. Teague." Colin did shorten the length of his stride, for he had noticed his teacher and mentor was not as spry as he was when he had first put himself under the older man's teaching.

"This has to be one of the hottest summers on record."

Teague expected no answer and he received none. He glanced over at his pupil, Colin Winslow, noting that he was slender but strong, with not one bit of spare flesh on him. He wore no hat, and his chestnut hair was ruffled slightly by the breeze. Teague noticed that as usual, the young man was deep in thought. It was something he had seen in Colin from the beginning. *This boy is almost like a machine—or better. His memory is sticky; everything that touches it is implanted there forever. I don't see how such a young man can cram so much knowledge into his skull!* He had always admired the young man's ability to keep silent until he had something important to say.

As the pair walked farther, they saw a man beside the road filling a coarse sack with some type of weed.

"Hello, Egbert," Teague said pleasantly. He knew the tall, thin man well, for he was a familiar figure in these parts. Egbert Thornton made a good living by collecting herbs and plants of all sorts and selling them to the pharmacists and physicians. "What have you been up to today?"

Egbert turned and grinned up at them, exposing a wide gap between his front teeth. The sun had freckled his face to the point where it looked as if he were speckled with orange paint. "Why, nothing unusual, Doctor." He glanced at Colin and said, "Now, Mr. Winslow, you know a great many plants and herbs, I'll be bound you don't know these."

Colin glanced at the weed and shrugged. "That is orach. Some people call it 'stinking orach.' And stink it does, like old rotten fish. It grows on dunghills, and you will notice that it is a little bit early. It usually comes around in June or July. It's used as a universal medicine for any disease that ails a birthing mother; it cools the womb, for as you know the heat of the womb is one of the causes of hard labor. It can make barren women fruitful. And if you love health and ease, keep the juices made of this herb always by you."

Teague laughed at the sour expression on the face of the herb collector as Colin rattled off the so-called healing properties of the herb. Phineas knew the information came right out of the bible of apothecaries, *Pharmacopoeia*. It never ceased to amaze the old man that Colin had practically memorized the massive volume. "There you are, Egbert. Let that be a lesson for you!"

Colin smiled. "It sounds impressive, but it's just a stinking weed, good for nothing, really."

Egbert glared at Colin angrily, then wheeled and went back

to jerking the plants out of the ground and stuffing them in his leather bag.

Teague laughed at the man's anger and said, "Let's hurry on now, but I must give you a warning. You are going to get into trouble."

"How is that, sir?"

"You must learn to be more careful of your words. Truth is wonderful, but it can be overused without discretion."

Colin turned his eyes on Teague. "No, it can't. Truth is truth no matter how you say it."

"Ha! Have you ever heard of Sir Thomas More? All he had to do was tell one little lie to Henry the Eighth, and he could have had not only his life but any title he wanted."

"He was a great man, Dr. Teague."

"And now he's a dead man! You want to know why? Because he told the truth and got his head lopped off as a reward."

"Would you have lied?" Colin asked, puzzled.

"What a fool question, boy! Of course I would have lied! One little lie to save my life? More was a fool."

"What would you have had him do?"

"I would have had him do what any logical man would do."

"And what is that?"

"More could have lied to Henry, then gone into his room and shut the door. Then he could have confessed his sin to God."

"That would not have been right!"

"It would have kept him alive. God would have forgiven him. Why, that's his business."

Colin sighed, for he had become accustomed to Teague's philosophy. "Sometimes I think you're a scoundrel, Dr. Teague."

"No, I do what I have to do to get by, and you need to learn to do the same."

The two trudged on and when they reached the outskirts of London, Teague said abruptly, "You've made enemies, Colin. Some of them powerful men."

"I've done nothing to hurt anyone."

"You have done too well in your profession."

Startled, Colin threw a quizzical glance at Teague. "How is that possible? A man should do the best he can at whatever he sets out to do."

Teague did not answer, and his mind went back in time as he reviewed the swift progress Colin Winslow had made. He had fulfilled all the requirements to become an apothecary, and he had done it in little more than a year. Ordinarily an apprentice served his time under a licensed apothecary for six or seven years. Colin had simply waded through and memorized in one day what it usually took men a month to accomplish. He was, Teague thought, the ablest student he had ever encountered. *Once he sets his mind to do something, it's as if everything in the world ceases to exist.*

Teague had attempted many times to warn Colin about success that comes too easily or too quickly, and now he tried again. "You don't understand human nature, Colin. Men don't like to be outdone by younger people. They like to be in what I call an *inner ring.*"

"An inner ring, sir?"

"Yes, once a man gets his qualifications as an apothecary, or even as a physician, he wants to make it more difficult for others to get to where he is. He doesn't want to share his triumph. That is the reason why there are so many barriers to overcome when becoming a physician or apothecary." Teague saw the young man was deep in thought. "Don't you see, Colin? It's human nature for men to be jealous. I think your Bible says that, doesn't it?"

Colin shrugged. He knew the Bible well; in fact he had memorized much of it, but he was still only a nominal member of the church. He had often tried to defend his position, but Teague had apparently touched on a soft spot because Colin just grunted, "I don't know what you are talking about, Doctor."

"Then I will make it so plain even an ignoramus can understand it! You are smarter than any of the apothecaries. Why, even now you know more than most of the physicians! It was easy for you. You did it too fast. Do you know how that makes them look?"

"No, I don't."

"It makes them look stupid."

"What would you have me do? Less than my best?"

"Learn how to look ignorant. I know your head is as stuffed full of facts as an egg is with meat, but that won't help you if you get cut off at the knees. Try to make them feel better, at least. I know that many are stupid, mean, and petty, but try to make them feel superior rather than inferior to you."

"I will try, sir."

The sun was low in the sky as the pair entered the city. Colin looked around and wrinkled his nose. "I don't see why a city has to stink. Why can't they take better care of it? This is awful."

"Why, of course it is," Teague said. "It is part of the curse."

"The curse? What curse is that?" Colin was accustomed to Teague throwing out remarks like this. Many times they were connected with religion, although Teague professed to have none.

"Why, Adam and Eve had the only clean world, Colin. Didn't you know that?"

"Of course I do."

"Well, they managed to get themselves thrown out of paradise and then started off fouling the earth in every way, and all their offspring did the same."

"They certainly fouled up London," Colin grunted. As always the street was full of garbage, for people threw it out the window, that and night soil as well. There had been some talk of creating a channel—a ditch, more or less—that would run through the center of the street and carry off the refuse. Hogs were rooting around, sniffing at the garbage.

"No wonder people are sick so often, living in all this filth," Colin remarked.

"Well, if there had been a better way, I'm sure old Galen would have mentioned it."

"Galen was wrong about many things."

"Shush! Don't be saying such things, Colin! I have warned you before. You well know I have little respect for Galen, but the quickest way to get your head lopped off, professionally speaking, is to challenge the founders of medicine."

"They were ignorant."

"No matter; men today insist they are right because they were the first."

Indeed this was the condition of medicine, and it irritated Colin greatly. Galen, the most prominent of physicians and one of the founders of medicine, had written a huge book. Colin had soaked himself in it, but he had not read far before he realized there were inconsistencies in Galen's work, as there were in the works of the other founders of medicine. But he quickly discovered that the writings of the founders were like the Bible to physicians. Their treatments were apparently handed down from heaven, because the ones who challenged the founders were called renegades and usually shunned.

They reached a large stone building, one of the three hospitals in London. When the two entered, Colin shook his head. "They don't even keep the hospital clean."

Teague nodded but didn't comment. He shared Colin's opinion of some of the useless "cures" set forth by the early physicians.

They said nothing more as they made their way down the hallways. They often visited the hospital to do what they could for the patients. The great stone building was poorly lighted by high, dim windows. The hallway opened into long rooms with rows of beds. Colin noticed that two or three or more patients were put in the same bed with no regard for the diseases they might have. Some of the patients did not have beds but lay on piles of straw—men, women, and even children. The place was indescribably dirty and overrun with vermin. Terrible odors of filth and disease destroyed any hope that patients might be cured.

They passed through an arched doorway, and Dr. Teague moved to stand beside a man lying on a wooden cot. "How are you today, Williams?"

The patient's eyes had been closed, but now they fluttered open. He was lying on a gray blanket, blood-soaked bandages around his legs. Colin did not need to touch the man's brow to see that he had a fever. Teague went through the motions, but it was obvious to both of them that the man was dying. His legs had been crushed when a large stone had fallen on him, and his will was the only thing that was keeping him alive. Phineas Teague said little, for the patient was only half-conscious.

After doing what little they could, Colin said bitterly, "This place itself is enough to make a well man sick!"

"It's all they have, though."

Colin did not respond until they had turned the corner and headed down another corridor. "Someday I am going to have a hospital much better than this one."

"You'd better hurry and get rich, then, because that would take a lot of money. Come now, and try to keep your mouth shut about such things."

"Why should I?"

"Because this next patient is under the care of Doctor Regis Perry. He's one of the prominent physicians of London and more importantly, he's head of the Royal College of Physicians." Teague spoke with a wry, sarcastic note in his voice. "You know the College of Physicians, don't you, boy? Ordained by God and manned by angels."

Colin knew that Phineas Teague had carried on warfare with this organization for some time. He also was aware that in 1512, just after the succession of Henry VIII, Parliament passed an act regulating the science and cunning of physics and surgery. Indeed, medicine had fallen to the depths, for most doctors were ignorant and illiterate. It was not until 1518 that Henry VIII himself overrode the act of Parliament and issued a charter that took power to regulate medicine in London, and gave it a new body, the Royal College of Physicians. This college could issue licenses to those who were considered learned and skilled enough to practice. They could impose fines on those who practiced without a license. The college was financed by these fines, and the word of the Royal College of Physicians was as unchangeable as the Ten Commandments.

As they stepped into the room, Colin's eyes went to Dr. Perry. He had seen him before, and for some reason the sight of the man disgusted him. Perry was short, stocky, and muscular. He had huge hands with thick fingers, and his head was perched on a short, stubby neck. He looked, in fact, like a butcher.

"Well, Teague, it's you," Perry said with a thick, rasping voice. His hands were bloody, as was the apron he wore.

"Good afternoon, sir," Teague said. "How is the patient?"

"I'm doing the best I can. She is not responding well."

"What have you prescribed for her?"

"I have tried a cooling medicine, red lead. And along with yellow lead oxide, I have thrown in some carbonate, together with some zinc oxide."

"Powerful medicine, indeed," Teague said blandly and glanced at Colin with a warning look in his eyes. Colin said nothing, but he had to bite his tongue. He knew that doctors used such terrible so-called cures mixed with camphor, wax, and oil of roses. He watched as Dr. Perry rubbed the ointment into a cloth and placed it on the tumor on the woman's breast. *That won't help any more than a rotten apple.*

Something in Colin's face must have shown his disgust and

disapproval, for Dr. Perry glared at him. "Do you have something to say, Winslow?"

"No, sir." Colin managed to smooth his face and thought, *I'm becoming an excellent hypocrite! Might as well stab that poor woman in the heart with a dagger, for all the good he is doing.*

"This is the treatment that Galen prescribed," Perry snapped. "I've heard rumors that you do not believe in Galen, Mr. Winslow."

Hating himself, Colin replied, "You are mistaken, sir. I believe that he was an innovator and the forerunner of all good physicians everywhere."

"See that you hang on to that thought, Mr. Winslow!"

Teague seized Colin's arm and led him away. As soon as they were outside, Colin burst out, "What an idiot!"

"Of course he's an idiot! But he's president of the Royal College of Physicians! If you want to learn how to get ahead in your profession, you must learn to smile and to agree with people as needed."

"I'm not sure I can do that, Dr. Teague."

"You can do it, Colin. I've had my wars with them. But I still haven't been stripped of my license."

"I am surprised at that also. How do you account for it?"

"Why, the Lord is looking after me."

"You don't believe in the Lord."

"You wound me to the heart." Teague laughed shortly. "What makes you think I don't believe in God?"

"Because you make fun of him."

"No, I make fun of those who use God as an excuse to do as they please."

Colin pondered that for a moment and said, "I'm not sure I believe in God."

"Why, you go to church every time the doors are opened."

"Going to church does not make you a Christian any more than going to a stable makes you a horse."

"What a thing to say!" Teague said, but he smiled. "Jesus was a humble man, was He not?"

"He was."

"And I am sure you have read in the Scripture that 'God opposes the proud but shows favor to the humble'?"

"That is in First Peter."

"I thought you might know it. That is your job, boy: stay humble and learn your art and your science. One day things may change, but for now the College of Physicians takes the place of God to us."

"Not for me!" Colin asserted. "I will never say a thing like that."

The two had argued before about religion. Teague maintained he had none, but Colin had seen the lives of his parents and knew that their religion was real. It grieved him that he had not found it. Now he said stubbornly, "I *will* become a physician, and I *will* tell the truth!"

"Well, may the Lord help you, because the College of Physicians won't! Come now. Let's see the rest of these patients."

"Colin, a messenger brought this. It's from your parents."

Colin took the folded paper from Teague and opened it. He scanned it, and when he looked up, Teague saw fear in the young man's eyes. "What is it?"

"It's my sister, Adara. She's very ill."

"What are the symptoms?"

"She's got stomach pains and a high fever."

"That could be any one of many different maladies. I know you must go to her, Colin. I'll take care of our practice. How old is your sister?"

"Just seventeen."

Teague put his arm around Colin's shoulder, the first time he had ever done so. "Go at once, my boy!" He hesitated, then said, "It's at times like these I wish I were a man of God."

"So do I, Doctor," Colin whispered. "I want to pray, but I can't."

"Your parents are godly people. They'll pray for her."

Colin stared at Teague and said bitterly, "That's not the same thing, is it?" He turned and left the room, and Teague watched him go, sadness in his eyes. "Poor boy! I wish I could pray, but why would God listen to a sinner like me?"

"Can't you do *anything*, Son?"

Colin looked down into the face of his sister, which was pale and twisted with pain. She had lost so much weight that her body was shrunken, and her face was skull-like. He had been beside her for twenty-four hours, ever since he had arrived at Stoneybrook. He had not slept, and he had tried every treatment he'd ever heard of, but all to no avail.

"I've done all I can, Mother." He choked as he spoke, and leaned down and embraced Adara. She was in a deep coma. He held her, and the tears ran down his cheeks. Finally he laid Adara's thin body down and straightened up. "I'm sorry, Father," he whispered.

Brandon could not speak, and the agony in his eyes revealed the torment of his soul. Adara, their only girl child, had been his pet, and now he was losing her. He cast a helpless glance at Colin, and his lips twisted as he tried to speak. Colin had known only strength from his father, but now the terrible weight of grief drained him of all his courage.

Dr. Morgan was in attendance, sorrow on his features. He was a thin man with silver hair. He had been be the Winslows' physician for many years, but now he, too, was pale. "I brought her into the world," he whispered. "Never did I think to see her like this!"

Colin wanted to turn and flee, but that was not an option. He well knew that his parents looked to him for help, and his soul seemed to knot in a hopeless fear. He tried to pray, but could not. His parents prayed, and the pastor of their church came and added his prayers, but all that Colin could do was stand and be destroyed by the first real tragedy of his life.

The end came at dawn the next day. Adara opened her eyes, and for that moment, she had knowledge of what was happening to her. She looked up into Colin's face as he leaned over her and cried, "Brother—help me!" Colin held her hand but could only weep. He leaned over and kissed her cheek, then stepped back. He was aware that his parents were saying their last farewell. He had wept until there were no more tears, but as he heard the faint voice of Adara fade away, he cried, "Oh, God! Help me! I want to save lives, but I can't do it unless you help me!" He turned then and went to stand beside his parents, and the sight of his sister's dead face was like a dagger in his heart.

8

May 15, 1581

D r. Regis Perry, head of the Royal College of Physicians, the most powerful medical organization in England, was a thickset man with a square head set on a neck so short he did not seem to have one. His arms were bulging with muscle, and in a farmer's clothing he could easily pass for one of that group. Perry had a bulldog face with a lantern jaw, and small eyes set rather close together. They were a muddy brown, but when he grew angry they glowed as with a subterranean heat. However, his eyes at the moment were hiding that anger, for he was unable to release it in the presence of his powerful visitor.

William Farley, the Right Honorable Viscount Withington, was not a large man, at least when he stood next to Perry. He had a tall, slender frame, dark hair, penetrating gray eyes, and an imposing manner. He was a man of great discernment, and he could tell in a glance that Dr. Perry was angry. He glanced over at the third man in the room, Dr. John Chadburn, the head of Oxford University. Chadburn was a small man with mild, delicate features and was at all times anxious to avoid confrontation. He seemed caught between the upper and the nether millstone, for the two powerful men who flanked him were both dangerous, influential, and not men to antagonize.

"I think, Lord Withington, you will have to understand that disease is not at any doctor's beck and call." Perry's voice was harsh and gravelly. He ran his thumb over his thick, choppy lips and attempted to make himself look as amiable as possible. "I understand your anxiety for your son, but you must learn to be patient, sir."

Lord Withington put his steady gaze upon Perry and said in a voice that was somehow ominous, "Dr. Perry, I brought my son, Leslie, to you because he was ill. He has been here now for three weeks and he has grown progressively worse. I am not a doctor, sir, but I do know my son, and I fear for him. He is a sick young man."

"I am sure Dr. Perry is doing his best," Chadburn said quickly. "Disease is a deceitful thing. If you would just be patient—"

"I *have* been patient, Dr. Chadburn. The treatments have not been effective. I have met with your chief physicians more than once, and it is obvious that they have not the foggiest idea what is wrong with Leslie. Therefore I intend to take a step I feel is important."

Alarm ran across Dr. Perry's blunt features. "What do you mean, my lord? We have the finest physicians in England."

"That may well be, but my son is not getting any better. I have a nephew, the only son of my brother, and he became very ill, and all the medical attention my brother got for him was useless. He was at the point of death. At that time my brother took the boy to Dr. Phineas Teague—I believe you know the man."

Instantly, Dr. Perry's face grew red. "I know him, my lord, but I could not recommend him."

"And why is that, Dr. Perry?"

"He has no respect for the forerunners and founders of the medical profession."

"That may well be. As I have said, I am not an expert, but as soon as my nephew came under Dr. Teague's care, along with that of his young associate, Mr. Colin Winslow, he almost immediately came back to health." A smile touched Withington's face. "It was a miracle! I thank the Lord for it. I also thank the Lord that Dr. Teague and Dr. Winslow were used as his instruments for the healing process."

Instantly, Perry snarled, "Winslow is not a physician, my lord!"

"I am not aware of the different categories you have set up. All I know is that my nephew was restored to health, while you have not been able to make my son any better; therefore I am going to take Leslie to these two men."

"Colin Winslow is a worse rebel than his mentor, Dr. Teague! He could kill your son!"

"I am not interested in a piece of paper that speaks of a man's qualifications," Lord Withington said. His voice had a thread of steel running through it. "I have talked to some of my friends who have had the same symptoms as my son, and several of them have received treatment from Dr. Teague and his associate. They all say Mr. Winslow, as young as he is, is successful in his work with Dr. Teague."

"It is very dangerous, I must warn you! Your son could suffer dreadfully if you put him in the hands of these two men! They have no respect for the great physicians of history. Why, they both had the gall to say Galen, the greatest of all physicians in history, was wrong on many counts!"

"Who is Galen? Is he practicing now?"

"Why, no, sir, he is not. He has been dead for many years. But his treatments are used by every reputable physician in the world."

Lord Withington said disdainfully, "Yes, the physicians who treated my nephew followed this authority, and the poor boy nearly died. It was only after Dr. Teague and Mr. Winslow treated him that he lived. My mind is made up. I thank you for your help and I will pay your fees, but I intend to see that my son is examined by Dr. Teague and his associate."

As soon as the door closed behind Lord Withington, Regis Perry unloosed a string of oaths such as John Chadburn had never heard. Chadburn waited until Perry had run down, then said, "If I were you, Dr. Perry, I would not take on Lord Withington as an enemy. He is a powerful man, so you should tread very carefully."

Perry's face grew as red as a furnace, for he well knew that Chadburn had great influence as head of Oxford; and he clapped his meaty lips together, for he well knew that Chadburn was right. He filed the incident in his mind and made a vow that moment that he would do whatever was needed to bring the downfall of Dr. Phineas Teague and his associate Colin Winslow, no matter what the cost!

"Not a bad old pile of bricks, is it, Colin?"

Colin had arrived with Teague at the Withington estate. They had been driving for what seemed like hours through the lands that belonged to the viscount, and now the driver halted the carriage in front of the imposing structure.

"It is more than a pile of bricks, isn't it, Dr. Teague?"

Indeed, Withington was most impressive. Colin stared at it, fascinated by the size. He studied the immense front lawn, which was decorated with fountains and hedges carved into fantastic states. Great gargoyles crowned the structure, which was composed of white towers that seemed to rise to the sky. "It's a huge place, Doctor."

"I never look at these places without thinking that they are nothing more than monuments to man's pride. Who would want a house with fifty bedrooms? Come, boy, let's see what Lord Withington wants. I hope we can give it to him! He is a good man to have on our side."

Colin leaped to the ground and waited as his companion descended slowly. They stood in a huge courtyard, a place of perfect symmetry, with skillful structures scattered everywhere. It seemed the stone leaves in the stone trees came to life.

"Shut your mouth, boy, before you swallow a bug," Phineas Teague grunted. "It's a house, just bigger than most. But when Lord Withington dies, he will leave it here, just as a peasant will leave behind his thatched roof. Come along now."

The two moved forward and climbed the steps, and as they reached the top, a massive door swung open. A tall servant in livery stood before them, saying, "May I help you, sirs?"

"I am Dr. Teague and this is Mr. Winslow. Lord Withington has asked us to call."

"Of course, sir. He mentioned that you would be coming. Would you step inside, please?"

The two were led down a wide hallway, then into a massive room with a high ceiling and large windows that allowed the summer sunbeams to illuminate the place. Carpets were everywhere, so thick they seemed to reach to Colin's ankles, and beautiful paintings adorned the walls. Rich velvet curtains were pulled back from the windows, revealing sumptuous furniture exquisitely carved.

Colin was still looking around when a man entered from the right. Colin turned and saw that Lord Withington was a tall man, somewhat imposing. There was an aura of power about him, a sense of authority that Colin had noticed in other men of influence.

"Dr. Teague, I believe."

"Yes, and this is my associate, Mr. Colin Winslow."

"You gentlemen are welcome to my home. I am glad you could come so quickly."

"We came as soon as we got your message. I assumed it was important. What can we help you with?"

"Gentlemen, would you sit down?" Withington waited until the two were seated and the servant left before he said, "I have one son, gentlemen. Leslie is nineteen years old, and he has been ill for over a month. I fear he's growing steadily worse."

"What has been done, my lord?"

"I have had him examined by five physicians, but none seem able to help him." Worry lines appeared in Withington's face and he seemed less assured. "No physician has been able to find what is the cause or the cure for my boy. I have a brother, Sir Winfred Farley. I believe you know him, Dr. Teague."

"I do indeed, sir. I attended his son in his sickness."

"That is what my brother tells me. He spoke so highly of you and Mr. Winslow that I sent for you at once. I fear I have wasted time with other physicians. They talk a great deal, saying things that no man could understand unless he has studied the medicine for a lifetime!" Withington said with frustration.

"I fear my profession hides behind difficult sentences and obscurities in language," Dr. Teague agreed. "I assure you I will tell you nothing but the simplest truth."

"That is what I have been told by my brother."

"What are your son's symptoms, my lord?"

The three men talked about the young man's symptoms and finally Lord Withington said, "I am anxious for you to see my boy. It seems almost hopeless. Day by day he loses strength and weight. My wife and I are terribly afraid."

"That is natural, sir," Teague said gently. He could be a harsh man at times, but toward those who were suffering or had a family member in danger he could be kind and patient. His voice became softer as he said, "I think it might be best that we see the young man before we make any decisions."

"Would you like for me to write down what I have told you, Dr. Teague?"

"Oh, no. My assistant here will remember every word you have said."

Lord Withington set his gaze on Colin. "That is a fine and unique gift for a physician."

"I trust that we will be able to help your son," Colin said quickly. He felt an instant liking for the man. He had known other powerful men of influence who were arrogant, but he saw little conceit in this man. "We will do the very best we can, sir," he added quietly.

"Leslie is probably asleep at the moment, but I would like for you to meet the rest of my family."

Lord Withington spoke to the servant, saying, "Ask my wife and daughter to come in, Wilkins."

Colin was studying Lord Withington's face and there he saw pain, fear, and helplessness. *No matter how powerful a man is,* he thought, *when death faces him or someone he loves, he is the same as the poorest peasant in England.* He and Teague rose as two women entered the room.

"This is my wife, Lady Withington, and this is my daughter, Lady Benton. This is Dr. Teague and his associate, Mr. Winslow."

Lady Withington was in her early forties. She was an attractive woman with a wealth of brown hair and warm brown eyes. At the moment he could see fear in them, but Colin also saw an attractive, gentle spirit.

"I welcome you, gentlemen, and I hope you will be able to help my son."

Lady Benton was a young woman, Colin saw, no more than twenty-five. There was much of her father in her and little of her mother. She stepped forward and extended her hand. Dr. Teague took it at once, bending over it with a polite kiss.

"I am so happy you are here, Dr. Teague. We are very worried about Leslie."

Colin did not expect her to speak to him since he was a mere assistant, but Lady Benton came at once and extended her hand. Colin followed Dr. Teague's example. He bent over it awkwardly and touched the back of her hand with his lips. When he straightened up, he saw that she was watching him in a strange manner.

There was something different about this woman. Her eyes were dark, and her skin was flawless. There was an exotic richness in her lips that most women did not have. Her figure was clearly discernible in the orchid-colored dress she wore. "We welcome both of you, and I pray you will be able to help my poor brother."

At that moment refreshments were brought in, and they all sat down while a serving maid passed around the drinks and a platter of bread and cold meats. "I thought you would be hungry after your long journey," Lady Withington said.

As they ate, Lord Withington said, "I must warn you, I have had a difference of opinion with medical men who may give you some problems."

"I am used to that," Teague smiled. "No doubt it was with Dr. Perry."

"You were expecting it, then?"

"We have crossed swords before. Our methods differ completely."

Colin did not join in the talk, but he listened avidly.

"Well, I am glad to hear that, because their methods were of absolutely no help! But I would not want to cause problems in your professional life."

"We are healers," Teague said. He took a bite of bread. After chewing and swallowing, he said, "We will do what we must for our patients, and the college must do as it pleases."

Lady Withington's voice was laced with fear. "I beg you, sir, save my son. You were able to save our nephew Simon, and I pray that you will have that same success with Leslie."

"Mother, I am sure these gentlemen will do everything in their power," Lady Benton said. Colin saw her eyes fixed on him rather than Teague, which disturbed him. After all, Teague was the physician.

Finally, Lord Withington said, "Wilkins tells me that my son is still sleeping, and you must be tired. Wilkins, show these gentlemen to their rooms."

Lady Benton smiled. "Before you take a rest, Mr. Winslow, I would like to hear more of your treatment of my cousin Simon."

The invitation was more of a command, and after the others had left the room, Colin stood before Lady Benton awkwardly. He'd had little experience with women, and this was the most beautiful woman he had ever seen. He knew that she was married to a nobleman, for she bore the title "Lady Benton."

"Come, it's so beautiful outside. I love this time of the year. Let me show you my roses."

"Certainly, Lady Benton."

Colin followed her outside through an intricate aisle of hedges until they came to a beautiful rose garden. He stopped and exclaimed, "I've never seen such colors in flowers!"

"My mother is a great lover of flowers, much more than I. I just enjoy them, but she adores them. Shall we sit?"

Colin waited until Lady Benton seated herself on the stone bench, then seated himself beside her. It was a small bench, barely wide enough for the two of them. Colin was intensely aware of the pressure of her arm against his. She turned to face him, and a smile crept across her lips. "I am surprised to see you are so young. No one told me this."

"Yes, my lady, I am nineteen."

"And yet Dr. Teague places such trust in you. I can see it in the way he spoke of you."

"I have been very fortunate, my lady, to study under Dr. Teague."

"Tell me about yourself."

"Myself? Why, there is not much to tell."

"Oh, come now! A handsome young physician such as yourself, you must have a great deal to say."

Colin was awkwardly speechless for a moment, for there was a lingering smile on Lady Benton's lips that was reflected in her eyes. At her insistence, he told her a little of his life.

When he was finished, he noticed she was watching him in a peculiar way.

"Most of the doctors I've known have been older men. That's why I was surprised to meet a young handsome doctor such as yourself—"

"My lady, I am not a physician."

Lady Benton only smiled. There was a sensuous turn to her mouth that fascinated Colin, and at the same time made him very nervous.

"Mr. Winslow, the physician has such an intimate relationship with his patients. I suppose you grow accustomed to such intimacy with your female patients." She laughed because she saw Colin's face redden. "Well, I did not think there was a man in England with a blush left in him! I like you for it, sir! I would guess that some of your female patients must have shown you signs of their favor."

Colin could not think of a single word to reply. She saw his awkwardness. Suddenly she reached over and covered his hand with hers. "I like you, Mr. Winslow! It's refreshing to find a truly innocent man in our country. You must tell me more about yourself; I am fascinated."

Colin stuttered a little, then asked a question that had been on his mind. "Is your husband here, my lady?"

"Oh, no. I lost my husband over a year ago. He was Aaron Caldwell, the Right Honorable Viscount Benton. He died in a riding accident."

"I'm very sorry for your loss, my lady."

"Thank you, Mr. Winslow. It was a hard loss, but time does heal all wounds. One must go on with life." She smiled and said, "Now, tell me of some of your victories in your practice."

When Colin entered his room he found Dr. Teague waiting for him. "Do I have the wrong room, Dr. Teague?"

"No, this is your room. I wanted to get a report of your meeting with Lady Benton."

"Why, she merely wanted to discuss possible treatments for her brother."

Teague had piercing eyes. Right now those eyes seemed to pin Colin to a board, as he himself had pinned butterflies and other insects.

"That is the first lie you have ever told me, Colin Winslow. I am sorry to see such dishonesty in you."

Colin dropped his head. "I—I don't know what else to say, Doctor. It's true, now that I think about it, that Lady Benton never asked about treatments during our conversation. I don't know why."

"Well, *I* do." Teague said abruptly. "I am not a man of God, but I remember a sermon I heard when I was younger. It stayed in my mind all these years. It is very simple. I don't know where it is in the English Bible, but it says, 'Let him that thinketh he standeth take heed lest he fall.'"

Colin straightened and moved his head slightly from side to side. "Yes, Dr. Teague, that's in the book of First Corinthians. But, sir, a woman like that wouldn't be interested in any man without a title."

Teague laughed rather harshly. "So you think all that women are interested in is titles? You are wrong—dead wrong! Some of them are interested in what a man brings to the bed with him."

Colin was accustomed to Teague's rough speech, but this still shocked him. "You can't possibly mean she has any immoral interest in me?"

"You are the brightest boy I have ever seen—and yet the densest in some ways! You know all the cures that go back two hundred years, but you can't see when a woman wants you." He shook his head and said, "Listen to this, my boy. Money, power, and women—these are the snares that destroy a man."

"They will not destroy me, sir!"

Teague threw up his hands. Clearly, Colin was blind to the danger he was in. "You did not hear a word I said!" he said with disgust. *"'Let him that thinketh he standeth take heed lest he fall.'* Just watch out for that woman. I've seen her kind before."

"Yes, sir," Colin replied neatly. After Teague left he shook his head. *Teague is not often wrong, but he has to be wrong about this.* He looked about the room and studied the expensive furniture, the hangings on the wall . . . but his mind kept going back to when Lady Benton put her hands around his. He had seen something in her eyes that somehow drew him. He shrugged his shoulders in a motion of impatience.

"I would like to see the record of what the physicians have done for your son, Lord Withington," Teague said.

"Of course. I insisted that they write them all down." He moved over across the room, opened the desk drawer, and pulled out a stack of papers.

"Here it is, Dr. Teague." Teague took the papers and Colin stood close beside him. The two men read through the documents. Instead of replying to Teague, Sir William asked abruptly, "What do you think, Mr. Winslow?"

Colin was surprised, for he had expected Dr. Teague to deal with Withington. He said briefly, "I think you can guess my thoughts, my lord."

"Just tell me, what do you see, Mr. Winslow?" Lord Withington demanded.

"I am sorry, Sir William, but what I see here is not the kind of medicine that Dr. Teague has taught me to practice."

"What do you mean?"

"They bled the young man four times, and once only two days between."

Lord Withington stared at Colin. "Isn't that common practice?"

"It is common practice and the old authorities all agree with it, but I see no value in it."

"Dr. Perry told me it was to bleed out the bad blood."

Colin could not help smiling. He did not know it, but he looked very young standing before the nobleman. "Bad blood, sir? No one has ever proved that there is such thing as bad blood. And if it did exist, how would anyone know that the blood bled out or taken by leeches was bad and not good?"

Lord Withington stared at the two men, then fixed his eyes on Teague. "Do you agree with this?"

"I do, sir."

"And look at this, my lord," Colin said. "Purging! I have never *seen* such purging!"

"But I understood that was common also."

"It is common because physicians know of nothing else to do. Galen, the old master, said that bleeding and purging are good for men, so we do it, even if we do not understand why."

"You amaze me, Mr. Winslow." Lord Withington laughed shortly and shot a direct glance at Colin. "Dr. Perry said you were a rebel."

"I think that is exactly what he is," Teague agreed slyly. "But you go to any physician and ask why purging and bleeding are helpful in ridding the body of disease, and they will give you long words and convoluted sentences. Which mean, in translation, *I do not know.*"

"And I am looking at the medications the physicians gave your son," Colin said. "Listen to this—'horn of unicorn.' There is no such animal as a unicorn, at least not known to man. What could they possibly have given him, perhaps the horn of a billy goat?" Colin began to grow angry. "Here it says 'the grease of a heron and the fat of a vulture.'" His tone grew louder as anger filled his face. "And listen to this. They gave your son, so they say, 'a bezoar stone.'"

"What in the world is that? I asked, but I could not understand the answer," Lord Withington said.

"It is supposedly the stone taken from the intestines of a

Persian wild goat. And look, rooster testicles, crayfish eyes! On and on they tried all these remedies not knowing what they were."

"I see you are angry, Mr. Winslow."

"I am, my lord."

"Well, what would your treatment be, sir?"

"That is for Dr. Teague to say."

"We would both say the same, my lord," Teague said flatly. "In the first place, no more bleeding and no more purging. Second, there will be no more of these harsh medicines that were poured down your poor son's throat. The things I would prescribe—and I think my young colleague would agree—are a good diet, very light at first, rest, and some very mild medication. That which has been tried and we know to be effective. No more bezoar stones, whatever the blasted things may be!"

"Very well, gentlemen. It shall be as you say."

Leslie Farley prospered almost immediately with the treatment that the two men set forth. He slept long hours, and without the terrible purging and bleeding he gained strength. His diet was very bland at first, but then increased in richness. He grew stronger, and the color returned to his cheeks. He was able to get out of bed after three days, and within a week was well on his way to health. Satisfied, Teague said, "I must get back to my practice, I am afraid."

Lady Benton said, "I would be afraid for you to leave, Dr. Teague—unless you could leave your colleague here with us. I still fear for my brother."

Teague's eyebrows rose. He said in a spare tone, "If you insist, Lady Benton."

Lady Benton did insist, and as Teague was leaving, the last thing he said as he got into his carriage was, "Be careful, boy!" He leaned out the window and grabbed Colin by the shoulder, pulled him close, and said fiercely, "That woman is a man eater!"

"I think you are mistaken, Dr. Teague. The only time I have ever thought so."

Teague shook his head and released Colin, then said, "God keep you, boy. I hope he will save you from the clutches of that woman. I repeat, she is a man eater."

The driver spoke to the team of horses, and the coach left. Colin thought, *Dr. Teague is a wise man, but he knows nothing of women. He has never been married or even had a sweetheart, as far as I know. He is mistaken about Lady Benton. He must be!*

9

May 29, 1581

The two weeks that Colin had spent at Lord Withington's home after Teague's departure had sped by so quickly he hardly realized it. Actually, for the first time in two years he was not working eighteen hours a day. His duties were light: only to visit young Mr. Farley, and the young man had improved so drastically that this became a mere routine.

The weather was exceptional for May. Flowers seemed to explode into vibrant colors, and the grass was so green it almost hurt his eyes to look at it. For the first few days of his extended visit, Colin went out alone for long walks, but soon he was accompanied by Lady Benton. She was an expert horsewoman and insisted that Colin, who was in no way her equal in this skill, accompany her. Often they left early in the morning and stayed out until noon. Twice she had the cook pack a lunch, and they shared the meal under a huge yew tree beside a crystal-clear brook. Those had been some of the best days of Colin's life, and he knew he would treasure them always.

Lady Benton seemed intrigued by Colin's profession and even more so by his phenomenal memory. She teased him considerably about that and other things—especially his love life, or lack thereof. "You *must* have had sweethearts, Colin," she said

one morning as they were riding their horses near the stream.
The brook made a sibilant whisper and glittered in the morning
sun. She moved her horse closer to his, so that they were very
close indeed. When he turned to look at her, she was smiling at
him and added, "Come now, what was your first sweetheart's
name?"

"I've never had a sweetheart, Lady Benton."

"I can't believe that! A handsome young man like you?"

"Well, you should see my brother, Adam, if you think I look
well. He's *very* handsome, and so is my father. I'm much
smaller, more like my mother. My father and my brother are
both strong men, and I'm not much in that way."

"I don't believe it."

"It's true. Adam is the hero of the family. He sails with
Drake, you know."

"Yes, you've told me that, and I'm sure he's a wonderful
sailor. Do you envy him, being the oldest son and heir to the
title?"

"Oh, no, Lady Benton. Adam is the man to carry on the
family name. We always knew that."

"And you aren't a bit jealous?" she asked with a slight smile.

"Why, no, not at all. I'm happy with what I am doing."

They traced the stream as it made a sweeping S-shape. Finally, as they stopped to water their horses, she said, "I think
you are a very honest man—except when women are concerned.
Now, you must let me give you some motherly advice."

Colin stared at her. "Why, you're not old enough to be my
mother."

"Well, then, some sisterly advice. You must be careful, for
there are clever women who would take advantage of your innocence." She continued to tease him, something she enjoyed
doing. Finally, when they dismounted, she reached out and took
his hand. He stood very still and didn't know where to look, for
he was indeed untutored in the ways of love. His heart had

always been set on learning, but this woman had affected him. As she held his hand, he shyly met her eyes and saw something in them that drew him and, at the same time, made him somehow ill at ease.

"I—I have grown very fond of you, Lady Benton."

"I've become very fond of you, also, and when we're alone I insist that you call me Heather." She squeezed his hand and moved closer, pressing against him. "We're good friends, aren't we, Colin?"

"Oh, yes!" Suddenly he blurted out, "You're the most beautiful woman I've ever seen!"

Suddenly, Heather laughed. "There! It took two weeks, but I finally got you to say what any other man would have said ten minutes after meeting me. I must take you under my wing, Colin."

"To do what?"

"Why, to teach you how to win the love of women. You are far behind in that, for love isn't something you can learn out of one of your books." She kissed him on the cheek. "There! Your sister gives you a kiss. Come now, we'll be late for our dinner!"

For three days after this encounter, Colin continued to relive that moment over and over. At times it seemed as if he could feel the touch of Heather's lips on his cheek, and he could not put her out of his mind. He tried desperately to shake off thoughts of her, but then would come a memory of how she had pressed herself against him, or how she would place her hand on his cheek with a smile. At times he recalled Teague's warning about her, but he would never allow himself to dwell on that. He had heard young men talk about the details of their love affairs, often in crude terms, but never had he been so confused about such things. He could not sleep for thinking of Heather and more than once almost decided to leave, but he found he could not tear himself away.

Lord and Lady Withington were grateful to Colin and interested in his life. One Thursday evening as the family finished dinner and were eating flavored ices, Lord Withington asked, "What's your goal in life, Mr. Winslow?"

"Why, to be a good physician and heal people."

"That's indeed a noble goal," Lady Withington said with a smile. "And you've made such wonderful progress—and so quickly!"

"Well, Dr. Teague has helped me. I could never have succeeded without his help."

"I am sure he has," Lady Benton said. "But you would be a success even by yourself with no help."

"Certainly you would," Leslie said. He had become fond of Colin, and the two had spent many hours together, mostly playing chess. Both of them loved the game. Colin had found he had a warm admiration for Leslie Farley.

A lively conversation went on for some time, and Colin consumed a great deal more wine than he was accustomed to. He became more excited as he talked, and the servants kept the wine glasses full. When he forgot to drink, it was Heather who reminded him, "Drink the wine, Colin, it's good for you. Doesn't it say that somewhere in the Bible?"

"I think that's in First Timothy, chapter five, and verse twenty-three."

"You know the Bible very well!" Lord Withington exclaimed. "That is an excellent thing in a young man."

Colin hesitated, then said, "I must tell you in all honesty, my lord, I am not a Christian."

"That surprises me! How is it that you know Scripture so well but are not a believer?"

"My parents are the best Christians I know. They read to me from the Bible from the time I was very young. And I read the Bible for myself as I grew older. I memorize things easily, and the Bible is in my mind—but not in my heart, I fear."

"Well, surely you will find God one day," Lady Withington smiled. "I will pray that you do."

By the time the meal was over and the family had excused themselves, Colin found that he walked unsteadily as he made his way to his room. He drank so infrequently that he didn't realize that he was actually drunk, perhaps because he was thinking of the wonderful time he was having with this family.

He entered his room and donned his usual sleeping costume, a simple pair of linen breeches cut off at the knees. He felt sleepy, but as he turned to the bed, he heard a faint knock on the door. He jerked around. *Who could that be this time of night?* Thinking it might be a servant coming to ask if he needed anything, he opened the door and was shocked to find Lady Benton. She was wearing a diaphanous blue robe over what appeared to be a very thin night dress and whispered urgently, "I have to see you, Colin."

Colin stepped back to let her in, then mumbled thickly, "Let me get dressed, Heather." He slipped into an old robe, then asked, "What is it, Heather?"

"I have to talk to you."

She stepped inside, and Colin saw that her eyes were fixed on him in a strange way. Colin was not thinking clearly, but he had a momentary fear of what would happen if Lord Withington found his daughter in the bedroom of a guest. He tried to think, but the wine had numbed his mind. "What's wrong, Heather? Is Leslie all right?"

"It's not about him, Colin. I have to have your medical opinion."

"But Dr. Teague is the one you should consult. I'm not actually a physician."

"No, Colin, I'm afraid to talk to anyone but you."

Colin shook his head, confused. He could smell the fragrance of her perfume, a musky scent. It seemed almost too thick, yet drew him somehow into a state of excitement. "What's the matter, Lady Heather?"

"Jane Forrest, my best friend, died four months ago."

"What did she die of?"

"Cancer. And I-I'm afraid I may have the same problem, Colin."

"Oh, surely not, Heather! Most physical symptoms we have, more often than not, turn out to be nothing."

Heather was watching him closely. Suddenly she reached out and took his hand. "No, I have this lump—here." Taking his hand, she put it on her breast. "You see? There is a lump there, isn't there?"

Colin had made such examinations many times, but there was something different about this. His mind was cloudy with alcohol and the fullness of her breast. The exotic perfume and the look in her eyes seemed to draw the power of speech from him. Her eyes fixed on him. Colin could not help but notice the smooth curves of her body beneath the thin night dress. "I—I don't feel any lump."

Pressing his hand tighter, she smiled, "You are a dear boy! I am so glad! I have been so frightened." Suddenly she put her arms around his neck and pulled his head forward. She put herself against him and kissed him. Colin Winslow, at that moment, was totally helpless. He tried desperately to resist, but somehow all of his defenses were down. He knew nothing but the smoothness and the fullness of the woman. Suddenly, Heather laughed, "You're a sweet boy, Colin. Love me!"

Then Colin cried out hoarsely and pulled her toward the bed. She laughed, and Colin Winslow lost himself in a desire such as he had never known. Once a thought came to him: *This is wrong!* But he quickly put away the thought.

Ten days had passed since Heather had come to his room, and Colin was besotted with lust. He had made love to Heather exactly five times. Over and over he relived each time. At night he would lie in his bed, unable to think clearly, for he was beside himself with love. He thought, *I love her, and I know she loves me!*

Late one Thursday evening, after the family had gone to bed, Colin slipped quietly down the corridor to Heather's room. He tapped on the door, and when it opened Heather smiled and whispered, "Well, it's my lover."

He slipped inside and shut the door. She came to him willingly, but he said quickly, "Heather, I have to tell you that I love you."

"Why, we've had a good time, Colin, and I think a great deal of you."

Colin shook his head. "No, it's more than that. I love you. You are the only woman I've ever known. I want us to be married."

"Why, Colin—!" Heather blinked with surprise. She tried to think how to say the truth without hurting his feelings. "That can never be, Colin."

"Why not? We love each other."

"Colin! You are so *innocent*! You don't love me."

"Yes, I do!"

"No, Colin, you love *love*. I remember what that was like when I had my first man. I'm your first woman and you are filled with delight, but we could never marry. Surely you see that."

"Why not?" Colin replied quickly.

Heather shook her head. "For one thing, I could never be the wife of a doctor, and you would never be happy with me. I'm spoiled, Colin, and am accustomed to expensive ways. Anyway, my father would never permit it. I have to marry for material reasons. I have to marry a man who has a title and land."

She saw that he was stricken, and at that moment, she felt very sorry for him. It had been a game with her, but he looked as if she had driven a knife into his heart. She put her hand on his cheek and said with compassion, "I'm so sorry, Colin! I didn't mean for this to happen."

Then the truth came to young Colin Winslow. "You used me!" He was stunned and tried to deny the thought, but couldn't. He heard her say, "We'll always remember our time together, but you need to find a young woman of your own class. She'll be wonderful, I'm sure."

Colin didn't hear the rest of what she had to say. Blindly, he left the room and went back to his own. He stood there trembling, knowing that he could never forget her words. The sweetness that he had felt for her turned to bitterness, and he knew that he would never trust another woman as he had trusted her.

10

June 10, 1581

"Something is wrong with that boy!" Phineas mumbled under his breath, probing into the interior chest cavity of a corpse. It was not as fresh as he would have liked. He and Colin had stolen it the night before, and for a moment Phineas looked disturbed. "Why can't a man have a nice, fresh corpse to work on once in a while?" he muttered. Almost viciously, he opened the corpse up wider; then his mind went back to his assistant. *Something must have happened to him. His mind is not on his work.*

As always, Teague was infuriated that there was a problem he could not solve instantly. He stared down at the corpse with his piercing hazel eyes. He reached up now and pulled at his wild silver hair. He looked for a moment like a man who was trying to lift himself off the floor by his hair. Finally he muttered, "The boy has to come out of it sometime! He has too good a mind to spoil."

For a time Phineas forgot himself, as he always did when he was dissecting a corpse. It was a matter he could never resolve, this miraculous thing called the human body. He remembered a line of poetry he had read once that simply said, "What a piece of work is man!" Phineas hated poetry, but he loved that line.

He had spent his life examining the mechanics that make up the wondrous creature that is man. He was not a believer in God, and this troubled him at times. He was faced with a dilemma: he well knew this miraculous fragment of flesh, bones, blood, and nerves, all functioning in a way that was marvelous indeed. How could this be? Could this be by an accident? Somehow, Phineas managed to not think very hard about that. Once, Colin had asked him, "Dr. Teague, if you found a clock with all its intricate workings would you say, 'My, this is miraculous, how this clock just came to be without a maker!'?"

Snorting viciously, Teague pulled at the corpse and pushed aside the errant thoughts. He well understood that if there was a clock, there *had* to be a clock maker. And if there was a man with all his intricate parts that were so marvelous in order, there *had* to be a man maker! For most of his sixty-seven years he had struggled with this problem. One of the reasons he was fascinated by Colin Winslow was the faith of the young man. He knew that Colin himself did not claim to be a Christian; nevertheless, he was adamant about defending the Scriptures and the concept of a God who made the world and everything in it.

Suddenly, a door opened and closed, and relieved to put away the theological thinking he frequently fell into, Phineas turned to see Colin, who had the most downcast expression he had ever seen on his face.

"What's the matter with you, boy? You've been glum ever since you returned from Withington."

"Nothing's wrong with me."

"Nothing? You think I don't know anything about human nature? You think I can't see when a man has been hit right between the eyes? Come now, tell me what's bothering you!"

"I tell you it's nothing. Now, leave me alone!"

Phineas stared at him. "Well, that is the harshest thing you have ever said to your dear friend. A dear friend who is me."

Colin chewed on his lower lip, and Phineas saw that his words had hit hard.

"I'm sorry, Dr. Teague. It's is just that things are not going very well for me lately."

Phineas positioned himself so he was able to look into Colin's eyes. A yellow beam of sunlight made a golden shaft as it came through one of the high windows and illuminated the young man's features. "If I ever saw misery on a man, it's on you." Suddenly a thought came to him and he said abruptly, "When a man is as down as you are, it can only be a woman. Is that it?"

"No!" Colin said harshly.

Phineas cocked his head to the side and stared at Colin. "Why so great and furious a *no*? If what I said was not so, a simple negative would have done. It *is* a woman."

Colin stared at Phineas and his voice had a sharp edge to it. "Are we going to work on this body or not?"

"Since you won't talk, we'll have to." Phineas hesitated, then put his hand on his young friend's shoulder. It was a physical expression of affection Teague rarely used, and Colin looked at him, surprised. "I'm sorry, my boy. I don't mean to pry into your problems. When a man has trouble, whether it is a woman, or money, or sickness, he doesn't need someone trying to arm his way into his misery. So whatever it is, I pray that you will get over it."

Colin suddenly smiled. It was a wry smile, but his eyes did brighten just the same. "You *pray* it will go away? I thought you didn't believe in prayer."

Phineas scowled and jerked his hand back. "There you are! I try to show a little consideration, and you say something as unkind as that. Of course I don't believe in prayer! It was just a figure of speech. Come now, let's get to this body. It's rank enough as it is, and it'll be worse by the time we get through with it!"

The members of the local chapter of the Royal College of Physicians were all equally uncomfortable. There were five of them, and they all had their eyes fixed on the head of the college, Dr. Regis Perry. No one spoke, and Perry grew irritated. "What's the matter with you men?" he angrily demanded. "I'm not asking you to do anything that doesn't need to be done. You know that Teague and Winslow have hurt us all."

Dr. Rowlins spoke up rather timidly. "But Dr. Perry, there is nothing that we can do about it. Dr. Teague is a world-renowned physician."

"I don't care about that! You all know how he has spoken of us. He makes no secret of the fact that he thinks we're all worthless as physicians."

Dr. Ralph Johnson spoke up. He was a heavyset man with dark brown eyes and a cruel mouth. "I agree with Dr. Perry. Something has to be done about those two."

"What can we do?" Rowlins asked.

"We can strike their names off the list of our membership," Perry said and grinned wickedly. His colleagues knew Colin had been operating under Teague's license.

"That would be acceptable to me," Rowlins grunted. "Every one of us should sign our names to that."

The meeting did not continue long. Perry was a bull-like man in appearance and was the same in his ways. He was accustomed to having his own way, and now, with Johnson supporting him, he was able to get the support of the other members.

"All right then, it's settled. I will draft the letter and get it off to Teague at once."

Rowlins suddenly reconsidered, then shook his head. "You can get rid of Colin Winslow, but you'd better not try it with Teague. He has the support of some very powerful men."

"I believe that is so," Dr. Thompson said. He rarely spoke at the meetings, but he sounded determined now. "We will lay ourselves into real trouble if we attack Teague."

"Well, so be it. We will eliminate Winslow. I wouldn't be surprised," Perry said with a cruel smile, "if Teague did not resign in protest. And that would be fine with me!"

Adam Winslow seemed to bring some sort of light with him when he joined groups or entered rooms. He had a mysterious quality that some people possess to attract all eyes. There could be fifty men in a room, but when Adam entered all eyes turned to him. Part of that force was due to his strong body and good looks. He was two inches over six feet, with golden hair and unusual hazel eyes that seemed to burn when he got angry. There was an energy in him that blazed, and other men seemed to pale in comparison.

"Well, Brother," Adam said with enthusiasm as he clapped Colin on the shoulder, "I'm glad to see you again."

"It's good to see you, Adam. When did you get in?"

"Two days ago. It was a good voyage, too. We took three prizes." As Sir Francis Drake's most trusted lieutenant, Adam would get his fair share of the booty. "Tell me, what have you been doing with yourself? Still determined to be a grubby doctor, I suppose."

"Actually, I don't think that's going to happen."

Adam blinked with surprise. He had never agreed with Colin's decision to become a physician; he would have preferred him to become a sailor like him. But he of all men knew that Colin had not the talent nor the frame nor the inclination to become a fighter.

"What do you mean? Have you decided on another profession?"

"Not really, Adam. It's been decided for me."

"Decided for you? Who did the deciding?"

"The Royal College of Physicians. They are the authority. A man has to be certified by them before he begins to practice medicine. I got a letter from them that said I have been dropped from their roll and cannot serve as a physician."

Adam growled, "Who do they think they are? They can't do this to my brother!"

"I'm afraid they can. I can never practice without a certificate."

Adam stared at Colin and had a rare moment of insight. He suddenly realized he had overshadowed Colin in every way. He was the oldest son and would inherit the title. He had made a fortune with his voyages with Sir Francis Drake and was rapidly rising as one of the stars of the Seahawks. He had a large ego, but at the same time he had a warm heart for his family. He saw that he had not shown any real consideration to this younger brother of his and said firmly, "Something will have to be done."

"Nothing can be done. They are the final authority on this."

Adam Winslow stood silently for a moment. He was a man of action rather than a man of thought. This situation displeased him, and he felt a glow of anger. "We will see about this!" he said grimly, then reached across and hugged Colin. With a determined grin he said, "Don't give up, Brother. If this is what you want, I will see that you get it."

Colin suddenly smiled. He felt the weight of his brother's arm and the strength of his muscular body, and he saw the light of battle in his brother's eyes. These were qualities that he could never have, but he was moved that at least Adam was sympathetic. "I don't think there is anything you can do, but I appreciate your willingness to try."

The Queen's Counsel was comprised of only men. Elizabeth sat at the head and the men she trusted to decide the fate of the British Empire sat around the long table. At Elizabeth's side, as always, was William Cecil, Lord Burghley, and everyone realized that Elizabeth would take no action against his advice. Across from him at Elizabeth's left was Sir Robert Dudley, the Earl of Leicester. He was the handsomest man in the room and the one many thought Elizabeth would choose as her husband. That had never happened. Cecil had once whispered to Walsingham, "She will never marry." When Walsingham had objected that it was entirely possible, Cecil said flatly, "No, she will never share her throne with a man. She is now ruler of England, and she will die ruler of England, without a man's help."

The rest of the men at the table were the powers of English government. At the farthest end from the queen, next to Sir Francis Drake, sat Adam Winslow. He listened now to Sir Francis as he urged Elizabeth to strike at Spain with every force that could be summoned. This was an old argument, and though Drake had plundered Spain's treasure ships, King Philip hesitated to declare war.

"That would mean war," Elizabeth said. "We have not the money for war."

Drake sat up straighter and challenged the queen as few men would dare to do. "My queen, we must strike Spain. If we do not, they will gain the power to strike first. They are even now building ships, and they aren't fishing ships, either!"

"No, indeed!" Adam exclaimed. He was the youngest member in the room and was not really a member of the counsel, but was there at Drake's request. "We could take their ships and more of their treasures and gain power over them."

Everyone in the room turned and stared at Adam. It was unheard of for a man so young to be so outspoken. Elizabeth, however, smiled. "You speak too rashly, young man."

"I beg your pardon, Your Majesty." Adam tried to look humble but failed miserably. "I only want to see you rule the greatest nation on the face of the earth. And to see you do that, we must defeat Spain."

The meeting went on for thirty minutes more, with Drake arguing for the first strike against Spain. Elizabeth, however, was determined to forbid it and finally dismissed the meeting, abruptly stating, "We will hear no more of this." She rose, and the men rose with her. They started to leave, but Elizabeth said, "Captain Winslow, a word with you."

Adam went at once to the queen. "Yes, Your Majesty, what is it?"

"How is your family?"

"Very well, indeed. They speak so well of you, especially my father."

"He is a dear man. I wish there were a hundred thousand like him in our kingdom. And your mother, is she well?"

"Yes, ma'am."

"I'm glad to hear it."

"Your Majesty, there is one matter that I hesitate to mention, but it means a great deal to my family."

"What is that, Captain Winslow?"

"It has to do with my brother, Colin. I believe you have met him?"

"Yes, I met him when he was younger. Now he is gaining quite a reputation as a healer."

"Exactly, Your Majesty. It grieves me to tell you that his career has been brought to a halt."

Elizabeth stared at Adam. "Indeed, how did that happen?"

"It's the College of Physicians. They have wrongfully excluded him, taken away his certificate. He can't practice medicine without it."

Elizabeth suddenly cursed. She was plainspoken always, but from time to time profanity came across her lips. She exclaimed, "I will not see your brother mistreated!"

"He has great talent. Anything you could do would be greatly appreciated by all of our family, Your Majesty."

"You tell your brother not to worry. I will see to this matter."

"Thank you, Your Majesty."

The queen left, and Drake came to stand beside Adam. He had to look up to stare at the tall young man. "What was that all about? Did she rebuke you for speaking so plainly?"

"No, it was something else entirely, Sir Francis. My brother is in trouble and she has promised to help him."

"Well, if she has promised, hang on to it. Sometimes she forgets."

"She will not forget this, Sir Francis!"

"You must bring Mary, Queen of Scots, to trial!" Lord Burghley said. He and Walsingham had met with Elizabeth before she had seen the full counsel. Both had been trying for months to get Elizabeth to see the danger her sister queen could cause her.

"I cannot attack a sister queen. She has her authority from God the same as I do," Elizabeth replied staunchly.

Walsingham sighed. "Your Majesty, she has forsaken her rights as a queen."

"Queens or kings cannot be deposed. They are chosen by God to lead their people."

"She has led her people to terrible straits. The Scots were happy to get rid of her. They did not worry about the divine right of royalty."

"That is their problem; that is what they have chosen. I'll hear no more of this." Then she suddenly smiled, for these were the two men she trusted most. "I know you think I am wrong in this, but you must let me have my way. Go now, Walsingham, I have more people to see."

Walsingham left, but Burghley remained. "What is next on my agenda, William?"

"You summoned the College of Physicians for a meeting."

"Yes, have them come in."

Burghley nodded at the soldier at the door. At once, he opened the door and a group of twelve men entered the room. They all bowed deeply, and the queen said, "I'll make this a very short meeting. It concerns the charges you have brought against Dr. Colin Winslow."

"He is not a doctor!" Regis Perry said abruptly. He had no

gentleness about him and he was accustomed to having his own way, but he was now facing a woman who *always* had her own way.

"Do you speak so to me, Dr. Perry?"

"I—I apologize, Your Majesty, but this man is dangerous."

"I will hear your cause."

Elizabeth sat for the next fifteen minutes listening to the charges, all of which seemed irrelevant to her. When they were finished, she finally said, "So, your chief displeasure is that this man is not a good candidate as a physician because he does not pay attention to *old* books and the *old* authorities?"

"That is right, Your Majesty. He has no respect for the most trusted authorities."

"Are the old authorities always right?" Elizabeth demanded.

"Perhaps not always, Your Majesty. But we must respect them."

"Respect, yes. But this man is doing great and wonderful new things that, it seems to me, none of you have thought of. I have made my decision. You will certify him completely." She paused and looked out at the men, who were struck by her words. Perry opened his mouth to protest, but one look at Elizabeth's face and he shut it instantly.

"I trust you understand me. There will be *no* unpleasantness toward Dr. Winslow. He will be given full accreditation. I command you, Dr. Perry, to make out the certificate and deliver it in person. Do you understand my orders?"

Perry swallowed hard. "Yes, Your Majesty." Indeed he did understand them. There was no mistaking Elizabeth, queen of England!

Colin looked up when he heard knocking at the door of Teague's house. "Who could that be, Dr. Teague?"

"I'm not expecting any patients, but you'd better go see. Someone is probably sick."

Colin rose and answered the door. He stared with astonishment at the man who waited there, then said, "Dr. Perry, will you come in?"

Dr. Regis Perry swallowed hard and managed to mutter, "Thank you, Mr. Winslow." He stepped inside and saw Dr. Phineas Teague, who was standing at a window. "Dr. Teague, how are you today, sir?"

Teague smiled. "Very well. Will you be seated, sir?"

"That will not be necessary. I have something for you, Mr. Winslow."

Colin watched as the man reached into the leather bag that was dangling from his belt and pulled out a paper. He saw that Perry's face was pale.

"This is your certificate to practice medicine," Perry said, and the words were obviously hard for him to utter. He held out the paper. "You are now a fully qualified member of the College of Physicians."

Colin took the paper and his face lit up. "Look, Dr. Teague, I'm now officially certified!"

Teague came over and glanced at the paper, then looked sharply at Perry. This made Perry very uncomfortable and he mumbled, "Well, sir, that is all I have to say. Good evening—and congratulations, Dr. Winslow." He managed to get the words out despite the fact that he was gritting his teeth ferociously.

As soon as the man was out the door, Teague shook his head in wonder. "That man has never done a kind thing in his life. What could have changed his mind?"

Colin's face glowed. "It had to be Adam."

"I don't understand you."

"I shared my problem with him about getting certified, and he said he would make it right. Obviously he took it to the queen, and she had a hand in this."

"Of course! Perry would never do this, except from a direct command of the queen herself." He put his hand on Colin's shoulder. "So, Dr. Winslow, as I may now call you, I have a command for you."

"A command?"

"Yes, go home. Your parents need to hear this. You need to talk to your brother and give him proper thanks. And you need some time off."

"I would like to go home," Colin said thoughtfully.

"Off with you, then. When you come back, we'll find some fresher corpses than the last one we had!"

11

June 30, 1583

Midsummer had come, and the sun scorched the earth even in the late morning. Colin, who had been home for several weeks, knew it was time for him to return and take up his work with Teague. He had discovered that his visit home had brought back painful memories of Adara, and tears came to his eyes often. He thought, *I wasn't kind enough to her. Now she's gone, and I can't do anything for her.*

Then one morning, when he was packing his clothes, his parents came to him and said, "We want you to have this, Son."

Colin took the money that his father handed him. He was surprised by the weight of it. "Why, what is this for?"

Eden smiled and put her arm around him. "We want you to have some money to spend on something for yourself. I'm sure you need instruments or something that will help you with your profession."

Colin shook his head. "You don't have to do this, you know."

"This is something we want to do. You never spend anything on yourself. Get some stylish clothes. Make a splash when you get back to the big city."

Colin reached out and took his father's hand. "Thank you, Father, and you, Mother. I'm sure I'll find a use for it."

"Where are you going this early?" Eden asked.

"I'm going out to see Meg. I haven't visited her since I've been home. If it won't offend you, I want to give her some of this money. I know she needs it sometimes."

"Do whatever you please. She is a good friend of yours." Brandon smiled. "People still call her a witch, but I notice that more and more go to her when they are sick."

"I'll be back in time for supper, but I think I must leave tomorrow morning."

Colin left the house and mounted his horse. He passed many of the field workers, who all smiled and greeted him. The men pulled at their forelocks and the women curtsied. He had always been friendly with all the servants and greeted them with a smile.

By the time he reached the woods, the sun was a quarter of the way up in the sky. He took several shortcuts to Meg's cabin, and along the way pulled some herbs he knew Meg would have use for. As he approached the door he called out, "Meg, are you home?"

The door opened and Meg Caradoc stepped outside. A tiny smile tugged at her lips. "Well, at last you come to see me. You've been at home a long time, and I've been waiting for you to come."

"I'm sorry, Meg, I should have come earlier. But look, I've brought some herbs for you."

"Come in the house, boy. Let's see what you have there."

Colin followed Meg inside and dumped the contents of the bag on the table in the center of the room. She plunged her hands in the herbs, pulling up samples and exclaiming with pleasure, "Pansies! I have been needing some of those. They've been scarce around here." She picked up another plant with sharp pointed leaves. "Borage. I've got a use for that. Old Andy Milton has got the pestilent fever. This will help him if anything will."

"Angelica, balm, and melancholy thistle," Colin added.

Meg looked up and smiled. "You've done well; you haven't forgotten your herbs."

"No, I haven't. As a matter of a fact, I use them quite a lot. You'd be shocked at what some so-called doctors feed their patients." He shook his head in disgust. "They use beaver glands, crayfish eyes, sparrow brains, duck livers, and other things too disgusting to mention."

"I expect they kill as many as they cure," Meg said with anger in her voice.

Colin laughed. "You're right about that. But I've been certified, Meg, by the College of Physicians. It was the queen herself who got me in."

"Well, she has more sense than I give her credit for."

"Oh, Meg, Elizabeth is a well-educated woman. I was surprised to find out she curses her fair share," he said with a hint of a smile. "All her royal maids and all the servants say her language would put a sailor to shame."

"Doesn't surprise me one bit. Her father was that way. Henry the Eighth was one to swear, he was. Now sit down." Meg turned to the fire and said, "I'm going to make you a meal you will never forget."

"Is it turtle soup?"

"No, I haven't had any turtles lately, but I have some duck eggs and a fat, juicy hare."

"Sounds good to me."

"While I fix our food, tell me all of what you have been doing."

As Meg prepared the meal, stoking the fire and stirring the contents of the large black pot, Colin told her what he thought might be fitting for her to hear. He did not mention Heather.

When he finally ceased, Meg turned and looked at him. "What is it you are not telling me, boy?"

"Why, nothing! I've told you all."

Meg came over and grabbed a handful of Colin's hair. She twisted her hand and put her face close to his. "I can see right to your brain, and farther than that to your heart. You've been through some kind of trouble."

Colin was amazed. He tried to free himself, but her grip was firm. "It's nothing," he protested. "Turn me loose!"

"I will when you tell me. But I vow I already know. It was a woman, wasn't it?"

Colin blinked with surprise, and with her eyes burning into him, he knew he could not lie. "Yes," he whispered. "It was a woman, and I made a stupid fool of myself!"

"Of course you did! Now tell me all about it." Meg released his hair, pulled up a three-legged stool, and sat beside him. "I want to hear. So tell me all."

"It's not fit for you to hear," Colin protested. "I haven't even told my parents."

Meg didn't speak. She simply leaned forward and pursed her lips. Her eyes seemed to glitter, and suddenly Colin found himself pouring out the whole story. He related how he had met Heather and how she had been too much of a temptation for him. He didn't go into details, but he did say in a broken voice, "I loved her, and she was just playing with me."

"Of course she was! She made a fool out of you, all right."

"That will never happen again. Wise men learn from their mistakes."

Colin started to see the memories as vividly in his mind as if they were happening right in front of his eyes. Anger burned inside him. "I will not be made a fool of ever again! I'm through with women forever!"

Meg laughed. "That is just a young man talking who's had his feathers singed. You'll find a woman who will be good for you. You just have to learn how to tell a good woman from a bad one!"

Colin felt relieved that he had shared his guilt with someone.

He knew Meg would keep his secret. He had his meal, and when he rose to go he put his arm around her. "I see you're wearing the earrings I got you."

"Wearing them! Like I said, I'll be buried in them," Meg said with a smile. She reached over and patted his cheek. "Go back now. I'm proud of you, and your parents are, too. They probably talk about you all the time."

"Oh, Meg, Adam is the one they should be proud of."

"No, not Adam, you! Go back to London, and get me another present."

"I'll do that," he said. He hugged her and felt the lean strength of her frame. He also saw tears in her eyes, which surprised him. "I'll be back for a visit soon, and we will have more time."

"Go with God, boy!"

Summer had gone, fall passed, and the winter now brought its bitter chill to the land. It was on December the tenth when a heavy snow fell, muffling the sounds of the wagon wheels and iron hooves of the horses. Phineas Teague was startled when a knock came at the door of his home and office. "Who would be out in this weather?" he grumbled. Getting out of his chair, he opened the door and looked at the couple who stood there. "What is it?"

"My name, Doctor, is Jude Tanner, and this is me wife, Kate. She needs a doctor's care." Tanner was a tall, bulky man with thick hands and a rough visage. His wife was a small woman, with black hair and well-shaped features.

"Well, come in, come in." Teague led them back to the living area that he and Colin had converted into a proper place to see patients. Their instruments were there, as well as an examining table. The smell of herbs and other medicines was strong in the room.

"What's the trouble, Tanner?"

Tanner looked down at the floor and removed his hat. He pushed his thick fingers through his tow-colored hair and mumbled something.

"What is that you say? I can't hear you, man."

"If you don't mind, Doctor, my wife would like to see your young assistant, Dr. Winslow."

Teague stared at the man, and anger began to grow in him. "Why do you want to see him when I'm standing here?"

"Well, sir," Kate said in a frightened voice, "my sister Irene was very sick and came here. You were gone, so Dr. Winslow treated her and made her all well, he did. I'm very much afraid and would really like to see him. If you don't mind, sir?"

"No offense, Doctor," Tanner added quickly.

"Well, by heaven, there *is* an offense! I've been practicing medicine longer than that pup has been alive! Sit down! I'll go get him since you think he is the only physician in the world!"

Slamming the door behind him, Phineas went down the hall and into the dissection room where he and Colin worked on their stolen bodies. "Well, Dr. Colin Winslow, you have a request."

Colin was bending over a cadaver, but he straightened up. "What is it, Phineas?"

"Some idiot woman who doesn't think I'm fit to treat her. She wants you."

Colin suddenly laughed. "Don't tell me you're jealous, Phineas!"

"Jealous! Not at all! Why would I be jealous of someone who was my student not six months ago?"

"You don't have to be," Colin said quickly. "You're a better doctor than I can ever hope to be."

"You're getting arrogant!"

"I don't think so," Colin said. He put down his instrument and laid his hand on Phineas's shoulder. "I owe everything to you, Phineas. Don't be upset."

Teague grew calm from Colin's words. "Well, blast it all, I'm shocked to discover that I have all this foolish pride."

Colin started out the door. "I'll see the woman."

"Wait a minute. I want to ask you something."

"What is it?"

"Are you over that woman who made a fool of you? You told me about that, and I told you to put it behind you—a young man's folly."

"I was a fool, but you can be sure that will never happen again. All women are fickle."

"Is your mother a bad woman?"

Colin blinked with surprise. "Of course not!"

"Well, do you think she's the only good woman in the world?"

"No, of course I don't think that. I spoke too hastily."

"That you did. Now go see if you can help that woman out there."

Two days had passed since Kate Tanner had been treated, and both she and her husband were relieved that her ailment was not serious. They were very happy with Colin and left singing his praises. The weather had grown colder, and Phineas had gone to visit an old friend of his at the university. Colin found himself walking back and forth in the house and thought, *I'm lonely. I need to do something.* He hesitated for only a moment, then made a decision. *I know what I'll do. I will go home for Christmas. It'll be good for me, and it will please my parents.*

Putting on his heavy coat and fur cap and a pair of thick gloves, he left the house. He took with him thirty pounds that he had saved from the bag his parents had given him on his last visit. He had spent little of it after giving some money to Meg, and now he was glad he was able to buy nice gifts for Adam and his parents. A pang came to him when he realized that this was the first Christmas that he wouldn't buy a present for Adara. He tried to ignore that thought and decided to buy a gift for Meg.

As he left the house, the bitter cold seemed to grip him with an iron hand. The snow was not falling heavily, but in tiny fragile flakes. Only a few people were out, so the streets were not crowded. He visited several shops but found no gifts that seemed appropriate. He was very cold and decided to come back earlier the next day. As he started walking home, suddenly the door of a shop burst open to his right and a girl came running out. A big, burly man was right at her heels, cursing and reaching out for her. He caught her in his large hands and began to beat her, a thing that Colin could not tolerate.

The girl cried out for help. Her eyes lit on Colin. "Please help, mister!"

Colin stepped forward, saying, "Sir, you don't have to beat the child."

The man turned to him. He was bald except for a small fringe around his skull. His eyes were cruel. "Mind your own business! She's none of your concern."

"She's only a child!"

"I bought 'er, and she's bound to serve for seven years. I'll do as I please with 'er!"

He started to drag the child back inside, and she begged, "Please, mister—help me!"

Colin moved without thinking. He tried to stop the man by grabbing his thick arm, but that didn't faze the brute. Before he could move, Colin was struck on his forehead and driven backward. The snow was so deep that it cushioned his fall, but he felt blood running down the side of his face. He started to get up, but a heavy boot struck him in the side. He had never felt such pain! It was like fiery lightning running through him. The man cursed and shouted, "That'll teach you to mind your own business!" Colin tried to get to his feet, but the pain in his head and side was tremendous. His eyes were fixed on the girl, and the look of terror on her thin face caught him.

Colin was often a man of impulse. He struggled to his feet. "You say you bought the girl?"

"Fair and square. I paid twenty guineas for 'er."

The girl cried out, "'e only paid fifteen!"

"I'll give you twenty-five for her."

The man grinned, his thick lips turning upward, revealing brown teeth. "Why, a swell gentleman like you I'm sure could pay more. She's scrawny now, but later she will be more interesting, if you knows what I mean." He smiled and winked crudely. "Once she gets a few years and puts on a few pounds, she'll be a juicy wench! I'll take thirty quid and not a farthing less."

Colin nodded. "Get her papers and you'll get the money."

"That's a deal. Don't you try to run away, girl! I'll find you and give you a few good ones!"

Colin closed his eyes, for the world seemed to be revolving from the pain in his head and side. He moved over to lean on the outside wall of the shop, barely able to breathe. The man quickly came out and handed him a paper. "I done signed it. This makes 'er your bound girl for seven years. You can do whatever you want with her. I'm glad to be rid of her. Now let's have the money."

Colin, moving slowly, fished the leather purse out of his coat pocket. He counted out the coins and handed them to the man, who laughed and went back into the shop.

The girl cried, "I'm gonna get my things!" When she came out with a bundle, she said, "'e tried to put his 'ands on me!"

Colin tried to straighten up but could not. "What's your name, child?"

"Twyla Hayden."

"How old are you, Twyla?"

"I dunno. Maybe twelve or thirteen, I reckon."

"We have to get out of this cold. I'm Dr. Winslow."

He moved away carefully, walking like an old man, and the girl walked beside him. "He tried to put 'is 'ands on me, 'e did! You bought me, but you better leave me alone."

Colin was hurting too much to say anything. He knew the blood was freezing as it ran down his cheek.

The girl asked, "Where we goin'?"

Colin could only gasp, "Home!" And he made it the goal of his life to reach that haven.

Teague heard the door open and looked up from his book. He was shocked to see Colin stagger in, his face covered with blood. Leaping from the chair, he caught the younger man as he began to fall. "What in the world happened to you?"

"Got beat up—"

Teague stared at the child and demanded, "Who are you, girl? What are you doing here?"

The girl looked up at him and kept her distance. "My master was a-beatin' me, and the doctor, 'e tried to stop 'im, and 'e got all beat up."

"And you helped him get here?"

"Yes, I did."

"Well, here is half a crown. Now get out of here."

"I won't! I belongs to 'im now 'cause 'e bought me for thirty guineas."

"You are too scrawny to be worth that."

"I belongs to 'im!" she insisted.

"Well, you can stay until I get the truth." He looked at the wound on Colin's head and said, "That is going to leave a scar. But you never were much to look at anyway. Come on. I'll sew you up."

Colin had the taste of laudanum still in his mouth, and he remembered vaguely that Teague had dosed him until he was practically unconscious. He tried to move, but there was still a sharp pain in his right side.

"You want somefin' to drink?"

Opening his eyes, Colin saw a girl, but his vision was still blurred. "Who are you?"

"I'm Twyla."

"What are you doing here?"

"You brought me 'ere. Don't you remember nothin'?"

Indeed, Colin's memory started to come back, and he said, "Water, please, Twyla."

He waited until she brought back a cup of water and drank it thirstily.

"That man sewed up your 'ead as good as any woman could sew up a shirt."

"More water, please," Colin croaked.

He waited until she brought more water, and then Dr. Teague came in. He looked at Colin with disgust. "You're making a career out of being a fool! You ought to have more sense."

"This fellow was beating the child," Colin argued weakly.

"What business is that of yours? You should've let him do it."

Twyla cried out and stepped forward. Her eyes were violet, a color that Teague had never seen before. "You got no 'art! You don't!"

"Keep still!" Teague snapped. "She can't stay here, Colin. You can sell her and get your money back."

Colin was regaining his senses and remembered what had happened. "She won't eat much," he whispered.

"No, I won't have it," Teague said stubbornly.

The girl moved closer to Colin and grabbed at his arm. "You won't do it, will you, mister? Sell me to someone?"

"No, I won't do that. Maybe I can find a nice family to take you in."

"No! You bought me and I'm not leavin'!" She glared at

Phineas and snapped, "You're not no gentleman! 'e bought me fair and square and I'm stayin'!"

"How old did you say you were, Twyla?" Colin asked.

"I guess twelve."

Colin turned and looked at the child for a long time. She was dirty and dressed in rags. Her arms and legs were like thin sticks. Her hair was black as a raven's wing, and her eyes were large and of a peculiar violet color. She was watching him closely, and there was a silent plea in her expression. Finally he shrugged and looked at Phineas. His voice was weak, but he said clearly, "Phineas, how much trouble can one child be?"

12

December 20, 1583

Colin had made a rapid recovery from his beating, though he was still sore. He would always have a scar on the left side of his forehead, but he made light of that. Somehow—and he was never quite certain how it came about—Twyla had become his nurse. She insisted on changing the bandage on his head, and she was an outstanding cook. Colin and Teague were pleased with this, for neither of them could cook. For two days Twyla fed Colin nothing but soft food and soup that was delicious, but soon she was cooking more substantial meals.

It was a Thursday morning, and a cheerful fire was blazing in the fireplace. It cast heat throughout the bedroom, where Colin was sitting in a chair soaking up the warmth.

"You think you can feed yourself, Mister?"

Colin turned to face Twyla, moving carefully not to strain his side. "I think so." He took the soup and tasted it. "This is wonderful, Twyla."

"Anybody can make soup, Mister."

Colin ate the soup while studying the girl carefully. She was dirty and apparently had no concept of bathing even her face. Her hair was as black as the darkest thing in nature, and those startling violet eyes seemed to bore right through him. She was as thin as a stick but apparently healthy and strong for her age and size. "Tell me about your parents, Twyla."

"I don't got none."

"You must have had at some time." He saw that the girl was glaring at him with something like anger. "What's the matter?"

"My ma was a dollywop."

This was, Colin knew, the common term for the lowest form of prostitute. Twyla stared at him defiantly, and Colin could not think of a thing to say. "What about your father?"

"I never knowed who 'e was." She used a vile term when she spoke of the man.

Trying to change the subject, Colin asked, "Where did you learn to cook so well, Twyla?"

"My ma left when I was six, and a woman and her husband took me in. She was a cook, and she taught me. She was the one that sold me to Clem Baxter." This was the name of the man who had abused her.

Phineas came in, and at once Twyla got up and left. Her dislike of him was obvious. Colin knew she was still angry with Phineas for saying she should be sold.

"Well, let me see how that wound looks." Phineas reached out and seized Colin's head, twisting it around and glaring at it as if it was some sort of enemy. "Oh, I did a good job there, but you're going to have a scar. A man ought to have a scar here and there to mark his foolishness."

He reached down and began probing at Colin's ribs. When he reached a particular point, Colin took a sharp breath. "Careful, that hurts!"

"You should be glad you didn't get those ribs broken." He shook his head and went over to the fire, backed up to it, pulled up his coattails, and sighed. "This feels good. It's colder than a well digger's rear out there."

"The fire is nice."

"What about that girl? You can get around now. Are you going to sell her?"

"No, I'm not."

"She's in the way!" Phineas snapped.

"She cleans the house—as well as she can for a girl who never kept anything clean—and she can cook. She won't be any trouble. She's just a child."

"She's a female child, and that can be trouble at any age. And she is dirty as a pig! I'll wager she's never had a bath in her whole life."

"She hasn't had many opportunities." Colin related what he had learned of Twyla's background and Phineas said, "She'll probably bring disease in here. We'll both probably die of it."

"I wish you would look on the bright side of things! She's cooked the best meals we have had in a long time. We can make her take a bath and clean up."

"Bath or no bath, she'll cause trouble."

"No, she won't. Now leave her alone."

Two days after this conversation Colin's parents arrived, and both were shocked at his appearance. His forehead was still purple from his bruises, and the thread that Phineas had used to sew him up was dangling. "What happened to you, Colin?" Eden cried.

"Well, I got on the wrong side of a fellow."

"It looks as if you were run over by a carriage, and the horses, too," Brandon said.

At that moment Twyla came in with a bowl of soup, but she paused abruptly, staring at the strange couple.

"Come in, Twyla, I want you to meet my parents."

Brandon and Eden turned and looked at the child, waiting for an explanation. "Who is this child?" Brandon asked.

"I'm 'is bound girl, I am. I belongs to 'im. 'e bought me," Twyla said.

The news seemed to shock both of his parents. Colin at once began a lengthy explanation. It did not suit Twyla, however, and she interrupted to say, "The man that owned me tried to 'urt me, and 'e put his 'ands on me. The doctor 'ere tried to 'elp me. 'e got knocked down and kicked, but 'e paid for me so now 'e owns me."

"I don't *own* you, Twyla! I've explained that to you."

"That's wot the paper says. I'm bound, that means you own me," Twyla said curtly. She put down the soup, whirled, and left without another word.

Brandon scratched his head and looked dubious. "I don't know about this. What are you going to do with her?"

"I couldn't let that fellow have her. He was beating her mercilessly." He found himself telling them the story of Twyla's background. When he finished, he dropped his head and said with some degree of embarrassment, "I didn't know what else to do."

Eden walked over and put her hands around his head and kissed the good side of his face. "I'm proud of you, Son."

"Adam could have done better. He could have whipped that man."

"Adam wouldn't have thought about helping her," Eden said in her sweet and loving voice.

"No, I don't believe he would," Brandon said. "And even if he had whipped the man, she would still belong to him."

"Mother, would you do me a favor?"

"Of course I will."

"Take Twyla out and buy her a few things. She only has one dress, and it's only a rag. And see if you can get her to clean up a little bit. I don't think she's ever had a bath."

"I'll do what I can, Colin."

Later in the day, after Eden had taken Twyla out for some clothing, Brandon sat down and talked to Colin. His talk was mostly about Mary, Queen of Scots. "That woman is going to get Elizabeth killed."

"You don't mean that, do you, Father?"

"I certainly do! She has the morals of a cobra! There is evidence enough to hang her, if she were anyone else."

"You mean actual evidence?"

"Not enough to suit Elizabeth, but nothing will ever suit her."

"I can't believe Mary would harm our own Queen Elizabeth."

"That's because you don't really know anything about her. Pretty much everyone knows Mary was responsible for the murder of her husband. Then she married the renegade who killed him."

"Why did she come to England?"

"Because they kicked her out of Scotland. Elizabeth is going to have to face up to that sooner or later. She worries about Mary, and rightly so." Brandon's face grew stern then, and he said, "No one likes to see a woman killed, but Mary will be the death of our queen—unless she dies."

Eden was troubled about Twyla but never let her feelings show. The girl had no manners, and her speech was spiced with curses and vile language. She had no idea at all about making herself look better.

Eden took her to a dressmaker and bought her three dresses, one to take with them and two more to be picked up when they were finished.

"Wot do I want with three of 'em when I can't wear but one?" the girl said.

"Well, you can wear one when you go to church on Sunday, one when you work, and one for going to town," Eden answered brightly.

"I'm not going to no church, and I got a dress to work in." Nevertheless, Eden saw that the girl was pleased. "Why are you doing all this for me?" she demanded suddenly.

"Because I always liked to dress girls."

Twyla looked up with fear in her eyes. "What do you want me to do for all these things you're buying for me?"

"Why, nothing, Twyla. I just want you to look nice. I tell you what, let's go home and wash you up. We will fix your hair, and you will see how pretty you look and feel."

"You think Mister will like it?"

She had gotten in the habit, Eden had noticed, of calling Colin *Mister*. "I'm sure he will. Now, let's find you some new shoes."

"I never 'ad no new shoes."

The two spent several hours shopping, and during this time Eden pried the story out of the girl of how she had been abandoned and raised by her prostitute mother until she was six. She told of how she tried to keep her innocence from young men, and some not so young.

"You're going to look beautiful," Eden said as they headed back to Colin's home. "So let's get started."

Colin was standing beside the fire when the door opened. His father was at his side. Colin blinked with surprise when Twyla came in with his mother. She was still skinny, but looked older somehow. "You look very nice, Twyla. Did you pick out that dress yourself?"

"No. Your mum, she picked it out."

"She did a very good job. Your hair looks nice, too."

"She washed it. She washed me too."

Eden turned to hide her smile. Colin said quickly, "Well, you look like a different girl."

Colin's parents stayed for only a short time. When they came to bid him good-bye, Twyla was off in the other part of the house. "Are you sure you know what you are doing—about that child?" Brandon asked with some apprehension.

Colin replied the same as he had to Teague. "Why, Father, how much trouble can one child be?"

"More than you know," Eden said dryly. "But I'm proud of you for taking up for the child. You just be careful now. Watch over her."

"Of course I'll do that."

It was December the twenty-fifth. Twyla had worked all day fixing a Christmas dinner. She had made wheat bread of the finest quality, and a large turkey cooked in the fireplace. She had roasted several small birds, basted with butter. She had also made a platter stacked high with homemade gingerbread, a delicacy that Phineas had never eaten. They drank beer with the meal, and afterwards for dessert they had boiled suet pudding.

"This was the finest meal in all of England, Twyla!" Colin exclaimed while sitting back and smiling at her.

"It was good," Phineas agreed. "I don't know anything you could've done to make it any better." This was the first positive thing Phineas had ever said to Twyla.

She managed to smile and said, "I loves to cook for people wot likes it."

Phineas left sometime after dinner to go to bed for his afternoon nap. Twyla and Colin sat before the fire, soaking up its warmth. Colin said, "Here, sit down on this stool, Twyla. I have something for you."

Twyla stared at him with something like suspicion. "What is it?" she demanded.

"Do you see that sack over on the shelf? Bring it to me." He waited as she brought the sack over and tried to hand it to him. He pushed it back into her hands and said, "You've done very well. I had my mother buy this for you for Christmas. She was always good at picking out gifts."

Twyla took the sack and held it for a moment. "For me?" she said.

"All for you. It's Christmas! Open it now." Carefully, Twyla undid the drawstring and pulled out a box. Colin watched her as she opened it. She stared at the gift. "Do you like it?"

Twyla reached out and picked up the comb and brush made from mother-of-pearl. She did not speak for so long that Colin asked again, "Don't you like it?"

When Twyla looked, Colin saw that her eyes were filled with tears. "Thank you, Mister. It isn't bad to be owned by you."

Colin shook his head. "I don't own you, Twyla. You'll be my servant for seven years and then you'll be free."

She took the comb and ran it through her coal-black hair, then tried the brush. "I'll keep 'em always, Mister."

She got up and came over to Colin. She held the comb and brush in one hand and reached to touch Colin's scar with her other. "The old doctor, 'e says you'll allus 'ave that scar."

"Well, I'm no beauty, so it doesn't matter."

At that moment, the bells began to toll all over London and Colin smiled. "Merry Christmas, Twyla."

Twyla looked at the brushes and looked up at him. She gave him the first real smile he had ever seen from her, and then she whispered, "Merry Christmas, Mister!"

PART THREE

Twyla

(1584–1587)

13

May 24, 1584

Twyla moved around the room, making sure everything was in place, then walked to the fireplace, where she was cooking a stew. With a wooden spoon she stirred the stew, tasted it, and with a frown that made slight lines in her forehead, she muttered, "Don't got enough seasoning." She removed three bottles from a shelf and added to the stew from each of them. She put the bottles back, then began to walk restlessly around the room. All of the cooking and cleaning were done, and Twyla felt bored. A look of discontent on her face, she put her arms across her chest and muttered, "I wish 'e would come before the food gets cold."

From outside the house she heard the sound of someone chopping wood, and the faint voices of children at play. It was May now, the summer fully come. Twyla walked to the window and stared out at the scene. The house was set on a street that ran north and south, and she noted that the sun was already sinking low on the western horizon. The scene held a charm for Twyla Hayden. When she had first come to live with the two doctors, she had been tense, expecting nothing good from them, for she had learned to trust no man—nor any woman, for that matter. But that had changed, and now she smiled as she thought about how she had become a part of the household—and an important part, too. Neither of the men could cook anything, and both were horrible housekeepers. It was Twyla who kept the house neat and clean and who cooked the meals that pleased them so much.

Impatiently she moved to the ladder and climbed upstairs to her small room. A thin afternoon light filtered through the window, and she reached over to pluck a dress that hung from a peg on the wall. Quickly she slipped out of the plain dress she wore for rough work and pulled the other dress over her head. It was a struggle, for though the dress had fit her perfectly six months earlier, now she had blossomed so that her figure was beginning to stretch the fabric. A thought came to Twyla. *Maybe I'm older than thirteen. I'm swelling up like a woman!* The thought pleased her, and quickly she picked up the brush that Colin had given her for Christmas. She ran it through her black hair with a sense of pleasure, then put it back in the chest and went downstairs again.

As she stepped off the last tread, the back door slammed. She moved quickly to see Clyde Maddox, the handyman, who had entered with an armload of wood. He dumped it in the wood box beside the fireplace, then turned and grinned at her. He was a burly man with blunt features and a pair of faded blue eyes. "How 'bout a bite to eat, sweetheart?"

"I'm not no sweetheart of yours, and I'm not your cook, neither! You have to come back after the gentlemen have eaten."

"I'm not good enough, is that it?"

"You can't 'ave nothin' to eat," Twyla said firmly. She turned to walk over to the fireplace to look at the stew but then felt his thick arms go around her, brushing against her chest. She quickly pulled a pin that was stuck in the front of her dress and rammed it into the handyman's arm.

"Ow! That hurt! Why, you blasted little vixen! I ought to take a stick to you!" Clyde rubbed his arm angrily, then glared at her and said loudly, "You wouldn't 'ave stuck no pin in me if I wuz Colin Winslow, would you now?"

"Get out of here! You leave me alone!"

Maddox grunted and shook his head. Still rubbing his arm, he strode toward the back door. Suddenly, he turned and came at her. She held the pin up and threatened, "I'll run it right in your eye! Now get out!"

"It's gonna do you no good to play up to that doctor. He won't pay no mind to a servant girl. He'll marry him a rich woman, that's wot 'e'll do," he grunted, then stepped outside, slamming the door hard.

Twyla wanted to yell at him, but she was trying to learn to control the anger that sometimes rose in her. When she had first come to live with Colin and Phineas, she had often shouted, and both men had rebuked her for using the profane language she had picked up on the streets. Maddox's words had stirred her and somehow made her feel guilty. She knew that she did have an affection for Colin Winslow, for he was the first man ever to show her kindness. She moved to a chair and picked up the huge orange-colored cat, who grunted with surprise. As she held him close he said, "Yow!"

"Yow yourself, Arthur." Twyla rubbed her cheek against his silken fur. "I have to tell you things, because there's no one else to talk to." She suddenly realized that her speech had changed somewhat during the brief time she had spent in this house. It was smoother now, for listening to the two educated men had gradually affected her. She also had learned better personal habits and bathed regularly. She was a quick young woman, and her good behavior pleased both men. "You're the only one I talk to, Arthur. I dunno' what I'd do without you." She hugged the big cat for a moment, then put him down and continued to wait impatiently.

Ten minutes later she stirred the stew again. Then from a cupboard she took a piece of paper and laid it flat on the table.

She sat on a tall stool, dipped a pen into a bottle of ink, and began to draw. Quickly, the image developed beneath her hands. This was her one gift, the ability to draw things. She'd always had this talent, even as a small child. The sketch emerged and she looked at it with satisfaction. She held the paper up and said, "Look, Arthur, there you are. Aren't you beautiful?" She turned the paper over and began to sketch again, this time with more care. The pen scratched on the paper, and the outside noises faded into the background. Finally, she picked the paper up and studied it. It was a picture of Colin. She muttered bleakly. "Mister don't even know I'm 'ere, and 'e don't care."

A sound at the door caught her attention, and quickly she ran to the fireplace and threw the paper in it. She had never told Colin or Phineas that she could draw. She looked at Colin as he came in, noting his slumped shoulders and mussed hair.

"Hello, Twyla," he greeted her, his tone weary.

"Hello, Mister. Come sit down and eat before it gets cold. I thought you was never comin'."

"I had too many patients."

"Well, now you sit there and eat a good supper."

Colin slumped down in the chair, and Twyla put a wooden trencher loaded with vegetables before him. She went to the fireplace, got a loaf of fresh-baked bread, then dipped a full bowl of stew and put that before him too.

"Have you eaten, Twyla?"

"Not yet, Mister."

"Fix yourself something and eat with me."

Twyla was waiting for this, so she quickly prepared her food, sat down, and began to eat. She kept her eyes on Colin, who was thinking so deeply about something that lines furrowed his brow. She thought again how strange it was that he had taken her in. She had known nothing but harshness from men and she had expected the same from him, but he had been nothing but welcoming and grateful for the work she did. Now as she studied him, she thought again how handsome he was. He had chestnut hair with a touch of red, and his blue-gray eyes seemed to change according to the setting and the color of his clothes. His complexion was fair and his mouth was well formed, though wider than usual for a man. His face was V-shaped, beginning with a broad forehead, then tapering down to a prominent chin. He was not a strong man, not heavy with bulging muscles, but he was quick in his movements. She wondered again why he had bothered with her, for at times it seemed to her that he did not even know she was on the planet. This disturbed her even now, so to get her mind off it she said, "Tell me what you did today."

"Treated patients."

"What was wrong with 'em?"

She kept firing questions at him until finally he shook his head as if to shake off a pesky fly. "Don't ask so many questions," he snapped shortly.

"Well, *someone* 'as to talk around 'ere!" The temper she was learning to control flared. "I'm 'ere all day with no one to talk to except Arthur. Now tell me wot you did."

She saw her anger made him blink, then he chuckled lightly and smiled. "I guess I'm a little grumpy tonight. It's been a hard day." He related several of the cases he'd treated, then asked, "What did *you* do today?"

"Same thing I allus do, cleaned the house and washed clothes and cooked. I worked all day trying to make this house nice for you and spent all day making the best meal I could. It might as well be fodder! You don't care about anybody but your bloody patients! Maybe if I was sick, you'd talk to *me*."

Colin dropped his head and for a moment sat motionless, the food forgotten. Finally, he looked up and said, "I'm sorry, Twyla. I—I lost a patient today."

"You mean he died?" Twyla asked softly.

"It was a young woman."

Twyla saw the hurt in his eyes. She knew it troubled him deeply if one of his patients did not do well—especially if one died. Finally she said, "I bet you did your very best. You allus do."

"Well, today my best wasn't good enough." Colin looked up at the ceiling as if seeking an answer there. After a time, he lowered his head and looked directly in her eyes. There were times he would talk to her, but so often he was lost in thoughts that no one could tap. Now his voice was low. "I have been thinking, Twyla, about what she'll miss."

"What do you mean, Mister?"

"She'll miss falling in love, getting married, going to dances. She won't be having any children. She won't have any of that—and it was my fault."

"No, it wasn't!" Twyla said quickly. She wanted to go up to him and wrap her arms around him, but she knew that would be unseemly. "It wasn't none of your fault."

He gave a short laugh and said, "I don't know what I would do if I didn't have you here to encourage me, child. It means a lot to me."

Twyla wanted to tell him how much living in this house with him and Dr. Teague meant to her—to be plucked out of the hellish environment that she had grown up in and find a place of warmth and solace and peace. She thought every day about where she was now, a place where the two men showed her consideration such as she'd never known. All this was in her head, but she just could not say it, at least not now. *I'll tell 'im later* was her thought, but she wondered if she ever would.

After supper, Colin went into his room and changed clothes while Twyla cleaned up the dishes. Colin returned and sat down to read beside the candle.

Twyla was quiet for a time, then asked, "What's that you're reading, Mister?"

"It's a medical book—and a bad one at that. Here, look at this, Twyla."

Twyla instantly got up, walked over, and sat down beside him.

"Look how bad the illustrations are."

She gasped and said, "Who drew *these*?"

"I have no clue. Nobody with talent," he said with a chuckle, for he was amused by her reaction. "They don't look anything like bones really do. The fellow who drew these had obviously never seen an autopsy."

"You mean he never done what you and Dr. Teague do to dead people? Cut 'em up?"

"That's right. And it's obvious that he never really saw bones." He leaned back for a while, silent, then he turned to her and smiled. "You know what I'm going to do, Twyla? I'm going to produce something brand new. I'm going to write a book of anatomy."

Twyla looked confused. "What's that?"

"It will have in it every bone, every muscle, and every nerve laid out on a page so that young doctors won't have to go rob a grave or the gallows to get a body." He spoke with excitement, and Twyla listened intently. He continued to go through the book and point out the poorly drawn illustrations.

"There was a man once named Andreas Vesalius. He has always been a hero of mine. He loved to dissect things just the way I do. But back in his day, doctors didn't do dissecting. They depended on a man name Galen. But Vesalius was unhappy with some of the things the great Galen said, and one day he was dissecting a corpse and found out that it was not at all the way Galen had described it. He found out that Galen had never dissected a human being! He had only dissected monkeys and other animals. Now, is that a way for a physician to do research? No! Vesalius did something about it, and I intend to do the same."

At that moment the door opened and Phineas came in.

Twyla rose, saying, "Sit down, Doctor, I'll fix you something to eat."

"Thank you, Twyla, that will be nice. I'm famished."

Twyla left for a moment to get some milk from the next room. She overheard Phineas say, "That child is hungry to learn. She's done well. I was wrong about her in that way."

"Yes, you were. And yes, she has done very well."

Phineas said firmly, "You'd better be careful about her, though. I might have been wrong about her never cleaning herself up or never learning anything, but I'm sure she can still be trouble in some other ways."

"What are you talking about, Phineas?"

"I mean you must not do a wrong thing."

Colin's frustration was clear in his voice. "Why, she is just a child!"

"She's on the brink of becoming a woman. Mind what I say! Men are weak at best, and better men than you have been snared by a young woman."

Colin's face burned, for he had not freed himself from the guilt of his sin with Heather. It seemed that no prayer or effort could get that time out of his mind, and he could not answer his colleague.

Twyla came back in the room, and the two men grew quiet, not realizing she had heard the whole conversation. Phineas began to eat. He had a peculiar method—he shoved food into his mouth as if he were stuffing it into a cabinet to store for future use.

Finally, Colin said, "I've heard that the Seahawks have returned from a raid, and Adam was with them. Do you know when they got back?"

"Just this week. Came back with a load of plunder to give to the queen. They're having a big ball, and you should go. Adam will certainly be there."

"I believe I will. I'm very proud of Adam; as a matter of fact the whole family is."

Phineas looked at Colin. "It's you they should be proud of."

Colin shook his head. "I'm not the one bringing a treasure to the queen."

"And what if Elizabeth gets sick? Will she send for Adam, or for you? Let's have no more nonsense! Now, you should look like a prince. Where are your best clothes?"

As Colin entered the large room that was often used for dances and entertainments, many greeted him. His reputation had spread. He smiled and spoke to some, but to others he gave only cool greetings. These were the members of the Royal College of Physicians; they only feigned respect for him. The queen came in, and Elizabeth had never looked better. Her fine dress, studded with pearls and diamonds, glittered as she walked. As she entered, she turned and met Colin's eyes and gave him a warm smile, and Colin bowed deeply.

As soon as Elizabeth was seated, she lifted her hand, and the double doors opened. The Seahawks began to march in. At the head was Sir Francis Drake, the scourge of the Spanish Main. Immediately behind him, Colin saw his brother, Adam, dressed like royalty and smiling broadly. Behind them were men bearing chests of the treasures Drake brought back from his voyage. They put them down before the queen, and Drake said with a wide smile, "Here is your treasure, Your Majesty, straight from the pockets of the King of Spain!"

"I'm very grateful to you and the Seahawks, Sir Francis."

"We must hit them hard, Your Majesty! The easier we are on them, the harder they will make it on us."

Elizabeth did not respond, for she still wanted no wars. She had made it plain that if Drake were successful, that was one thing, but if he only made Spain angry enough to war, he would suffer for it.

After the presentations were made, Colin was watching as the queen spoke to Drake and to Adam. Someone called his name, and he turned and found Lady Heather Benton standing before him. She was dressed in a rich burgundy gown, her hair swept up and glittering with jewels. Shock ran through him, and all the wild emotions she had once stirred in him came rushing back. He could not speak for a moment, but she smiled quickly and said, "You're looking so well, Colin. And I hear such marvelous things about you."

"Thank you," Colin managed to say. "You—you look wonderful." Indeed, Heather was more beautiful than ever. Like the queen, she was dazzling. She spoke easily, praising his accomplishments. He finally said, "It's good to see you, Heather. I've missed you."

"Have you? I've missed you too."

This was encouragement enough to Colin, and his hope began to come back. "I would like to see you again sometime. Do you mind if I call on you?"

"Why, I think that would be fine." She turned to look at Adam, who stood with the other Seahawks. "The Seahawks have done well. They presented such bounty to the queen."

"We're all very proud of them, and my brother, Adam."

As they talked, Colin's hope continued to grow. Finally, Adam walked over to them. He looked tall and bronzed and extremely handsome. He spoke to Colin, but his eyes were on Lady Heather Benton. "Well, here you are, Brother. You're always working your wiles on the most beautiful women in the room!" he teased. "I beg, lady, do not put your trust in him, for he is a devil when women are concerned." He nudged Colin sharply, saying, "Introduce us, Colin."

Colin said with restraint, "This is Lady Heather Benton. Lady, this is my brother, Adam, as you well know."

Heather looked up at Adam, her eyes sparkling. "I've been such an admirer of the Seahawks! All England is so proud of your accomplishments."

Adam preened, saying, "If you can tear yourself away from my brother, I'll introduce you to Sir Francis Drake."

"Why, that would be wonderful!" Heather exclaimed. She slipped her arm through Adam's and they made their way through the crowd. Colin stood forgotten, and the happiness that had rushed through him left as quickly as it came. He could not bear to watch, for Heather was obviously taken with Adam. He left the room, not saying a word to anyone on his way out.

Twyla heard the door close and was surprised when she saw Colin come in. "It's so early! I thought you'd be home late."

"No, I've had all I can handle of balls."

He started for his room, but Twyla rushed to his side and tugged at his sleeve. "Mister, you promised to tell me all about the ball, about all the pretty dresses and the dancing. Please tell me."

"I don't feel like talking."

"But you promised!"

He heaved a sigh and said, "All right, fix me some of that good spiced ale you make and I'll tell you what I remember."

Soon he was sipping the hot liquid she had brewed for him. He told her of what the queen looked like with her pearls and diamonds on her dress and about the treasure Drake had presented. Twyla hung on his every word. "It must have been wonderful!" She had a dreamy look in her eyes as she asked, "Who else was there?"

"Well, there was Lady Heather Benton—" He broke off. "I didn't mean to talk about her."

Twyla knew something was wrong. "Why not? Do you know her?" Colin tried to change the subject, but she kept urging him to say more, made curious by the look in his eyes. He didn't say much, but Twyla soon learned that he felt deeply for the woman. When he finally in desperation let it slip that she had rejected him, Twyla said angrily, "She wouldn't 'ave you?"

"No! She used me, and then she threw me out!" Colin said bitterly. "When I saw her tonight I—I thought that we could find each other again. But she doesn't care a pin for me! She went off with Adam and forgot I was even there."

"Why, Colin, you're jealous of your own brother!" Twyla just realized she had used his name for the first time.

"No, I'm not!"

"Yes, you are. You still love that woman, or you wouldn't get so angry when you talk about 'er!"

"I don't care for her and I don't want to hear anything about it ever again!" Colin shouted. He got up and left the room, his face flushed.

Twyla stared at him as he left and muttered angrily, "Well, she's a bloody fool if she don't love you, Mister Colin Winslow!"

14

January 3, 1585

A beam of yellow light slanted through the windows. Tiny motes drifted through the amber rays that brought warmth into the coldness of the room. Colin was sitting at the table, carefully drawing on a piece of paper. His hand moved slowly and he bit his lower lip nervously. Suddenly, he straightened up and exclaimed, "Blasted paper! Blasted pen! Blasted everything!" Angrily, he crumpled the paper into a ball and threw it into the fire, muttering, "I just can't do it!"

Finally he stood and went to the window, watching as snow fell from a slate-colored sky. The flakes were as large as shillings and made a beautiful sight, softening the looks of fences and houses. Usually the sight pleased him greatly, but not now. When Twyla came in and asked, "What would you like for supper?" he snapped angrily, "What do I care? Fix anything you want." He had been trying for days now to make some anatomical sketches, but he had no talent for it.

Twyla snapped back, "You don't 'ave to shout at me! I'm not the one who's acting like a looney! You can fix your own bloody dinner!"

Colin turned and saw Twyla's red face, and he realized he

had hurt her. At once he moved over to her and put his hand on her shoulder, saying, "I didn't mean to shout, child."

"I'm not no child!" Twyla spat out at him. She was angry to the bone. Ordinarily it would have softened her to have Colin's hand on her shoulder, but now she had nothing but rage. "I'm not no child, Mister Colin Winslow! The way of a woman come on me nearly a year ago."

Colin stared at her in dismay. "I—I didn't know." A guilty feeling shot through Colin and he patted her shoulder. "I'm so sorry, Twyla. I know I'm full of faults, but please don't be angry with me."

Twyla slapped his hand away and shouted, "Keep yer bloody 'ands off me!" She burst out crying and ran blindly from the room.

Colin stared after her and ran his hands through his hair. With a sigh, he returned to his fruitless struggles to make the drawings for the book. He worked for an hour, but at the end he gave up in disgust. He got up from the desk and began pacing the floor. He had exhausted himself working on his book in addition to the busy practice he shared with Teague. The autopsies had been simple enough for him, for he was very clever in that way; his hands were strong and sensitive. Yet at the same time, it was impossible to make the bones, the muscles, and the nerves look realistic in drawings. He sighed, lowered his head, and whispered, "Lord, why can't I *do* this?" He got no answer and realized it was the first time in months that he had prayed. Actually, he prayed very little. His religion was a habitual thing, for his parents had brought him up in church. He knew he did not have the close relationship with God that they did. This troubled him, especially at times like these.

I need to get away from all this. I'll go home and visit the family. It was a sudden decision, but he knew it was right. Moving to the door, he called out, "Twyla?" and then waited until she appeared in the doorway. Her cheeks were wet with tears. "I'm so sorry I yelled at you. I'm sorry for everything." He saw that her face didn't change and said, "I'm going home to go visit my family. I was wondering if you would like to come with me." Her face brightened and the anger disappeared. Colin knew this was the way with Twyla. She could be filled with rage, but seconds later she would be happy and cheery as ever.

"Oh, yes!"

"All right, get your things. We are leaving today."

"In all this snow?"

"We are not going to let a little snow stop us." Colin had a slight smile turning up the corners of his mouth, for he was happy that he had made her feel better. "We'll have a vacation, just you and me. My parents will be excited to see you." Once again he was pleased because of the way the excitement changed her features. He realized her face, especially her eyes, were a window into her emotions.

He also suddenly realized that this girl had a beautiful face. He saw that there was a hint of her will in her eyes and in her lips. Her complexion was fair, with a tint of rose color in her cheeks that showed up when she was angry or embarrassed. The most exotic of Twyla's features were her violet eyes, set off by her black hair, the densest black he had ever seen. It occurred to him that she had grown up since he had brought her to live with him at his home. Still, he could see behind her composed expressions a little girl's eagerness.

"I'll get ready right now, Mister!" she cried, then wheeled and ran lightly toward her room.

The fire crackled and snapped as Brandon poked the logs with a heavy iron poker. The sparks flew like fiery stars up the chimney, and the heat filled the room. He and Eden were sitting in the parlor, the warmest room in the house.

"It is nice here," Eden said. "I don't remember such a long cold spell."

Brandon glanced at Eden and smiled. "The wisest thing I ever did was marry you."

Eden laughed, saying, "You never cease to amaze me, Brandon. You can be mean as a snake, and then you come out with something sweet like that."

"When was I ever mean as a snake?"

"Lots of times, but I have a way of forgiving." Eden said this with her teasing smile.

Brandon grinned back at her. "It's good to have a wife who ignores a man's shortcomings." He settled back in the chair and held his boots up to the fire. "I had a letter from Walsingham."

"What did he say?"

"The same thing he always says: 'Mary, Queen of Scots, is in conspiracy. She is the greatest danger England has.'"

"She's a prisoner. Elizabeth had her locked up the moment she came to England. What on earth can she do?"

Brandon gave her a sour glance. "She can still have Elizabeth assassinated."

"She would never do a thing like that!" Eden protested.

"She had her husband killed. What makes you think she would do less to Elizabeth?"

The two talked about the political situation in England, both well aware that England was on the razor's edge of war with Spain, and it would only take one incident to bring the Spanish down on their nation.

A tall servant appeared and said quietly, "Sir, Master Colin is here."

Instantly they got up and Eden said, "We've been expecting Adam, not Colin. Did he tell you he was coming?"

"He didn't say a word," Brandon said. "You know how impulsive he is."

Colin, accompanied by Twyla, entered the kitchen and was greeted by his parents. Eden gave Colin a kiss and he hugged her. Her eyes then turned to Twyla. "Why, my dear, you have grown since I've seen you!"

"Yes, you have," Brandon said. "It's good to have you here, Twyla."

"Thank you, sir. Thank you, Lady Winslow," Twyla murmured. Her face was pinched with cold, as was Colin's.

"Come to the fire and get warm," Brandon said.

They huddled close to the fire, and Eden had a maid brew some hot spiced ale for them. When they were warm, Eden said to Twyla, "You come with me. Let these men talk about unimportant things. I've got something *really* important to show you."

Eden led Twyla down the hall and up to the second floor, where she and Brandon shared a bedroom. There was still a fire burning so she didn't call a servant, but she put two small logs on and waited until they crackled merrily. Then she smiled, saying, "I can't believe how much you've grown! Pull up a chair until it gets warmer." She waited until Twyla sat down, then sat close to her. "Now tell me what you have been doing."

"The same as always. I cook and keep house. I try to keep the washing done. Just regular work, I guess."

"I'm sure you do more than that." Eden smiled a sweet smile, and a thought came to her. "I wonder if there is a young man pursuing you."

"No!"

Eden saw that she was troubled. "I'm sure there will be soon enough. Now, let me show you what I brought you up here for." She walked over to a heavy walnut wardrobe. She pulled out some garments and laid them down on her bed. "I knew that we'd see you sooner or later and that you would need some new clothes, so I've been getting you a new wardrobe."

Surprise washed across Twyla's face, and she whispered, "Lady Winslow, you shouldn't have done that."

"Nonsense! It's given me much pleasure. Now slip this on, and we'll see if it is too big."

Ten minutes later Twyla was standing before the fire, pleased with the new dress. "It's a perfect fit!"

"It certainly is! How old did you say you were, Twyla?"

She lowered her head and spoke in a soft tone. "I don't know, Lady. Fourteen or fifteen, I guess. I was never told exactly. I guess I could even be sixteen."

"Well, your figure has certainly blossomed since I saw you last."

Twyla looked down and ran her hand over the pale green material. It was the finest dress she had ever worn. It had a fitted bodice and a wide, low, square neckline. The long skirt opened in front to show a decorative kirtle, and the wide fur cuffs on the sleeves of the overgarment were beautiful. "It's so lovely!" Twyla whispered. "But it's too fine for me."

"Nonsense! Now, let's go down and let Colin and my husband admire you."

Eden led her back down the stairs and into the kitchen, where the men were still sitting at the table. As soon as they entered, Brandon jumped up and exclaimed, "Bless my soul! Look at that girl!"

Colin could not speak, and Eden saw that he was shocked. Brandon was praising the dress and how wonderful Twyla looked in it, but Colin stood staring. Eden looked at Twyla and saw that she was disappointed that Colin had said nothing. "Don't you like Twyla's new dress, Colin?" Eden asked.

"What? Why, of course I do! I'm so impressed that I'm speechless. Yes, Twyla, I like your dress very much indeed!" He added uncertainly, "I just don't know enough about young women to see that you needed new things."

Eden said with satisfaction, "Well, now you know, so you can see that she gets new clothes as she needs them. Oh, Colin, did your father tell you that Adam will be here soon?"

"Yes, he did. I'll be glad to see him," Colin replied, then added, "I thought I'd go see Meg while we're here."

"I had a feeling you would be doing that," Brandon said with a grin. "You two are always in some sort of conspiracy, it seems."

"No conspiracy, sir. She was my best friend growing up."

"Can I go with you, Mister?" Twyla asked suddenly.

"Why, Twyla, it's freezing out there. You ought to stay here and thaw out."

"I wish I could go. You've told me so much about Meg, I'd like to meet her."

"Well, if you like. We will need some fresh horses, I think. But we won't go until the weather breaks."

"We have fresh horses," Brandon said. "You take this young woman and go visit your friend anytime you like."

Meg was stirring the soup in a black pot suspended over the fire. It gave off a delicious aroma. She suddenly heard a voice calling from outside. At once she put the spoon down and ran to the door. As soon as she opened it, Colin came, in grinning widely. Before she could even speak, he grabbed her, lifted her off the floor, and swung her around. He hugged her warmly, and when he put her down, Meg said with a laugh, "Don't be so rough with an old woman!"

"You're not old, Meg. You never were." Colin smiled. "I'm so glad to see you. I've missed you."

"Did you now? Well, I'm glad to hear it. How long have you been here?"

"Just a week."

Meg looked at the young woman who hung back uncertainly at the door. "And who is this? Don't tell me you have brought a wife back with you?"

Meg saw Colin was shocked by this statement. He stared at Meg, swallowed hard, and said, "Oh, no! This is Twyla. She takes care of Dr. Teague and me—and a very good job she does! Twyla, this is my good friend Meg. You have heard me speak of her often."

"I'm glad to know you, Twyla." Meg went over and shook her hand and stared at her intently. "So you take care of this young fellow and his mentor?"

"Yes, I do the best I can."

"I'm sure you do a very good job indeed. Now come on inside, for I've got a treat for you."

The two sat down in two rough chairs. Meg went to the fireplace and spooned out helpings from the black pot into wooden bowls. She set the bowls in front of them along with two wooden spoons. "Try that," she said, "while I get some for myself."

Colin glanced mischievously at Twyla. "Don't ask what this is. It could be anything. Meg thinks all meat is good to eat."

"You mind your manners, Colin Winslow, or I'll take a stick to you!" Meg snapped. She came back with a bowl for herself and took a seat, saying, "This is turtle soup, and it's wonderful."

Colin tasted the soup and exclaimed, "This is as good as ever!"

"It is good!" Twyla said. "I've never tasted anything like it."

"The first time I met Colin, he was just a boy. He had a turtle and I made him give it to me."

"That's right. You cooked it, and I had my first taste of turtle soup." He ate hungrily, as did Twyla. As soon as they'd finished, Meg got up to get them some more of the delicious soup and some ale. "That ought to warm your insides. Now, tell me what you have been doing with yourself."

Meg listened as Colin spoke of his progress as a physician, but she was watching Twyla. The girl said little, and Meg had trouble guessing her age. Finally, when Colin had finished catching Meg up on all of his news, she demanded, "Well, what about yourself, Twyla? How in the world did you end up waiting on this ungrateful boy?"

"I'm not ungrateful," Colin protested.

"Yes, you are. *All* men are ungrateful," Meg said with some playfulness in her voice, but Colin noticed a ring of truth in her declaration.

Meg listened as the girl told in detail how Colin had saved her and ended by saying, "So I belong to Mister for seven years—well, less than that now."

Colin said vehemently, "I don't own you, Twyla! I wish you would stop saying that!"

Meg laughed and pulled a lock of Colin's hair, saying, "He's a devil with young women, so you'd better watch yourself."

Colin quickly said, "You know that is not true, Meg."

Twyla said quietly, "He'd never hurt me, not Mister!"

As the two sat talking, Meg saw that the Twyla never took her eyes off Colin. *Why, the poor child is smitten with him! And he's as blind as a bat!*

Meg pulled Colin aside as Twyla was getting her warm cloak. She whispered, "Be careful, boy! If you do this girl harm, you are no man and never will be!"

Colin said with exasperation, "Why, Meg, I would never harm Twyla!"

Meg shook her head. "See to it you don't. Don't you dare break her heart."

Colin stared at her without understanding, then saw that Twyla was ready. The two left the house, and as soon as they were mounted, Twyla asked, "What was Meg saying to you?"

"Oh, nothing important."

"It looked important to me. Now, what was it?"

Colin tried to think of a way to answer. "She just wanted me to be good to you."

"What did she mean by that?"

Colin saw that Twyla was more observant than he'd thought. Even now she was watching him steadily. "Well, she warned me not to be to be, well, too affectionate to you."

Twyla glared at him. "She didn't need to say that to you. You never are affectionate to anyone except your mother."

"Why, Twyla, you know how I appreciate the care you give Dr. Teague and me."

Twyla started to answer, then pursed her lips and shook her head. This troubled Colin, but he didn't know how to go on with the conversation.

They rode quickly, and when they arrived back at the house Adam was there to greet them. He looked big and strong, and his face was lit up with a huge smile. He came at once and grabbed Colin, saying with excitement, "I've got big news for you, brother!"

"What is it, Adam?"

"I'm getting married!" He laughed and added, "I'll wager you'll never guess the name of my bride. It's Lady Heather Benton! She has won my heart." Adam struck Colin lightly on the arm. "She speaks so well of you, but then her whole family does. Apparently you will have no problems with your sister-in-law. Wish me joy, Colin."

Colin had trouble speaking and could only say, "I hope you will be very happy." He soon excused himself to go to his room.

Later that afternoon he surprised his whole family by saying, "Twyla and I must get back."

"But it's too cold," Eden said. "Stay a while longer."

Colin shook his head. "We must get back."

Adam protested, but continued speaking of Heather and how happy he was. "I've never been so happy! You must find yourself a young woman, Colin. Fall in love with her and marry her. Then you'll know what true love is!"

Twyla rode silently beside Colin all the way back to the house. It was a long trip and very cold. When they arrived, Teague was there to greet them and noticed Colin's strange and distant manner. This bothered him, for he knew Colin better than anyone did—except Twyla. When Colin went to his room, Phineas asked, "What's the matter with Colin?"

"His brother, Adam, is going to marry a woman named Lady Heather Benton."

"Oh, my! That's too bad!"

"Why is he so upset about it?"

"Well, I shouldn't be telling you this, but maybe you need to know, Twyla. We were called in to treat Lady Benton's brother, and after he grew better, I left but Colin stayed for quite a long spell with her family. When he returned, it was as if he'd been shot in the heart. Colin had been totally bewitched by that awful woman! I thought he had gotten over her rejection, but perhaps a man never forgets his first love."

Twyla said quietly, "I know. Colin told me what happened. He's still in love with that woman, and now she's marrying his brother! I wish I could help him."

"No one can," Teague said bitterly. "Men can be fools where women are concerned!"

15

April 3, 1585

Phineas Teague straightened up to ease his aching back, looked across the cadaver that lay on the table in front of him, and studied Colin's face. Teague was not a man of much emotion, at least that he allowed others to see, but he had grown attached to his young friend. As he studied his former pupil, Phineas felt a sudden gladness. *Well, in my old age, I don't have a son of my blood, but at least I have this young fellow!* The thought pleased him, and he wondered for a moment if there was any way that he could put these emotions into words. But a lifelong habit of keeping his feelings to himself was too strong, so instead of speaking of his affection, he said briskly, "Well, we did all we could to save this poor fellow, didn't we, Colin?"

"I suppose so, but I was hoping he would make it," Colin said quietly.

They leaned over the corpse and stared at a small piece of tissue, an organ that Colin had lifted with his scalpel. "I still don't know what this thing is," Colin muttered. "I don't know what it is for, but it's in everyone. It must have *some* function. I've looked in every book I can think of all the way back to Hippocrates, but none of them even mention this."

"Small wonder," Phineas said dryly, then he reached out and touched the small organ. "Most of the old masters never even opened a dead body. You know, Colin, I keep thinking this tiny organ here had something to do with his death."

"He did complain of a terrible pain in his stomach. Somehow, even though I can't prove it, I *know* this thing killed him."

The two men studied the small bit of flesh, and finally Colin said, "Phineas, we need to do autopsies on other people who've had the same symptoms as this man."

"That would be risky, as you well know. Most of the members of the College of Physicians hate us already. They aren't about to give us any information, nor will they let us see the bodies of their patients that have died."

Colin had a quick thought. "Do you remember any of your patients who had the same symptoms as this man and then died?"

"I've been thinking about that." Phineas stroked his chin thoughtfully, then nodded. "I can remember a few with like symptoms, but I didn't do autopsies on them, so there is no way of telling what the cause of death was."

Colin shrugged his shoulders. "We doctors don't know as much as we should, do we?"

"Well, we know more than we did. Look at all those silly teachings of Galen. Speaking of books, how is that book of yours coming?"

"The text is fine, but it will be worthless without illustrations. The trouble is I'm no artist. None of my drawings looks authentic."

"So, hire an artist then."

Colin laughed, saying, "I doubt I could find one that would be willing to draw pictures of the insides of bodies. Most want to paint flowers, or pretty faces."

"You'll find someone. Don't give up, my boy."

❧

Colin leaned over the table, holding the quill firmly in his hand. He was making a sketch of one of the bones in the human arm and having a hard time of it. His brow was furrowed, and he shook his head, muttering, "I'll never be able to do it!" Suddenly he was interrupted by a knock on the door. Sticking the quill in the ink pot, he rose and walked to the door. When he opened it he saw a young man he recognized as James Laurence, a blacksmith from the village. "Come in, James."

"Thank you, sir."

Twyla entered the room and James greeted her warmly, "Good afternoon, Miss Hayden."

"Good afternoon to you, James."

Colin wanted to get back to his attempts at drawing, so he said rather shortly, "James, do you have a medical problem?"

"Why, no, sir. I don't."

Twyla said quickly, "Come with me into the kitchen, James, and sit down. I want you to try this spiced ale I just made. It's got ginger and cinnamon and just a little bit of honey."

"Thank you, Miss Hayden. It sounds delicious."

"Would you have some, Dr. Winslow?"

"No, I don't have time for that."

Impatiently, Colin waited until the pair went into the kitchen. He walked back to his desk and began to draw, but Twyla's and James's voices distracted him. They were talking of music, fairs, and other events that were taking place.

Finally, after an interminable time—or so it seemed to Colin—he heard the door open, then close. He got to his feet and turned to Twyla, saying sarcastically, "He's gone, then?"

"Yes, he's gone."

"I thought he would never leave!"

"Well, he didn't come to see *you*."

"Why did he come, then?"

"He came to see me."

Colin stared at her in shock. "Why would he do that?"

Twyla's cheeks colored slightly. "You think that it's impossible for a young man to come just to see me?"

Colin was already angry with himself for his failure to do the drawings for his book, and without meaning to he snapped, "Well, he can't call on you!"

"And why not, Mister?"

Colin tried to think of a reason that would not sound absurd, and finally blurted out, "You're too young. That's why."

"James doesn't seem to think so."

"Well, I don't like this whole thing."

Twyla turned to face Colin squarely. She had a tremendous capacity for strong emotions, and now she felt anger from the top of her head down to the tips of her toes. Her lips came together in a tight line. "I know what it is. It's because you own me, isn't it?"

"I never think of myself as owning you, as I have told you many times! But anyway, I don't know this James well, and he might not have good intentions." Then he blurted out, "Young men are dangerous."

Suddenly, a wry smile came to Twyla's lip. "Are you dangerous to women, Mister?"

"Of course not!"

"No? What about Heather Benton?" She knew as soon as the words left her lips that she had made a mistake.

Colin stared at Twyla, unable to answer. Finally, he said stiffly, "I don't own you. Let the young man call on you if he wants." He abruptly left the room, and Twyla could not remember his being as upset since she had come to live with Colin and Dr. Teague. "I shouldn't have mentioned that woman," she whispered to herself. "He feels bad enough, and I made it worse."

For a week, the tension between Twyla and Colin was almost a physical thing. Twyla tried desperately to undo her words, for she knew she had been wrong to utter them. A week passed, and as she got ready to go to market, she decided to get Colin to go with her. She walked through the house and found him staring at the book in front of him. "Mister, would you please go with me to the market? I have to buy quite a few things and it would be too much for me to carry."

Colin had a stubborn look on his face. He opened his mouth to refuse but instead got to his feet. "All right." He was tired of the barrier of tension between him and Twyla. He saw no signs of anger in Twyla; he realized the anger was only in him.

The two left the house, and Twyla did her best to cheer Colin up. She had always been able to do that. She was surprised when Colin mentioned Adam.

"Did I tell you that Adam is coming by to see us?"

"No, you didn't."

"He's been at home, but he's going to visit us before he goes back to his ship. I expect him sometime this week."

Twyla said no more on the subject. She knew that Colin was unhappy about his brother's upcoming wedding, although he had never said anything about it to her.

They passed by a pub, and as they did, two soldiers came out. One of them was a large man who said, "Well, this is a pretty one, isn't she, Sid?" The soldier put his hand in the small of Twyla's back.

"Better watch out, Barrett. She's got a man with her. He may take you to task," the soldier named Sid jeered.

Barrett sized up Colin and laughed, saying, "I don't reckon this pretty boy will hurt me. Will you, fellow?"

"Take your hands off of this young woman!" Colin said aggressively.

Barrett had blunt features and bulging muscles, and he wore a sword at his side, as all soldiers did. He wrapped his arm around Twyla's waist and said with a laugh, "You run along, sonny. This young lady's going to keep me company."

Colin stepped forward and tried to remove the man's arm from Twyla's waist. Sid simply pushed him back and grinned broadly, saying, "You better watch out, Barrett. He's getting mad. He'll probably cut you in two."

Barrett chuckled. "He don't even have a sword. What are you, some kind of clerk or something?'

"He's a doctor!" Twyla cried. "Now turn me loose!"

"A doctor, is he? Well, if I ever get sick, I'll know where to come." He grinned at Twyla and hugged her tighter. "You and me, we have things to do."

Colin stepped forward and struck at the soldier. He hit him in the face, but his blow didn't even move the man.

Barrett turned with surprise, and Sid laughed. "Don't let him insult you like that, Barrett. Meet him with any weapons he chooses."

Barrett's face was red. "I don't like being hit, Mr. Physician. You have to prove you're a man now. I've been in a duel or two. You can choose your weapon: sword or pistol?"

Twyla jerked away from the man and took hold of Colin's arm, trying to pull him away. "They're drunk, Colin. Don't listen to them."

"If you're any kind of a man you'll meet me next Friday," the large soldier said abruptly with a slight smile on his face. "Meet me at dusk in the cemetery. What'll it be, swords or pistols?"

"Swords!" Colin said. He wasn't sure why he said that—he'd had little enough experience with one.

Barrett laughed loudly. "Remember, next Friday at dusk in the cemetery. If you're not there, I'll find you and take a horse-whip to you right down the middle of this village." With a cruel smile he looked at Twyla and said, "Then I'll find something for me and this young lady to do together."

"I'll be there," Colin said firmly.

Twyla pulled at his arm, and when they were out of hearing distance she said, "You just ignore him, Mister. He is only a drunken soldier."

"I can't do that."

Twyla was shocked. "You can't fight him!"

"I have to."

Twyla argued with him all the way home. Stubbornly, Colin said, "I'll fight him, and that's all there is to it!"

As soon as they were in the house, Twyla told Dr. Teague what had happened. Teague said instantly, "Don't be a fool, Colin! Fighting is his profession. You're no good with a sword."

"I probably am a fool, but I'm going to do it." He turned and walked away.

Twyla turned to Teague, pleading, "You have to stop him, Doctor! You must, or he'll get himself killed."

"I'll do the best I can, but I've noticed that as easygoing as Colin is, there's a stubborn streak in him. I don't see it often, but I see it now."

"We have to think of *something*," Twyla said. "I couldn't stand it if something happened to him!"

"Nor could I. I'll think of something to be done."

Friday morning came, and Twyla had slept little. She went about the house mechanically doing her chores, and Colin stayed in his room. Twyla walked into the room where the two doctors made up their medicines and found Dr. Teague, who was measuring medicine out into bottles. As she watched him an idea suddenly arose, and she asked, "What's in that bottle?"

"This is oil of basil. It's good for the croup."

Twyla pointed to another bottle. "And this one?"

"That's a compound good for rubbing on open sores," Teague answered.

She picked up a large brown bottle and asked, "What is this?"

"Well, that is what we give people when we have to do some surgery on them."

"You mean it makes it not hurt?"

"It's like liquor, but a lot stronger. The person passes out." Teague shook his head. "It's really very dangerous. If you give too much it can be fatal."

"How much would be too much?"

Teague picked up a small tin cup. "Half of this cup would be enough to knock an ox down. I wouldn't give a patient even half of that. Why are you asking all these questions?"

"No reason." Twyla didn't say any more. Her mind was made up to go through with her plan.

Teague was staring at her. "You're up to something. What is it, girl?"

Twyla hesitated, then decided to trust the old man. "I thought if I could give Colin a drug to make him sleep, he couldn't go to fight that stupid duel—and he wouldn't get killed."

Teague laughed aloud. "You are a devious young woman— but you could kill him if you give him too much. Here, I'll mix you up a dose that will make him sleep like a baby!"

It was after four o'clock when Colin came out of his room. His face was pale as he said, "I have to go pretty soon, Twyla."

Twyla said quickly, "You must eat something. You've haven't eaten all day."

"I'm not hungry."

"Just a little bit to give you some strength." She pulled him to the table, and he sat down. She put some cold beef in front of him and some fresh-baked bread. He ate a few bites and she said, "Here, try this. It's a new kind of wine."

"It smells like it's full of spices."

She smiled, saying, "That's why it's called 'spiced wine,' Just try it."

Twyla watched as Colin drank the wine. "Very good," he said absently. He drank from the flagon until it was gone; then he sat there for a few minutes, saying nothing. "I know you think I'm insane," he finally said. "I don't know why this is so important to me. I think it has something to do with Adam."

She looked puzzled. "How could this have to do with him?"

"He is always the one who gives pride to the family. He can fight in battles at sea—I haven't ever done anything. He is able and I'm not."

Twyla pulled up a chair beside Colin. "Tell me about what you and Adam were like when you were children. Here, have some more wine," she said as she refilled his flagon.

He took another swallow of the wine and began to talk about their childhood. Twyla noticed that his speech was getting slower and becoming slurred. Finally, he blinked his eyes. "I'm getting sick, Twyla."

"You'd better lie down until it passes."

Colin got to his feet and started toward the horsehide sofa. He was weaving when he got there, and he muttered, "The room is spinning around."

"Lie down, Colin. It'll pass." He lay down, and Twyla put his legs up on the sofa. She watched as his eyelids fluttered, then closed. He was stumbling through words, trying to speak. Finally he quit, his breathing slow and regular.

"He'll hate me when he wakes up," she whispered, "but at least he'll be alive."

Thirty minutes after Colin lay down, there was a knock at the door. Twyla went to the door and saw Adam. "Well, Miss Twyla, how are you?"

"Oh, Captain Winslow, something terrible has happened!"

"What is it? What is the trouble?"

"It's Mister Colin. He is supposed to fight a man, and I know he would get killed."

Adam stepped inside, having to duck his head because of the low doorway. He listened as she told the story. He leaned in closer and stared at her with surprise. "You say you drugged him?"

"I couldn't think of nothing else to do."

Adam's lips turned up in a smile. "He hasn't been drunk in some time, I suppose."

"But he'll hate me!"

"He'll be alive and not hurt; that's what counts. I'll take care of this fellow he's supposed to fight. Where are they supposed to meet?"

"The man said at the cemetery at dusk," Twyla quickly answered.

"Well, it's about that time. I'll be back after I take care of this." He turned and left. Twyla felt a sense of relief. *Adam is strong. I know it makes Colin feel bad that he is not a man like this, but I'm glad he is not.*

The village was quiet and most of the citizens had gone home, seeking the warmth of their fires. A few people hurried along the main street. The two soldiers, who had been drinking heavily, were laughing as they approached the cemetery. "Here, have some more, Barrett," the short one named Sid said, offering his companion the flagon.

"That's right, Sid. I'll need some liquid courage to face that man-killing doctor," Barrett said sarcastically.

The laughter went on, along with more rude jokes about Colin Winslow. Finally, Sid said, "Here comes somebody, but that isn't the doctor."

"That's not him—he's too big," Barrett said.

The two stood and watched as the large man approached. He was over six feet tall and strongly built. He had a sword at his side, and his eyes were a steel blue. "Which one of you is Barrett?"

"That's me."

"My name is Winslow."

"You're not the doctor I had trouble with. Where is he?"

"He's indisposed. I'm acting as his representative." Adam drew his sword. "I'm Captain Adam Winslow of the Seahawks, second in command to Sir Francis Drake. I've been killing Spaniards, but I'm tired of that. So now I'm going to kill myself a worthless drunk soldier. Draw your sword!"

Barrett took one look at the fierce intensity in Adam's eyes and began to back away. "I didn't mean no harm, sir."

Suddenly, with a lightning-quick movement, Adam touched his sword right over Barrett's heart. His voice grew harsh as steel. "You lay a hand on my brother, you scum, and I'll cut pieces off of you an inch at a time! You understand that?"

"Y—Yes, sir. Come on, let's get out of here," he said to his companion.

The pair scurried away, and Adam began to laugh. "Not a fight in the bunch of them! Well, it's a good thing I came."

The room seemed to be swimming, and Colin felt as if he were rising out of a dark pit. His vision was blurry, but a candle outlined the figure of Twyla, who was sitting beside him. "What—what happened to me?"

"I couldn't help it, Mister! I had to do it!"

Colin sat up and immediately felt sick. "Get me some water, will you, Twyla? My lips are dry as a bone."

She rose, went to the kitchen, and came back soon with a cup filled with water. He drank it thirstily and he said, "It's time to go."

"It's too late. Look, it's dark outside."

"What happened to me? Did I get sick?"

Twyla knew she had no choice but to confess. "I got some

medicine that makes people sleep. I put it in the wine. That's what made you so sleepy."

"I'll still have to face that soldier," Colin said. "You just put it off."

"No, Adam came. He went in your place."

"Adam? Where is he?"

"He had to leave already. He came back here after he went to the cemetery, but his ship was due out. You don't have to worry. Adam scared those men so bad they'll never show their faces again."

Colin dropped his head. "Like I've always said, he's the strong one. I'm the weak one."

"Please don't hate me, Colin, and don't hate Adam. He loves you and he does whatever he can to help you, just as you would help him as a doctor if he got sick."

Colin was still woozy, but he said, "I'm glad you were able to stop me from going, even if the method was rather harsh. And I'm glad Adam was able to get that man off my back." He saw that her face was tense and she was close to tears. "But the next time you want to stop me from doing something, don't give me any drugs. Just talk to me."

Twyla whispered, "I did talk to you, but you wouldn't listen. I won't use the medicine again." She hesitated, then said, "As long as you behave, that is."

Colin reached out and ran his hand down her black hair. He suddenly felt better. He had not run away from the fight. "Next time you want to keep me from making a fool of myself, just hit me over the head with a stick. It couldn't feel as bad as this." He smiled weakly as he said, "Don't worry. I'll try not to be a bother to you anymore."

"How could you be a bother to me?" Twyla said softly. She saw that he was smiling, and this lifted her spirits. A rose color stained her cheeks, and her lips were caught in an uncertain, crooked smile. Whatever mistakes she had made, there was a sweetness and gentleness about her, Colin noticed. As his hands smoothed her hair, she held her head straight and looked at him, a quiet longing in her violet eyes. "I didn't want you to get hurt," she whispered.

"I'm glad to have someone to look after me," Colin said. "I hope you always will."

16

January 3, 1586

Over two feet of snow had fallen, cloaking the dead woods and the brown earth with a pristine blanket. All afternoon the sun had come out from time to time from behind tawny clouds and struck what seemed to be flashes of diamonds in the whiteness. The far-off low hills in their sullen haze brooded over some brutal thought and hunched down, seeming to seek shelter from the piercing cold.

Night had fallen now, and Colin went to the window and peered out. The faint crescent of the moon gave only enough light for him to see the white landscape. He drew his shoulders together against the sharp, pinching cold that pervaded the house. It seemed to him for a moment that the world was a dead ball moving through dead space. Suddenly the house shook as a gust of wind came out of the northwest. Colin looked up, startled, for it was as if a giant hand had taken the house and moved it roughly back and forth. He stood there as the wind whistled a long, low whine.

The snow began to pile up on the cold, dead world, and it seemed to Colin at that moment that the tremendously heavy stillness of the night was crushing him. He shivered slightly, and the shadows outside the house seemed to be filled with small stirrings as a faint sibilance whispered out of the freezing cold. Colin gave one more glance outside and saw a handful of stars; then one single star fell and made a faint scratch on the heavens. For some reason this depressed Colin. He turned, shoulders hunched against the cold, and moved away from the window. He came to stand over the dead ashes in the fireplace, staring at them. For a moment he thought of building up the fire, but he was weary to the bone and decided not to. Uncertainly, he stood there not wanting to go back to a cold bed, then sighed and moved to a horse-hide-covered chair. He looked at the drawings that lay on the table, then put one finger out and traced an illustration. He noted that his finger was white with cold and that it trembled slightly. The depression he'd felt before returned, and he shoved his hands beneath his armpits and tried to warm them.

"What are you doing up this time of the night?"

Startled, Colin looked up to see that Twyla had entered the room. She was wearing a heavy robe that he had bought for her. She also wore fur-lined house shoes. Her black hair seemed to glisten, and her eyes watched him carefully.

"What are you doing up, Twyla?"

"I heard you thumping around. Why don't you go to bed?"

Colin did not answer. He was studying Twyla and thinking how strange it was that she had grown up from a twiggy adolescent into a beautiful young lady in so short a time. Even though she was shrouded by the heavy robe, he could see the traces of her womanly form.

"I'm not sleepy, but you should go to bed," he said wearily.

"Where is Dr. Teague?"

"I don't know. He went off on some errand."

"At this hour? You don't think he has a woman somewhere, do you?"

Colin tried to smile, but his face was stiff from the cold. "I doubt that. He is a mysterious fellow, but a little old for chasing women."

Twyla did not reply. For a long moment she stood looking at his thin face, then asked, "Have you eaten today?"

"I ate some bread and cold mutton."

"When was that?"

"Sometime this morning. I don't know."

"I'll fix you something."

"No, you'd have to build a fire." He saw that she ignored him, and he was too tired to argue. He watched as she gathered the small sticks that they used for starting fires. She made a small pyramid out of it, then went to the lamp and lit a twist of paper. She carried it back to the fireplace, knelt down, and held it against the small pyramid. She waited until it caught, then carefully piled pieces of rich pine on it until it crackled brightly. The twigs burned as if they were soaked in oil. She stirred the small fire, sending myriads of sparks up the chimney, then piled more durable wood on it. Soon the warmth of the fire reached Colin and he said sleepily, "That feels good."

The heat radiated from the fireplace with a cheerful sound. For a time, Colin shut his eyes and welcomed the warmth that seemed to soak into his very bones. He heard Twyla move closer to him and had almost dozed off when he heard her say, "Here, drink this."

Opening his eyes, Colin saw that she was in front of him with a flagon. "What's that?"

"It's a posset."

Colin took it and stared at it. "What's a posset?"

"It's something that I've been working on. Nice spiced pottage of milk. It's curdled with some wine. It's good when it's hot, and I've put some honey in it to make it taste good."

Colin seized the warm cup. He tasted it. "Mmm, that's good!"

"Next time I'll put some ginger in it, or maybe some cloves."

Colin drained the cup and handed it back. She refilled it. "Drink some more. It'll warm your insides."

Comfort and warmth spread through Colin as he drank the second posset. He stared for a time at the fireplace with its popping sparks and bright colors. "What have you been doing all day?" he asked in a tired voice.

"I went to church."

"Did you like the sermon?"

She turned and gave him a long look. "Not much. I don't understand religion, Mister. What does it all mean?"

Colin stirred uneasily. "Why do you always call me 'Mister'?"

"It's proper, that's why. I can't call you 'Colin.'"

"I don't see why not."

Twyla turned and faced him. The heat was filling the room, and she allowed the robe to fall open at the top, exposing the woolen garment she wore underneath. "Because I'm your property."

Colin threw his hands up in a gesture of despair. "Twyla, I've told you a hundred times that's nonsense. If you say that one more time, I'll—!"

Colin broke off, and Twyla demanded, "What will you do? Beat me?"

"I might do just that!"

"No, you won't."

"How do you know?"

"Because it's not in you to beat anything." It was something she brought up frequently. "Why did you save me from that awful man?" she asked abruptly as she continued to stare at him. A small dimple appeared at the corner of her mouth, and he was aware that she was annoying him on purpose. He saw the light that danced in her eyes, and at the same time he saw her will and pride visible in those eyes and in the corners of her lips. "Why did you buy me?" she demanded again.

"I don't know."

"I know. You felt sorry for me."

"Maybe I did."

Twyla fell silent for a moment. Then she moved over and spooned some stew out of a kettle hanging above the fire into a wooden bowl. She came back and put it before Colin, and he ate it hungrily. "You're a fine cook, Twyla."

"Yes, I am." She refilled his cup twice after he had emptied it, then sat down and ate some stew herself.

She put the utensils away, then came and sat down on the floor, her back to the fire. "Tell me how you were when you were a boy."

"Why would you want to know that?"

"I'm nosy. All women are nosy."

"You're right there!" He began to speak, for he had long noted that she loved to hear about his boyhood days. He found pleasure in going back in his mind and finding the memories that lingered there. Finally, he grew sleepy and rose to his feet. He picked up three large logs and put them on the fire. "That ought to last until morning. I'm going to sleep in here where it's warm."

"So am I."

Twyla got up and left the room. She soon came back with covers. He was sitting in the chair, dozing off. She put one of the blankets over him, and then wrapped herself up and lay down close to the fire.

"You'll burn yourself up, Twyla."

"No, I won't. Now you go to sleep."

Her admonition was scarcely needed, for Colin was too sleepy to move. He started to protest, but fatigue struck him almost like a blow, and he leaned back in the chair. Twyla watched him for a time, until he moved restlessly and threw the blanket off his shoulder. Quickly, Twyla arose and reached for the blanket but then stopped and stood, looking at Colin. She reached out and touched his hair, then withdrew her hand quickly. She sighed, put the blanket over him, then went back to lie down before the fire.

❧

January had passed, but there was still some snow on the first of February—a light layer, just enough to cover the ground. Twyla had fixed a hot meal for Colin, Dr. Teague, and herself, of beer, bread, and fish. The beer was warm, for she had let it sit out and had added some cinnamon and other spices to it. She was glad to see Colin drink it heartily. "It's been a long day," Colin said.

Dr. Teague, sitting across from him, nodded. "Aye, it has." He looked weary, for they had seen patients all day long and a few after it had turned dark. Teague scratched his chin, which he had neglected to shave. "Colin, we have to have a new body."

"We can't do that. The ground is frozen."

"That's no matter."

"It will be when we try to dig it out."

"You've not heard? They caught a murderer over in Loxley. They hanged him today. You know, at the crossroads? You wait until midnight, then go get him."

Colin stared at Teague. "It's freezing out there."

Teague cackled, and his small eyes glinted with humor. "A man's got to suffer. That's what the Bible says."

"Where does it say that?" Colin asked quickly.

"It says it in half a dozen places. 'Man is born to trouble as the sparks fly upward.' That is the Book of Job. So, your sparks are going to fly tonight. We've got to have that body."

Finally, Teague went to bed. Twyla was clearing the table and doing the dishes. Colin grumbled, "I'm not going to do it."

"Good! It's not a good idea."

Colin waited for her to argue more, for it seemed she had reached an argumentative stage. He went over to a shelf and pulled a book down, and Twyla said, "Good night, Mister."

"Good night, Twyla."

Colin went back to the table and sat down. Twyla had made some small honey cakes. From time to time he reached over and broke off a piece of cake and chewed it. He studied the book for three hours. He then got up and sighed, "Of course I'm going to do it. That old man can make me do anything." He put on his heavy coat and a pair of boots that reached nearly up to his thighs, and then pulled a fur cap over his head.

He went outside and hitched the horse to the sled the servant used for hauling wood. "Get up, Hector. If I've got to freeze to death, you have to do the same." Hector nodded his head and slobbered his reply, then moved out from the yard, dragging the sled behind him.

Twyla had not gone to sleep, for she had known full well what Colin would do. She was a hardy young woman and rather daring, and she had decided to follow him. She donned her warmest clothes and waited in her room. Finally she heard the front door close, and moving to the window she saw the horse pulling the sled from the house. Quickly, she threw on her coat and pulled a wool cap over her ears and went downstairs. She opened the door and noticed that the moon was very bright. It was an old moon that looked as if it had been pitted by a thousand stones. Then, as she watched, a cloud came and covered it up.

The snow masked the sound as she moved along. A large hunting owl soared over her head. She heard nothing as the shadow crossed her face. She looked up, startled, as she saw the huge bird sail over until it dropped. She heard the sound of a scuffle, a squeal of terror, and then finally silence. *He got something to eat.* She hurried to catch up with the sled. Twyla had no trouble following them, for she could hear Hector's soft hoofbeats punching through the snow. She was a bit nervous, and being out at midnight and in the darkness frightened her. She made her up her mind to make sure Colin was in sight in case she needed him. It proved to be difficult to stay close to him. She had no trouble knowing which way he was headed, but keeping up with Hector was harder than she'd anticipated. To make things worse, he chose to go down a small, little-known path instead of staying on the main road.

Thirty minutes later, she was falling far behind. A cloud cloaked the moon again, which made the darkness almost complete. She knew that Colin was just ahead, although he was keeping out of sight. He had turned down a sharp bend just a second ago. She stepped into the curve, and suddenly a dark form emerged. Arms clamped around her, and she let out a squeal and was dragged to the ground. Fear was rising in her. "Let me go!" she cried.

The arms seemed to relax their grip and she heard a familiar voice say, "Twyla, what are you doing out here?"

Twyla wriggled herself free and stood up. "I wanted to go with you. I knew you'd never take me with you, so I followed you."

"You go home right now!" Colin ordered.

"I won't!" Twyla replied stubbornly.

"You are always saying that I own you, so if that's true, I'm telling you to go home right now."

"I won't do it! Own me or not, I'm going with you."

Colin looked desperate. He struggled with whether to turn around and take her all the way home, which would take forever, or to bring Twyla with him to steal a dead body. He became frustrated. "You are a troublesome brat!" he said angrily, then turned and moved to catch up with Hector, who had not stopped plodding down the trail.

Twyla hurried along behind Colin, saying nothing. Neither of them spoke until a half hour of silence had passed. Then he moved forward and grabbed the lines, saying, "Whoa! Whoa, Hector!" Twyla moved forward to stand beside him. They stood there in the semi-darkness, then the clouds that cloaked the moon moved. Twyla gasped, for there, high against the sky, was a body that was twisting slowly in the breeze. She couldn't see much, nor did she want to.

Colin shook his head and said, "We've got to hurry." He moved toward the body and, clambering up a slight hill, he managed to reach up, put one arm around the body, and with his knife cut the rope. The body came loose, and he couldn't catch himself. Falling over backwards, the body fell on top of him. The stench of death was in his nostrils.

"Are you all right, Colin?"

"Yes," Colin grunted. She noted that he was still angry with her. Colin shoved the corpse off and stared at it. He then grabbed the body by the armpits, pulled it to the sled, and loaded the unseemly burden. "Let's get out of here," he said sternly.

Nothing could have pleased Twyla more. She kept pace with him, and when they were in sight of the house he finally broke the silence. "Well, we did it. You got your own way. Are you happy?"

Twyla didn't answer for a moment; then she said, "I'll help you carry him in."

The corpse was not a large one, but heavy enough that Colin could use the help. They struggled inside the house, then to the small room the two doctors used for autopsies. With a grunt, they lifted the body and plumped it down on the waist-high table. Twyla shoved the feet over and stared down at the dead face.

Her gaze surprised Colin. "What are you looking at? He's just another dead man."

Twyla seemed to be hypnotized by the man's features, which were twisted and worn with the warfare of survival that most peasants knew. "He was just a murderer," Colin said quietly. "Don't fret yourself."

Twyla didn't answer for a moment, then said, "His mother probably loved him, Colin. His mother probably never thought it would end like this. When he was just a baby, don't you think she had hopes he would amount to something?"

Colin did not answer. He had long since learned to harden his emotions against feeling anything for the bodies that he stole. "There's no way of knowing that," he said finally. He was shocked at her emotion. She was a strong young woman, yet he saw her still staring at the man's face.

"He deserved better than this," Twyla said quietly.

Colin moved forward and put his hand on her shoulder. "You're probably right. There is a lot of sadness and grief in the world. Come on, it's late. Go to bed."

She removed his hand, then turned and gave him a look that puzzled him. She said sadly, "All right, Mister, I'll go." He watched her as she left the room. She didn't look back as she disappeared up the stairs that led to her room. He stood there confused, thinking about why the whole thing had troubled him. He had stolen many bodies with Teague at his side, but this had been different. He went to his own room, undressed, got in the cold bed, and lay there shivering. He thought for a long time about Twyla and her words. *His mother probably never thought it would end like this.*

Twyla was excited about the trip to celebrate Adam's wedding. She noticed, though, as the time grew near that Colin grew more unhappy. She knew better than to ask him what was wrong.

The days went by, and finally on May 21, Twyla stood in the church at the wedding, watching as Adam and Heather were united in marriage. She was standing just across from Colin. Glancing at him, she saw that his face was set in an angry look. Twyla then knew with certainty: *He's still in love with her.* The thought pierced her. Sympathy came for the young man who had picked her out of nothing and protected her. Anger came to her, then, as she stared at Heather. There was a lightness about the woman she had perceived on their first meeting. She was beautiful and witty, and she pleased Adam. *Colin doesn't need a woman like that!* She resolutely turned her gaze away and didn't look at Colin until the service was over.

It was a time of celebration, but Colin was having none of that. She joined him at a table laden with food, but he took nothing.

"Have some of this wine, Mister." She held up a cup. "They'll be very happy."

"I'm sure they will!" The words were filled with bitterness. He turned abruptly and walked out of the room.

Twyla watched him go and felt sadness for him, but anger at Adam and Heather. *They don't even know how this is affecting him! They don't even care!* Something heavy was added to her heart that day. *Colin will never look at another woman. That woman has spoiled all the gentleness and goodness he had to give to a woman!*

17

August 1, 1586

D r. Teague entered the room abruptly. Shutting the door behind him, he moved over to where Twyla was mixing something on the table. Plopping himself down in a chair, he studied the ingredients, then demanded, "What are you making?"

"Buttered loaves."

"Good! Be sure you make enough. That Colin is a hog; he barely leaves enough for me."

Twyla laughed. "You're a glutton, Doctor, and so is he. Now you be quiet while I work."

Teague watched as the young woman mixed mutton fat, currants, spice powder, and salt and then kneaded it into a special bread dough rich with eggs and sugar. Picking it up, she cut the loaf into three pieces, fried more butter, and shoved sugar between every piece. She placed it on grill called a spider over the coals, and at once a wonderful smell permeated the air. Teague asked, "How long will it be?"

"You're not getting any of these until after supper tonight."

"Don't torment an old man, girl! I've worked hard today. I'm starving."

"No matter, you'll have to wait."

"Oh, you could spare one of those buttered loaves. You have plenty."

Twyla shook her head. "We are going to have a good supper, and I don't want you to spoil your appetite." She glanced down at Teague's hands, which were filthy. "You're not going to get any buttered loaves until you wash those hands."

"I washed them yesterday."

"Dr. Teague, you've been cutting up a dead body, and now you're going to pick up buttered loaves? That will probably poison you. Now go wash." Twyla pointed toward the porch.

"All right, but it's a waste of time." Teague limped off into the room. He stopped to look outside. It was August now and very hot. The heat from the fire had caused perspiration to accumulate on his forehead and drip down his face. He was already sweating from cutting up the corpse, but the fire seemed to intensify the heat. *I hope that bossy girl won't make me change my clothes, too!* He left, went out on the back porch, washed his hands, then returned to the large room. Sitting down, he asked, "How old are you, girl?"

"I don't really know."

"Of course you know. Come on, tell me."

"I'm either fifteen, sixteen, or seventeen."

"Did they tell you how old you were when you were small?"

"No one told me because no one cared." The harsh statement seemed to linger in the air. Then Twyla turned and said in a troubled tone, "I'm worried about Colin."

"Why are you worried?"

"Come, now, Dr. Teague, you've watched him. He hasn't been the same since Adam got married."

"Men don't get over women like they get over coughs."

"You think he will be that way all of his life? He's so unhappy!"

Teague said with a sly smile coming across his lips, "Give me a piece of that buttered bread and I'll tell you."

Twyla studied the old man and then broke a generous portion of the dough. She dipped it in a small pile of sugar and spice, then handed it to him. She watched as he took a bite hungrily. He chewed with pleasure, then swallowed and said, "That is very good! But about Colin, it's not just that woman who's got him down, even though she broke his heart. It's that book he's been working on, too."

"I thought he was through with it."

"He is as far as the text is concerned, but it has to have something more than words."

"Like what?"

"Like illustrations, pictures. For example, you can't just describe a heart; you have to *show* it. There are different valves, the shape of it, all the connections between the vessels."

Twyla listened for a time and the old man rambled on. Finally, when he got up to leave, she said, "We'll have supper early tonight." As soon as he was gone, she stood resolutely and thought, *I know what I can give him for his birthday. And that Heather Benton can't give him anything like this!*

"This supper was the best I've ever had!" Teague beamed and patted his stomach, which seemed swelled to the bursting point. "I am going to go to bed and try to do some digesting."

"Thank you, Dr. Teague."

Colin looked up and watched Teague leave. He tried to smile, for he knew that Twyla had put a good deal of work into his birthday supper. "This was a fine meal, Twyla. You're a wonderful cook."

"You didn't eat very much."

"I'll eat some more later."

A silence fell across the room. Suddenly, Twyla said uncertainly, "I got you a present, Mister."

"Why, you shouldn't have done that, Twyla!"

"I wanted to. I didn't have any money, but I got something

you would like." She turned and left the room, and came back almost immediately. She was carrying a stack of papers nearly an inch thick. "At least, I hope you'll like it," she said as she watched his face.

"Let me see."

Colin reached out and took the bundle of papers. He saw that they were all drawings. For a moment he stared at them in disbelief. "Where in the name of heaven did you get these, Twyla?" he demanded.

"They're mine. I drew them."

"You drew these?" Colin stared at the girl, then shook his head in awe. He began thumbing through the papers. "You have this artery just how it should be—even the nerve that goes to the eye. Look at it, Twyla, you've got it just right!"

He went through the stack, crying out with each fresh discovery. Finally, he looked up and exclaimed in wonder, "Twyla, you never told me you could draw like this!"

"I never told anybody.'"

"This is wonderful! You have a gift. Don't you see what this means?"

"Not really. What does it mean, Mister?"

Colin laughed and stepped toward Twyla. He put his arm around her and hugged her tightly to his chest. "Why, this means I can finish the book! You can do all the drawings. They're better than any I've ever seen."

"Please, Mister, you mustn't hug me."

"Why, of course I must! After all, you have just given me the best birthday present I've ever had. Come now, how did you do it? Sit down and tell me."

The two sat down again and Twyla said, "I went into where the bodies are when you and Dr. Teague weren't there. I just drew what I saw. I don't know what any of it means, of course."

"You don't have to know what the things mean. They're true

to life." Colin continued thumbing through the drawings. The sound of rustling paper filled the room. He kept pointing out things to her, his eyes bright with excitement. He suddenly took her hand in both of his. "Twyla, because of you I can finally get my book published. It will make us famous."

"Not me, sir, just you."

"Don't be modest now. We're going to be working together very closely. You can draw the things I lay out for you so we can have a complete book."

Twyla's eyes sparkled. "Yes, Mister," she whispered. "I can do that."

Colin opened the door and stood there, confused for a moment. "Why, Sir Francis! Come in!"

Francis Walsingham stepped inside the door. As usual, he was dressed in rather plain dark clothing. He didn't care much for frivolous clothing such as the other nobility wore. Colin had often thought that he looked like a huge, dark, ominous bird of prey with his dark hair, dark eyes, and dark clothing. "Why didn't you send for me? I would've come at once."

"I didn't have time, Dr. Winslow."

"Please come in and sit down. Let me give you something to drink and eat. Something to wash the dust out. It's hot out there today."

Colin found a pitcher of ale, poured it into a pewter flagon, then handed it to Sir Francis. He drank it quickly, and Colin filled it up again.

"Something has come up, Doctor, that I need some help with."

"What can I do for you?"

The head of the secret service of England was not a man to share secrets. There was always a mysterious air about him. Sir Francis glanced around the room, assuring himself it was empty. He leaned forward and whispered, "Mary, Queen of

Scots, has a servant named Renee Billaud. She is an older woman, and Mary is very fond of her. Elizabeth just received a letter asking our queen to send a physician to attend to her servant. Mary suggested that she would prefer you."

"Of course I'll be happy to do what I can. Do you know what the woman's trouble is?"

"No. I know only that she is not doing well at all. She might not live, so I think time is of the essence."

"I will go at once, sir."

"Just a minute. Don't be in such a rush." A slight smile turned up the corners of Walsingham's lips and he said, "It's not only a matter of treating the woman. You are aware that Mary is a thorn in Her Majesty's side?"

"Yes, Sir Francis, I'm aware of that."

"I've been trying for ten years now to get the evidence that there are plots to assassinate Queen Elizabeth and put Mary on the throne. I know she's guilty," he said grimly. "But the queen will not listen. She demands something solid."

"You asked my father to do this. You even asked me once, but it doesn't seem to do any good."

"You may find something this time. She's grown careless. You'll be with the old woman constantly. Mary's servants will be there, and visitors will be coming and going. You are a sharp fellow, Dr. Winslow. You have a mind such as I've never seen. You go do what you doctors do, then do what my men do. Find some evidence that that woman is out to gain the throne of England and Elizabeth stands in her way."

Colin didn't hesitate. "Yes, sir. I'll do my best."

"Good man! Now let me tell you how to contact me if you find something . . ." Colin took in all that Walsingham said. It was not a task that he had sought or liked. Indeed, he had always liked Mary despite the rumors. But Walsingham had put the task in terms he couldn't deny, for Elizabeth must live.

✳

Colin made a fast trip. He pulled his horse in front of Chatley, a house in the same county as Tutbury Castle. Chatley belonged to the Earl of Essex, and Walsingham had thought it wise to move Mary from Tutbury to Chatley. Colin's mind was moving quickly as he considered how to carry out Walsingham's instructions. He was greeted at the door by a pair of armed guards and announced, "My name is Dr. Colin Winslow. I'm the physician Her Majesty has sent for."

One of the guards nodded and motioned him inside. He left, but was gone only a short time, and Colin said nothing to the other guard. Finally, the tall guard returned and said, "Her Majesty will see you, sir."

Colin followed the man into the house, which was very large and ornate. There was dark furniture and portraits of the Essex line. He was directed into a hall, where another two guards stood. They stepped to one side, and one of them opened the door. Colin nodded, then went inside. The door closed behind him and he saw Mary standing beside a window, looking out. She turned to greet him, and he felt as always the power and force of this woman. She was forty-four now, but looked much younger. She was dressed in a dark green gown studded with jewels. Her hair was done up in a French fashion, and it flashed with diamonds that were intertwined among the locks.

"Ah, my dear Dr. Winslow, at last."

Colin stepped forward and kissed the hand she extended. Her hand closed on his as she pulled him closer. There was a magnetism about this woman that was almost frightening. Colin knew her history. He believed she was able to do almost anything with any man she wanted—with the exception of Sir Francis Walsingham!

He smiled and replied, "It's good to see you, Your Majesty, but I understand your servant is very ill."

"Yes, and she is very dear to me, Doctor. Come, you must help her."

"What are her symptoms, Your Majesty?"

Colin listened carefully as the queen spoke. Finally she paused, and from what she said he was not optimistic. "Perhaps I can see her now?"

"Of course. They allow me to keep her with me and my ladies. We take care of her, but now you are here."

Colin followed the queen across the spacious room. The sick woman lay on a bed underneath a window that spread the summer light on her face. He looked down, then bent over. "Madame, I'm Dr. Colin Winslow. I've come to care for you."

"This is the finest young doctor in England, Renee," Mary said. "He has been a friend to me for many years, as was his father. Do all that he says, for we must get you well."

Renee Billaud's eyes were open, but there was an aura of death about her. Colin had seen many patients with the shadow of death on them, and it was with a sinking feeling that he examined her carefully. The queen excused herself, and finally Colin straightened up. "We will have to help you get better, Madame."

"I will not live," she said in a very quiet and exhausted voice.

"We must be positive. I'll make some medication for you, and you must take it." He saw that the woman had given up. She had a lump in her stomach that he knew instinctively was a large tumor. There was no way to operate. Indeed, there was nothing to be done but to try to ease her pain.

Colin turned and went to where Mary was waiting for him. She came forward immediately to meet him, asking, "What do you think, Dr. Winslow?"

"She is very ill, Your Majesty."

"I know. It breaks my heart. You must stay here and do everything you can."

"Of course."

"Look, let me show you this." She walked across the room to an oak door and opened it. Inside was a room no more than ten feet square. It contained a single bed, a chair, and a table. A large window allowed sunlight to come in. "This is for you so you will always be available to my Renee. You'll do this for me, won't you?"

"Of course I will, Your Majesty. I must warn you she is very ill. But you know that."

"The good God, He knows all of this. I, along with all my women, am praying for her. We say our rosaries many times a day. But I feel much better that you are here. Please do what you can for her."

"Of course I shall, Your Majesty."

As Colin bent over Renee, he knew that her time was very short. He had been at Chatley for nine days, and he had seen the woman sinking deeper into the darkness that clouded her. Death was draining her spirit. All during the time Colin was caring for her, he had noticed that many visitors came into the queen's chamber. At first, Mary had seen to it that she spoke to them privately, so Colin was able to learn little. But as the days passed, the queen became less careful. It was almost as if he had become like a piece of furniture. He always looked busy by mixing medicines and potions, and Mary seemed to have forgotten him.

She is certainly carrying on some sort of plot. I need to find some evidence for Sir Francis—but how can I do that?

He was well aware that Sir Francis examined any message or letter that came from Mary. Without appearing to, Colin made note of every person who came, every bit of mail, and every message that came or that Mary sent—as much as he actually saw, anyway.

It was late on a Thursday night, and he had been sitting beside the sick woman for hours. He knew by this time that she might die at any minute. He leaned forward and studied her face, then asked softly, "Can you hear me, Madame Billaud?"

The eyes fluttered. Then the woman opened her eyes and whispered, "Yes. I must go to meet my God."

"I think you must, Renee. We all must at one time or another. Shall I get your priest?"

The woman didn't answer. Her eyes closed, and Colin thought she had slipped away. Then her breast heaved and she began to speak. She spoke in French. Colin was happy that he knew French, for she said, "You must be careful, Your Majesty. If you don't find a hiding space all will be lost—" She spoke rapidly, and Colin leaned in to hear her more clearly. Much of what she said made little sense, but finally he heard her say, "The hiding place for your messages, it is not good. It will be found."

"No," Colin whispered. "It's too carefully hidden."

"It's not. The first place the spies will search is the chest, and they will find the compartment and all will be lost."

The chest! A secret compartment! Instantly, Colin knew that he had discovered something. He gave a quick look at the dying woman and then moved across the chamber. The queen's sleeping chamber was off to one side, but she wasn't yet in bed. He went over to a large chest that he had noticed before. It was ornately carved of a dark wood. Carefully, he ran his hands over the exterior; then, holding his breath, he lifted the lid. It moved silently. He saw that it was filled with articles of clothing and coverlets. Despair seized him, for didn't know where to start. He laid the lid back and searched quickly. He could find nothing, and started to lower the lid. Suddenly, his hand touched something. It was on the underside of the lid. He lifted it back, and by the dim light of the single candle, he saw that there were carvings. Quickly, he ran his hand over them; then he apparently touched something, for there was a click that sounded like thunder to him in the silence. Instantly, he saw that a catch had been released and a secret drawer opened. He pulled out a series of papers, then moved over to the candle and began to read.

He read rapidly, for he knew that if he was caught, all would be in vain. There were only three papers, but he knew as soon as he saw them they were the evidence that Walsingham needed. They were written in Mary's own hand and laid out the plan to assassinate the queen of England! He knew that he could not take the papers out, for Mary would know instantly they were gone. He memorized the contents, then replaced the papers in the secret compartment and closed the lid. He went back, making no sound, to the dying woman.

Less than an hour later he sent for Mary, who, in turn, brought a priest. Colin stood back after informing Mary that this was the end. He watched as the priest performed the final rites. When it was over, Mary came over and held her hand out to Colin. He took her hand and saw that she was weeping. Mary said, "I knew it was hopeless, but I had to try everything."

Suddenly, Colin's heart skipped a beat. He knew that he held this woman's life in his hands. He knew also that she had done evil things, but at that moment she was nothing but a lonely woman who had had a miserable life. And now something more ominous lay ahead of her. He bowed and said, "I wish I could have done more."

Early the next morning, Colin left Chatley. He went at once to find Walsingham. He had been told he was at Richmond Palace. There was some difficulty getting in to see him. When he finally did, Walsingham looked at him with his piercing glance. "Well, what did you find?"

"I found what I wish I had not. "

"Is it evidence?" Walsingham asked eagerly.

"It was letters that Mary wrote agreeing to a proposal by a group of men to kill the queen. I can quote them for you, but you will need the papers themselves for all the details."

"Where are they?"

"In a secret compartment in a large chest in her room."

At once Walsingham moved to the door, and a large dark-haired man came immediately to stand close to him. He whispered something to the man, who left immediately. Walsingham came back to stand before Colin. He put his hands on the young man's shoulders, saying, "This is a noble thing you have done. I pray they will still be there."

"They should be. Mary is brokenhearted over the death of her servant. I don't think she will do anything until after the funeral."

"Finally we will have an end to this thing! Come, I want you to write down everything that those papers say." He put a piece of paper in front of Colin. Suddenly he saw something in Colin's face that made him stop. "You don't regret helping your queen, do you?"

"I feel sorry for Mary."

"She is not a woman to feel sorry for. She is an assassin."

"Perhaps so, but I only saw a woman."

"You are too soft. Come now, write all this down; then you can go back to your doctoring."

18

October 24, 1586

Colin and Dr. Teague stood looking down at Brandon. He grinned up at them, and though he was pale and his voice was weak, he seemed cheerful. "Well, *two* doctors! Couldn't you get three or four more?"

"You've got the two finest doctors in England, or anywhere else for that matter. Now, be still. I must finish examining you, Lord Stoneybrook," Teague snapped.

"You're not through?" Brandon began coughing, and Colin poured him a glass of water. "Blasted cough! I don't know why you have to examine me anymore, Dr. Teague. You have poked and prodded me until I feel like a specimen in a laboratory."

"That's the way we doctors have to do it," Teague answered. "We have to make the disease worse than it is so that we can charge higher fees."

Colin paid no attention to the conversation going on between his father and Teague. His mother had written that his father was very ill, and he and Teague had left at once. They had arrived at Stoneybrook two days ago, and both had been shocked at how weak Colin's father was. His mother had tried to prepare him for this, but Colin soon discovered that it was one thing to have a patient you don't know and another to have your own father as one.

"I think I'll make another potion while you finish examining the patient, Dr. Teague," Colin said.

"Don't bring me any more of that vile-tasting medicine! Make it taste better, Son."

Colin hid a small smile. "I'll try." He left the room, and instantly he was met by his mother, Adam, and Heather. Adam had a worried expression on his face. "Blast it all! I can face an enemy ship that outguns me, but I feel as helpless as a pup when sickness comes. How is he, Brother?"

"It's hard to make a diagnosis," Colin said. "There's so much sickness going around right now. I hope it's not the sweating sickness." This was a disease that had swept over England, characterized by profuse sweating and a tremendously high fever that usually killed the patient.

"Do you think it could be that, Son?" Eden asked quickly. She moved closer to Adam and held his arm tightly. "I've been so worried about him."

"I don't think so. These things always seem worse than they are. Most of the time patients get better with no doctoring or medicine."

Adam said grimly, "That doesn't say much for your profession." He kept firing questions until finally he said, "I've got to go."

"Must you leave?" Heather asked.

"Yes. I've got to attend Mary's trial." He turned to Colin and slapped him on the back. "I can't tell you how proud I am of you, Colin! It was you who exposed that conspiracy."

Adam didn't notice that his brother took no pride in this. Colin dropped his head and said in despair, "I wish I hadn't had to have anything to do with it."

"You had to do it. Your queen's life was at stake. Did I tell you that I was at Babington's execution?" Anthony Babington had been the mastermind behind the plot that Mary was involved in to kill Queen Elizabeth. "It was a fine execution," Adam said with some savor. "Elizabeth isn't much for harsh punishment, but she was furious at Babington for hatching a plot to take her throne. She demanded the most painful execution that her executioners could think of."

"What could be worse than hanging?" Eden asked.

"Hanged, drawn, and quartered. That's what Elizabeth insisted on." Adam seemed excited as he talked about it. "I was there. They hung Babington but cut him down before he was dead. Then the executioner took his knife and cut open his stomach. I was close enough when they pulled his entrails out, and I heard the villain say, '*Parce mihi, Domine Jesu.*' Got no idea what that means, but if he was praying for mercy, I hope he didn't get it! I must go." He leaned over and kissed Heather noisily, then left, calling for his horse.

Eden shook her head. "I don't see how he could watch something so horrible. I guess he is used to violence in his raids with Sir Francis Drake. I'm going in to sit with Brandon." She turned and left.

Heather at once said, "I need to talk to you, Colin." She took his arm and drew him into a larger room. As she turned to him, he was very much aware of the curves of her body in a rather revealing dress. Her perfume was almost like incense.

"What is it, Heather?" Colin said, annoyed, and not wanting to be this close to her alone.

"Tell me how your father is really. I know you may be shielding your mother. Is he going to live?"

"I hope so. Dr. Teague and I will do the best we can."

Heather moved closer, so close she was almost leaning on him. She looked up at him and he saw in her eyes something he didn't understand. He had never gotten over his attraction to this woman, no matter how she'd broken his heart, and he well knew he should now turn and flee, but he couldn't.

"Do you ever think of when we were together, Colin?"

Her question shook him. He wanted to shout, "I never stop thinking about you!" but he only said shortly, "No, of course I don't!"

Heather reached out, and this time the soft curves of her body brushed against his. "I shouldn't say this, but I've never forgotten those times."

"You have a husband now, Heather, and he's my brother."

"Adam's a great captain, but he's no lover. He's rough, Colin, not gentle like you." Disgust passed over her face. "He uses me! And I can't love him as—" She didn't finish her sentence. Instead, she reached up and put her arms around his neck to pull his head down. "I'm your sister now," she whispered. To Colin her embrace was not sisterly. As she kissed him, he hated himself for his feelings. He knew it was wrong, but he found himself unable to pull away as he knew he should . . .

Twyla passed by an open door and halted abruptly. She saw Colin kissing Heather, and this made her furious. *I thought he had more sense than that!* She left at once, seething with anger, and found Teague. "I'm going home, Dr. Teague."

"Now? We just got here."

"I wish we'd never come!"

"Why, we had to come, Twyla. Colin's father is ill."

"It's not good for Mister to be here."

Teague was quiet, and then had a moment of clarity. "Because of his old love affair with Heather? Oh, that's ancient history."

"No, it's not. That woman doesn't love her husband. She married him because he'll have a title when his father dies, and she'll add it to the two she already has. I'm going home."

"You can't go by yourself. Let me go speak with Colin." Teague found Colin, and one look revealed that the young man was in a deep depression. He said, "Twyla wants to go home. She can't go by herself. I've got to go with her."

"Why is she in such a rush to leave?"

A quick reply almost left Teague's lips, but he was able to hold it in. Colin saw that Teague was staring at him in an odd way, and finally the older man said, "Sometimes an old fire burns down. You think that it is dead, but there is a spark left in there. I've known that spark to catch and start another fire that burns the whole house down."

"What are you talking about, Teague?"

"You're too stupid to understand me. I'm taking Twyla home. You don't need me here."

Colin shrugged; he was preoccupied with thoughts of Heather.

The days passed slowly after Twyla left, and Heather missed no opportunity to make her desires known to Colin. Memories of their affair came to him, and he would recall with startling clarity what it was like to hold her in his arms. The desire to do so again was almost overwhelming.

Adam came home three days later and gave them the report of the trial. "She's going to be found guilty," he said with evident satisfaction. "You ought to go to that trial, Colin. Father is better now."

"No, I've got to get home. My practice, you know."

By now, Brandon had gotten much better. He was up walking around and had gained his color back. Colin never knew exactly what the illness was, but that often happened with patients. He gathered his things together, said his good-byes to his parents, and prepared to leave. He was met at the door by Heather and Adam. "They're going to execute that woman," Adam said. "You should be there. After all, it's pretty common knowledge that you were the one clever enough to get evidence to convict her."

"He doesn't want to do that, Adam," Heather said.

Adam looked surprised. He couldn't imagine such a thing.

"Heather, work your wiles on him. Make him do the right thing, like you do me. You can convince me to do something I hate and make me think I like it and that I thought of it myself."

Ignoring him, Heather leaned forward and kissed Colin on the cheek. "Come back soon."

"That's right, Wife. Draw him back here again." Adam clapped Colin on the shoulder, saying, "We'll go see the execution of Mary, Queen of Scots, together."

Colin left, but before he headed for home he made a visit to Meg's place. As usual, he had brought her some herbs and some small gifts. She took them with a smile, then sat him down, fed him, and began to bombard him with questions. "Where's that young woman, Twyla, you brought last time? I thought she was visiting here with you."

"She had to go home."

Meg caught the hesitation in his voice. "What about that other woman? Your brother's wife, Heather?"

"She's still here."

The hesitant reply put Meg on her guard. She was good with herbs, but even better at reading people. She could see their ulterior motives and what went on in their hearts. *If I ever saw guilt on a man's face, there it is! It's that woman—he's never gotten over her!* "I want to tell you something, Colin. You've been successful, but you need God."

"I know I do. I have for years."

"If you won't go to him, he may come to you, maybe in a most unpleasant way. I've known God to knock men and women flat to get their attention." She leaned forward and put her hand on his cheek. "Better you put yourself in God's hands, Colin, than force him to bring you down. He knows how to make a person hurt. Remember what I say, now."

"I will, Meg. I know I need God. I just don't know how to find him."

✗✗

For some reason, Meg's warning remained clear in Colin's mind after he got home. He was busy with his work but worried about Twyla, for she was cold toward him. He was aware she knew of his passion for Heather, but of course he did not feel he could speak to her of it.

One Friday morning, Reverend John Davis, the pastor of the local church, stopped by and made a request. Davis was a tall, portly man with a good-natured face, and Colin had always liked him. "Dr. Winslow," he said, "there's a poor fellow who's to be hanged tomorrow. Would it be possible for you to go by and give him what comfort you can?"

"Why, Reverend Davis, I'm no man for that! You know I'm not a Christian."

"I know, and ordinarily I'd never think of asking you such a thing, but somehow as I was praying for the poor chap, I got a strong feeling that you might be able to give him a little cheer. I don't say that impulse is from God, mind you, but when I get such a strong feeling, I give it the benefit of a doubt. If it troubles you, Dr. Winslow, I'll find someone else."

Colin's first impulse was to refuse, but he suddenly said, "I'll at least go talk to him. What's his name?"

"Charles Evans. He feels that since he's been waiting to be hanged, he's found God. He'll tell you about that. Thank you, Doctor, for your time."

Colin thought about the visit to the condemned man and could not understand in the least why he had agreed to go. He was troubled for the rest of the day and slept poorly, but he went the next day to see the man.

The pastor had made arrangements for Colin to go into Evans's cell, and as soon as he stepped inside and the steel door clanged behind him, he was greeted by a tall man with intense blue eyes and a warm smile. "I'm Charles Evans, sir."

"My name is Colin Winslow, Mr. Evans. The pastor asked me to visit you."

"Fine! Fine!" Evans said. "Sit down, sir, and since my time is short, I must tell you what has happened to me." Colin listened as Evans told of his misspent life, relating how he had killed a man in a robbery and how he'd been sentenced to hang. He spoke in a cheerful fashion and finally said, "This will sound strange, Mr. Winslow, but actually the best thing that has ever happened to me was getting a death sentence!"

"I—I don't understand that."

"Why, if I'd gone on with my life in such a sinful manner, I'd have died and would have gone to meet God unprepared. Now instead of living a miserable life and then spending an eternity in hell, why, I'm going in a few moments to meet my Lord Jesus! What a thing that will be! To spend eternity with him who died for me!"

Colin sat transfixed as Evans, filled with a joy that Colin had never seen, spoke of his newfound salvation. Evans spoke for a long time, then gave his visitor a direct look. "I must ask you, Mr. Winslow, have you ever been converted? Are you one of God's redeemed saints?"

Colin's voice failed him, and finally he could only whisper, "No, sir, I am not."

Evans spoke with eloquence for twenty minutes, urging Colin to call on God in the name of Jesus—and then the door opened, and the jailer said, "It's time, Evans."

Evans stood, and Colin stood with him. He asked, "Aren't you somewhat afraid, Mr. Evans?"

"Put your hand here on my heart." Colin did so, and Evans said, "Do you feel a weak heart, sir?"

"No, it's as strong as any heart I've ever felt."

"It's time for me to meet my savior, Mr. Winslow, but I beg you, don't let yourself fall into hell. Call on Jesus!"

And then the jailer pulled at Evans's arm, leading him out of the cell. Despite himself, Colin followed. He stood and watched as the hangman put the noose over Evans's head and heard Evans cry with a strong voice, "Blessed are the dead that die in the Lord!" Colin did turn away then, with a choking cry and tears running down his face.

For almost a week after Colin's traumatic visit with Charles Evans, he had difficulty sleeping. Over and over he relived the scene with the condemned man. His phenomenal memory had recorded every word Evans had said, as well as a clear vision of the happiness on his face. Tossing and turning, unable to sleep, night after night Colin rose with despair and walked the floor, his nerves raw with an emotion he had never known.

Both Teague and Twyla knew something was deeply troubling Colin, but he refused to answer their questions and cut them off so sharply that they ceased trying to help. Desperately, Colin tried to bury himself in work, but he was so distraught that Teague said with disgust, "Colin, you're no good for our patients! You're going to kill one of them. Take some time off—and don't come back until you get rid of whatever demon is gnawing at your insides!"

Colin finally left the village and wandered aimlessly over the countryside, sleeping at inns, but he found no peace. After ten days he returned, worn and exhausted, to his home and was met at the door by Dr. Teague. Something in the old man's face struck him, and he demanded instantly, "What's the matter, Teague?"

"It's Twyla, Colin. She's very ill."

"What's wrong with her?"

"She has a terrible pain in her stomach and a fever. One of those things that's hard to diagnose."

Colin was silent, for both men had seen people die from symptoms like these. "Let me talk to her."

"She's in bed. I don't know what to do, Colin. It's one of

those cases where whatever you do seems wrong. She's not getting any better, I know that."

Colin hurried upstairs at once to Twyla's room. He was shocked at her appearance—her skin was crimson with fever, she was wet with perspiration, and she looked gaunt. "Twyla," he said, "how are you?"

"I'm fine," she whispered, but her voice was very weak.

"I know better than that. Teague's worried about you. Let me check you over." During his examination he was well aware that Twyla was not herself. He tried to talk to her about his family. They all sent their regards. He didn't mention Heather, but Twyla asked, "How's your sister-in-law?"

"Why—very well." He knew his face had turned red and tried to cover his embarrassment by saying, "I don't think this is serious. Don't worry. Dr. Teague and I will get you through." He waited for her to answer, but she turned her face away.

He got up and left the room and found Teague. "I don't like this. These sicknesses are hard to pin down. We'll have to stay close."

Two days went by and Colin was miserable. Twyla had steadily grown worse. For a time he thought it was the sweating sickness, but as the illness continued Colin realized it was something else. The pain in her abdomen had increased and the fever kept spiking. She had no appetite and sweated profusely. Colin spent much of his time beside her, but finally he decided to take a walk. He didn't know when, but at some point he began praying. Colin had said prayers before, but he'd never had a great deal of confidence in his ability to pray. He suddenly thought of Charles Evans, and a fierce desire rose in him for the assurance the man had even in the face of the gallows. He cried out to God aloud, something he had rarely done. "Oh God! You've got to heal this young woman!"

Colin stopped dead-still in the snow-covered landscape and noticed the world was white and pristine. He found a fallen tree and sat down on it. He began to search his mind for a medical treatment for Twyla, but he knew that he and Teague had done everything they could. He was very afraid their treatments would not be enough. He had seen death hovering over Twyla.

He began to speak to God aloud again. He spoke haltingly, not knowing how to put his desire into words. He finally cried, "Oh, God, I've run from you all my life—but if you'll only let Twyla live, I promise I'll serve you as best I can!"

He waited, but nothing came. No voice from heaven, no sense of comforting peace. He spent an hour praying before he decided it was time to go back into the house.

When he opened the door, he saw Teague drinking ale in front of the fire. He admitted, "I'm afraid for Twyla, Teague."

"You have good reason to be. She isn't getting better."

"I've been praying, something I don't do a lot of, but I promised God I would serve him if he let her live."

"That's a fool thing to do!"

"What are you talking about? I promised to serve God!"

"You promised to serve him _if_ he did something for you. God's not like that. I thought you knew that, boy! He's a sovereign God. He demands everything a man has. You're selfish to try to bargain with God. You're saying, 'God, if you give me what I want, I'll give you part of myself.'"

"I didn't say that! Not exactly."

"That's what you meant, though." Teague stood up, walked over, and grabbed Colin by the front of his coat. "The only deal God will make with you is this: you give him _all_ of yourself. You tell God that even if the woman dies, you'll still serve him. That may get God's attention. You're not going to back him into a corner, so don't be a fool!"

Colin stared at his friend. He knew there was a great deal of wisdom in this old man, even though he didn't say much about God. He waited until Teague left the room, then threw himself down in the chair in front of the fire. His mind was swarming with disjointed thoughts, but after a long time it began to clear. *Teague's right. I can't force God to bargain.* He sat there until finally calm began to envelop him. He began to murmur a prayer. "God, I ask you to save Twyla. But whether she lives or dies, I'm going to serve you the rest of my life!"

For another thirty minutes Colin sat wondering what had happened to him. He knew the decision had brought to him a peace he had never known before. He continued to pray, "Lord, show me what to do. I'll do anything you ask of me." Almost immediately a thought came to his mind and he got up and said aloud, "It doesn't sound logical, but if this is what you want, I'll do it."

He went to Teague's room and knocked on the door, then entered without an invitation. Teague was wrapped up in the warmest clothes he had and was covered with blankets. He was lying in the bed, reading a book. "What do you want now?"

"I think God has spoken to me. I'm not sure about this, but let me tell you. You know that organ, that little thing that we kept noticing in people who had the same symptoms but then died?"

Instantly, Teague jumped out of the bed, throwing the covers back. "What are you saying, boy?"

"I think God is telling us we need to cut that organ out. It's crazy, I know. We don't know what it is or what it's for. I don't think anyone knows, but I believe it's what kills people sometimes. We have seen three people who died with symptoms like Twyla's, and when we did the autopsies, the organ had burst!" Colin took a deep breath, then said evenly, "We've got to operate *now*."

"I'm with you, Colin Winslow. I think she will die if we don't." Phineas came over and put his hand on Colin's shoulder, and his eyes grew soft. "Wouldn't it be something if God spoke to a pair of fumbling doctors like you and me?"

Colin said, "I'm going to ask Twyla if she'll let us operate."

"Go, boy! Go!"

Colin went into Twyla's room. She looked up at him with feverish eyes. He took her hand. "Twyla, I've not been a praying man, but I've been afraid for you. God has given me an answer. There's an operation that I believe will save you. I won't go into the details, but if we do it, I think you'll be all right."

"If you don't do it, I'll die?"

"You might. But this idea is something I believe God gave me."

Twyla put her other hand on his and smiled with her eyes. She was smiling for the first time since Colin had gotten home. "I've wanted you to be a man of God for a long time. Whatever God tells you to do for me, you do it."

"How is it you know God, Twyla?"

"Your mother—she helped me become a Christian, Colin."

Colin blinked with surprise, for only rarely had she called him by his given name. "You called me 'Colin.'"

"Yes. I'm going to call you that from now on."

"I'd like that. Well, I'll go get ready. It will hurt, but not much and only for a little while. Then, bless God, I think you'll be well." He saw hope light a fire in her eyes, then turned and left.

He found Teague waiting for him, and said, "She's agreed to the operation, but it's got to be warm in here and I have to be quick. To help ease the pain, we'll give her all the laudanum we dare."

"There it is," Teague whispered hoarsely. "Look at it, Colin! It's in bad shape and about ready to burst! Take it out."

Quickly, Colin moved his scalpel and almost at once removed the organ—whatever it was. He put it to the side quickly and began to sew the wound together. It had taken almost no time, and Twyla had not uttered a word. He put his hand on her forehead. "All done." He whispered. "How do you feel?"

"It didn't hurt. Not much."

Colin said, "We'll just wait, but I believe God is going to give you back to me."

Twyla smiled then, for she liked the sound of what he said. "I'm glad you did it, then. You're a good man, Colin Winslow!"

The next day Twyla was much better. Her fever had gone down and she had almost no pain. "I feel so good, Colin!" she said. She was sitting in a chair by the fire, eating some broth. Colin was sitting across from her and noticed the color in her cheeks.

"You know, I've heard about miracles my whole life," he said. "I always wanted to see one—and now I have!" Colin thought for a moment. "It's a miracle you're well, but just as great a miracle that Colin Winslow has found God—or at least God has found Colin Winslow. I'm going to serve him all the days of my life, Twyla. I'm never going to turn away from him."

Twyla didn't answer. The only sound was the fire crackling in the fireplace. As the two sat looking into one another's eyes, there was a feeling of contentment that Colin Winslow had never known. He knew he had chosen the way of God in his life!

PART FOUR

The Wind of God

(1587–1588)

19

March 20, 1587

"How would you like to go to the fair over in Boxton?"

Caught by surprise by Colin's invitation, Twyla looked up from the embroidery she was doing. "Why, I think that would be nice. I haven't been to many fairs."

"We'll go, then. We need a little relaxation, and you've been working too hard."

Twyla felt a gush of pleasure and thought, *I think after he saved my life, he became more conscious of me as a woman.* She put the embroidery down and turned to face him. "I don't suppose I'll be able to thank you enough, Mister."

Colin eyebrows rose in an expression of surprise. "That's what doctors do."

"No, it was more than that. It was a miracle of God."

"I think you're right, Twyla. It frightens me sometimes when I think of it. I might've killed you, experimenting like that."

He smiled, and Twyla thought again of what a finely formed face he had. There was a neatness about him, and a regularity of his features that was pleasing. "You're different since you've made your peace with God."

"I should've done it years ago." Colin reached over to the

table and picked up a copy of his book on anatomy. "The book is doing well. You know what I'd like to do?"

"What's that?"

"I want us to do a revision of it. Put in more illustrations, more detail, and I want you to do the artwork, of course."

"It would a pleasure for me to do it for you."

"I've been meaning to give you something." Colin stood up and walked over to a chest that was in a corner of the room. He opened it and took out a leather pouch, then came back. He was smiling now and said, "This is for you."

Twyla took the bag that he gave her, opened the drawstring, and looked inside. "Why, this is money!"

"Yes."

Twyla poured the golden sovereigns into her hand and gasped. "What's this for?"

"It's your pay for doing the illustrations on the book."

"You don't have to do that. I was glad to do it."

"I know you were, but it's only fair. I looked everywhere for an artist and there was one right under my nose. Shows what a thoughtless fellow I am."

"You're not thoughtless," Twyla said quickly. "I never let you see any of my drawings." Twyla fingered the coins. She looked up at Colin and said, "I've never had anything like this before."

"You'll have to be careful, Twyla."

Twyla blinked with surprise. "Careful about what?"

"About men," Colin replied quickly.

"What are you talking about?"

Colin laughed, reached over, took her hand, and squeezed it. "You're a woman of property now, and men are going to be after you for your money."

Twyla tilted her chin up and stared at him. "So you think a man will only be interested in me for my money?"

"Blast! I didn't mean to say that. I only meant that some men marry women for their money."

Twyla didn't answer but carefully slid the sovereigns back into the bag.

Colin asked, "What are you going to do with the money?"

Twyla held the bag out for Colin. "I want to pay off my bond."

"Oh, Twyla, that never meant anything to me! As a matter of a fact, I've got another gift for you." He went back to the chest and returned with a piece of paper in his hands. "Here, this should make you very happy."

Twyla looked at it for a long time, then whispered, "This says that my bond is all paid, but I never paid it."

"Why, I never intended you should. I just wanted to look out for you until you got old enough to look out for yourself."

Twyla held the paper reverently. She stared at it for a long time, and when she looked up, Colin saw tears in her eyes. "I don't know what would have become of me if it hadn't been for you. I thank God every day for you, appearing out of nowhere and saving me. You and Dr. Teague gave me life in more ways than one."

Colin was touched. He reached over and patted her on the shoulder. "Mind what I said. You're a young woman now, and you'll have to treat men carefully."

Twyla studied his face for a moment, then sniffed, "I suppose I can handle that as well as you handle the women who come after you."

"What women?"

Twyla almost burst out that she knew he was still in love with Heather, but she had judgment enough not to do that. She got up from the table with the bag of coins in her hands, saying, "We'll spend this at the fair, Mister. Now, what would you like for supper?"

Thomas Burke had come calling on Twyla, and as always she was glad to see him. She had known him now for more than six months. His family had recently moved into the neighborhood, and Thomas was the oldest son. He was a small young man with light blond hair and sparkling blue eyes. He had a quick sense of humor that pleased Twyla. Thomas had traveled a great deal with his family, for his father had been an official of the court and an ambassador for the queen. Twyla had been surprised when he returned to see her several times. Now as he sat with her, she asked, "Tell me more about Italy."

"It's full of Italians."

"Well, that's silly. Of course it is! What does the country look like?"

"The big cities in Italy are like big cities everywhere. They're dirty, nasty, filthy things that stink."

"But they have beautiful buildings there. I've seen paintings of them."

"The buildings aren't really pretty. As a matter of a fact," Thomas smiled, "all big cities look better from a distance than when you're in them. You know that's true with London. When you get far off, it's not a bad-looking place. But when you walk down the main street, it's full of garbage, trash, and even hogs rooting around. Big cities aren't like you."

Twyla looked up with surprise. "What do you mean by that?"

"I mean you look much better up close than you do far off. Just the opposite of the big cities." His eyes were laughing as he saw her beginning to protest. "I was only teasing you. You're an attractive woman from far off and up close as well."

"You shouldn't be talking like that to me."

"You should be talked to like this every day. I'm here to tell you that no matter how many suitors you have trailing around you, I'm getting rid of all of them. Give me a list, will you? I might have to fight duels with some of them."

"You're just foolish, Thomas," she said, though his teasing pleased her. Finally she rose and said, "You've got to go now."

"Oh, one of my rivals is coming?"

"No such thing." Twyla smiled. "My master is coming home soon with Dr. Teague. They've been working at the hospital."

"Master? I thought you told me he arranged for your freedom."

"He did, but I still serve him and Dr. Teague."

"You don't need to serve anyone." Thomas suddenly moved closer and took her hands in his. "You should never have to serve anybody. Why, if we get married, you'll have a maid just to do your hair and another maid to do the washing and the cooking."

"What would I do with myself all day if everyone was waiting on me?"

"You'd be making yourself beautiful for your husband. We'd be the handsomest couple in all of England."

His words gave Twyla a shock, and she whispered, "You shouldn't be talking to me like this. I'm only a servant."

"And I'm only a man. You have a jewel of great price that is difficult to find in this country."

"And what is that?"

"You have innocence, a quality I greatly admire in a woman." He reached forward and pulled Twyla toward him. Twyla had been kissed before by young men, so she recognized what was in his eyes. His lips fell on hers, and his arms tightened around her waist. She half surrendered, but at the same time part of her held back. Suddenly the door opened, and Twyla turned her head away from Thomas and pushed him back. She glanced toward the doorway and saw that Colin had entered and was looking at her sternly.

"Mr. Burke has been visiting," Twyla said quickly.

"Yes, I see that," Colin said with sarcasm in his voice.

Thomas Burke was flustered. He said quickly, "I must be going." He turned to Twyla and bowed, saying, "I'll look forward to seeing you on Thursday."

"Yes, it was kind of you to stop by."

As soon as the door closed, Colin said, "I'm disappointed in you."

Twyla felt a twinge of guilt. "I'm sorry that you should be, but it was just a kiss."

"I've tried to talk to you about men." Colin seemed to struggle for words for a moment, then said, "Men sometimes take advantage of young women."

Twyla knew this far better than Colin imagined. But she pretended to be ignorant. "What do you mean, 'take advantage'?"

"They do things that aren't right."

"What things?"

Colin opened his mouth to speak, but a blank look spread across his face. He stared at Twyla and added uncomfortably, "They just do things they shouldn't."

"Yes, so you said, but what sort of things? Maybe you should instruct me so I'll be on my guard."

As a physician Colin had little difficulty speaking plainly to his female patients, yet Twyla had the power to make him feel considerable confusion. He had watched her grow up from a skinny child to a beautiful young woman, but now he discovered that it was far more difficult dealing with a young woman than with a child. Colin had been aware of the attraction Twyla had for other men, and he had talked to Teague about his concern, saying, "You need to have a talk with Twyla and her ways with men."

Teague just stared at him. "Talk to her yourself. She's your servant."

Now Colin made up his mind. "Sit down and we'll talk about this."

Twyla sat down and watched as Colin drew a chair and sat opposite her. For the next ten minutes she watched him struggle to explain the dangers that a young woman faced from men. Of course she had learned such things as she was coming into her teens. Men had been attracted to her, and she learned early how to handle them. *Why, he thinks I'm innocent as a baby!* For a moment that irritated her, but then her sense of humor came into play. *Let him be uncomfortable, then, giving his explanations.* When he faltered, she pressed questions on him about intimacy. She was amused to see how discomfited he was to speak of such things.

Their talk, such as it was, was interrupted by a knock on the door. Colin had really told her nothing, but he was obviously relieved. "We'll speak of this later. I must see who's at the door." Colin stood and opened the door to a tall man dressed in rich attire.

"I'm looking for Dr. Colin Winslow."

"I'm Dr. Winslow. How can I help you?

"I have a message for you from the queen." Without another word, he pulled a thin sheet of paper from a purse he carried at his side.

Colin took the letter and noted that it was sealed with the royal crest. "Thank you," he said, then watched as the man mounted his horse and rode away. Closing the door, he looked at the paper.

"What is it, Mister?"

"I wish you would call me something besides *Mister*," he said absently, then broke the seal. He unfolded the paper and scanned it quickly, then looked at Twyla, saying, "It's a command. I am to be at court next week."

"What for?"

"It doesn't say. But I'll have to go, of course."

Twyla was intrigued. She had seen Queen Elizabeth twice when she'd passed through London, carried on a litter. Twyla knew that Colin and his family were on friendly terms with the queen, and she said, "You'll have to get some new clothes." Then she teased again, "We didn't finish our talk about what I must do when men try to steal my virtue."

An expression of embarrassment came across Colin's face, and he said stiffly, "I think I made myself clear enough. Just stay away from men, especially that fellow Burke."

"Oh, you're ordering me to stay away from him?"

Colin suddenly realized that he'd overstepped his bounds. "I—I didn't mean to order you around, Twyla. I'm sure you will show good judgment. You usually do."

"I'll be careful. Now, let's see about getting you a new suit made to meet the queen in."

The large room was full of counselors and noblemen, and Colin felt out of place. He watched as Queen Elizabeth, who was sitting on a raised dais, spoke to various men. It was a collection of the highest-ranking officials of Elizabeth's court, most of them men who wanted the queen's favor.

Elizabeth seemed to have forgotten that she had sent for him, for she didn't call his name. After an hour Colin was ready to leave, for he cared little about political affairs and what was going on at court. He was interested in one person, however: Sir Francis Drake, who stood at the queen's left hand, along with Walsingham and other officials. Drake was the talk of England as well as Spain. He had raided Spanish ships until Philip of Spain had put out special orders to capture *El Draco*, as he was called. Drake didn't look the role. He was of no more than medium height. His face had a triangular shape to it, and what appeared to be a weak chin was covered by a sharp beard. But his gaze could pierce a man like an arrow. Several times Elizabeth asked his opinion, which he rapped out with little ceremony.

Colin heard his name and looked up, startled, to see Elizabeth peering at him with a half-smile on her face. "Come forward, Dr. Winslow," she commanded.

Embarrassed at the attention, Colin made his way to stand before Elizabeth. He took her hand and kissed it, saying, "Your Majesty, you're looking well as usual."

"Is that your courtier opinion or an official medical diagnosis?"

"Both, Your Majesty." Colin looked up to see the queen smiling at him. She wasn't a beautiful woman, although she reveled in the young men who gathered around to tell her so. Her best feature was her complexion, but she was getting older and the bloom that had been hers in youth was fading.

"So, you have come at your queen's command."

"Why, of course, Your Majesty."

"Have you no idea why I've summoned you here, Dr. Winslow?"

"No, your Majesty, unless you have an ache or a pain."

Elizabeth laughed heartily, then said, "Not at the moment. I have something to give you." She stood and advanced until she stood facing Colin, then said, "Kneel, Colin Winslow."

"Kneel?"

"Yes. That means get down on your knees." She said this dryly as Colin dropped to his knees and kept his eyes on the queen. She held out her right hand, and Robert Dudley removed his sword and handed it to Elizabeth. "You've done much good service for your patients and have been my faithful servant. I dub thee Knight Commander of the Order of the Bath."

Colin felt the light tap of the sword, first on one shoulder, then the other. He looked up and saw that Elizabeth was pleased.

"I've surprised you."

Colin rose, shocked but able to say, "Yes, Your Majesty, you have."

"You are a knight now, but I have something more substantial. Give me the paper, Mr. Secretary." She took the paper that Lord Burghley handed her, then offered it to Colin. "This is a physical token of our appreciation. It's a fine house, and it's close enough to the outskirts of London that if I get sick you can be here in minutes. Now rise, Sir Colin Winslow."

Colin came to his feet, took the piece of paper, and looked at it in wonder. He hardly knew what to say. "I'm entirely undeserving of this, Your Majesty, but I'm truly grateful, from my heart."

"You will now be the court physician. That gives you a great deal of power among your peers, the other doctors in England." Elizabeth paused and her eyes narrowed as she added, "Many people want power, and it's a deadly weapon that can hurt the one who wields it. Be careful, Sir Colin, to use this power wisely. Do not let it make you a tyrant."

"I'll do my best to follow your instructions, Your Majesty."

Colin was at once surrounded by many who came to congratulate him. The first to come was Dr. Regis Perry, the head of the Royal College of Physicians. He had done all he could to ruin Colin's career, but now he had a smile on his lips that didn't reach his eyes. "Her Majesty has made a wise choice, Sir Colin," he said. "As head of the Royal College of Physicians, I welcome you, one in whom we all delight."

Colin was intensely aware of how little he delighted this man, but Elizabeth's words were ringing in his ears. "I'm always at your service, Dr. Perry. I'm grateful and appreciative." Perry was shaken, for he had expected at the very least to be snubbed. He saw that this was not to be, and he begged, "Sir Colin, I've been hasty in my judgments of you in the past. I trust you will forgive me?"

"There's nothing to forgive, Dr. Perry. We'll do good work together. Feel free to call on me anytime."

As he left the palace, Colin's mind was on the new house. His first thought was how much this would please Twyla. He hurried home as quickly as he could, and Twyla met him at the door. "Good news!" he said, then suddenly he put his arms around her and lifted her up and spun her around.

She knew his hug was not romantic, so she said only, "Why, what is it, Colin?"

Colin put her down and said, "You can't call me Mister any longer. I'm now Sir Colin Winslow. The queen knighted me!"

"How wonderful! You deserved it."

Colin saw that her eyes were sparkling and her lips were wide with a smile.

"And look! The queen has given us a new house!"

"A new house? Did you buy it?"

"No, the queen gave it to us. I will serve as the court physician. There's a small house for you. We'll have to hire servants, and you'll need a maid and a cook."

"What will I do with myself?"

"You'll be nice to me. That will be your full-time job." He paused, then said, "My parents will be proud of me."

Twyla smiled, saying, "They're already proud of you—and so am I, Sir Colin Winslow!"

Colin had dreaded telling Teague that he was leaving for London, but Teague was pleased, saying, "You're going up in the world, young man. I'm proud of you."

All during the month of March, Colin was fiercely busy. Now that he was the court physician, he had multiple calls for his service. Like his predecessors, he didn't answer most but assigned them to young assistants who had come to him seeking positions. He was amazed at how differently people treated him now that he had a title. He paid little attention to that, but he used every spare minute with Twyla to outfit the new house. It was a large house that required at least half a dozen servants, but money was coming in from the book now and the practice was booming.

In the last week of the month, Colin got a letter from his mother saying his father was not at all well and asking him to come to Stoneybrook. He showed the letter to Twyla. "I'm worried about Father. I've decided to go get him and Mother to bring them back here. There's plenty of room for them, and I can take constant care of him here."

"When will you go, Colin?"

He smiled at her, saying, "Well, at last you've stopped calling me 'Mister.' You've got to be good or I'll make you call me Sir Colin. Now, I'll go get my parents tomorrow, and you finish up on the house. By the way," he hesitated awkwardly, then said, "Adam and Heather will be coming to live with us for a time."

Twyla didn't speak for a moment, then hesitantly said, "Well, that will be nice."

"Adam needs to be near court along with Drake. They're getting ready to face a war with Spain. His house is too far away at present."

"There's plenty of room for everyone. When will they be here?"

"Within a week. I must get ready and go."

Twyla watched as he hurried away. She shook her head, for it displeased her that she would have to share the new house with Heather. She knew that the woman looked down on her because she had been a servant, and she also knew, from local gossip, that Heather was unhappy with her husband. Adam cared little for the social world of the court, while Heather wanted to go to every ball. She wanted Adam to fight his way up in society, but all Adam cared about was his career in the navy.

Twyla had heard, for some time, a great deal of gossip about Heather's personal life. Everyone, it seemed, knew that she'd had an affair with Sir George Beddington. He had no fortune, but he was a handsome man.

"Colin shouldn't have her in his house," Twyla muttered. "He's still in love with that woman, and she's nothing that a woman should be."

For two weeks now Twyla had been delighted to serve Colin's mother. She had always loved Eden and Brandon, and now that they were in the same house, she saw that they were made perfectly comfortable. This wasn't difficult to do, for there were plenty of servants. Though Brandon's health had been poor, he had improved greatly.

Twyla's relationship with Heather was not so happy. Adam was gone most of the time, for he and Drake were busy building a navy to meet the Spaniards. This left Heather with nothing to occupy her. Quite by accident, Twyla had discovered that the romance between Sir George Beddington and Heather was by no means dead. She overheard the servants talking about it and her first impulse was to speak of the affair to Colin, but she quickly saw that she must never say a word about Heather—at least until Colin was freed from his obsession with her.

But Heather had no hesitation about speaking to Colin about Twyla. She had not been in the house a week when she called Colin aside and said, "It's not fitting for you to be living in a house with Twyla. People are beginning to talk. You must get her out of here."

"What are you talking about?" Colin said instantly. "We're not living in the same house, as you well know. She's a fine young woman, and I'm very proud of her."

"You're vulnerable to women, as almost all men are," Heather said at once. "Don't you see the danger in living in the same house with her?"

"No, I certainly don't! We've been living in the same house since she was a child."

"Well, she's not a child any longer, Colin! You're alone together for much of the time. What if she draws you into an affair? She might have a child, and you'd be forced to send her away."

"You're talking nonsense, Heather! Twyla is a pure young woman!"

Heather moved toward Colin, putting her arms around his neck and pressing herself against him. "You're a target for an aggressive woman, and I'm partly to blame. I was your first woman, and I've never forgotten our love, and neither have you."

There was enough truth in Heather's words to send shame

through Colin, and the pressure of her body stirred old hungers. He drew away from her with a desperate fear that he would not be strong enough to resist her advances. "Don't speak of this again, Heather!" he said, then turned and left the room.

Heather slowly smiled, for she well knew that Colin was still drawn to her. She left the room, assured that there would be other times and that Colin would not be able to resist her.

20

April 15, 1587

Twyla found it easy to cook and listen to Thomas Burke at the same time. She'd made gingerbread so often that she didn't have to think about it. It was Colin's favorite sweet, so she'd learned to make it well. Compacted bread crumbs were the basis of the treat, and she added a stiff paste made with honey, pepper, saffron, and cinnamon. This she formed into a square shape and covered with box leaves, then impaled with cloves. She then put it in the special iron vessel she used to bake her pastries. The vessel was seated in a bowl of red-hot coals, and she also put hot coals on the top. She then came back to take her seat across from Thomas.

"I wish you would pay as much attention to me as you pay to your cooking," Thomas complained.

"Why do you keep coming to see me, Thomas?" Twyla asked. "Your father is rich and he'll want you to marry a rich woman. Also, I live much farther away now. It's a long trip for you."

Burke blinked in surprise. "Well now, that's coming right out with it!" he exclaimed. "That's what I like about you, Twyla: you say what you think. It gets a little tiresome having women falling all over you. Since I'll have a large fortune one day, I seem to attract them like bees to honey. Not you, though."

"How much money will you have? I might be interested." Twyla couldn't help teasing the young man.

He laughed and got to his feet. "You don't care about things like that." He came over and would have put his arms around her, but she put her hands on his chest and shoved him away. "Be off now, Thomas."

"I think we'd make a good couple. I've got money and you have beauty. What else is there?"

"There is one reason we could never marry."

"And what's that?"

"I don't have the feelings for you that a woman should have for the man she's going to spend fifty years in bed with."

The eyes of the young man flew open, and then he laughed with pleasure. "I can take care of that. After we're married I'll make you love me."

"Oh, you're impossible! Go along now. I've got work to do."

"I'll come and get you tomorrow. We'll go into the village, and I'll get you something pretty."

"I'll think about it."

As soon as Burke left, Twyla turned and looked over the large kitchen. It was at least three times as large as the old one, but she didn't like it as much. It lacked the coziness of the kitchen in Teague's house. She often thought of how it had been when just she, Colin, and Teague had shared the small house. Also, Colin had hired a cook and a housekeeper. Twyla had protested, but he had insisted, saying, "You've worked enough, Twyla. Now let someone else work for a change."

Moving to the kitchen window, Twyla looked out at the bright, sunny afternoon. A movement on the ground caught her eye, and she glanced down to see a group of sparrows engaged in a furious battle for the crumbs she'd put out earlier. She suddenly laughed and said, "Well, if birds can't agree, how can men have any hope?" She got a crust of bread, crumbled it, and threw it out through the open window.

Turning from the window, she went to a chest and pulled out her drawing papers. She was working on drawings for the new edition of the anatomy book. It gave her a feeling of pride that she had been such help to Colin. She hadn't been drawing long when the door opened and Colin entered. He wore a displeased expression and said at once, "I saw that pest walking down the street. Has he been here to see you?"

"No, I haven't had any pests here."

"He looked as if he came from here."

Twyla looked at him, her eyes wide with innocence. "No, the only visitor I've had is Mr. Thomas Burke, a fine young man admired by all. I wouldn't call him a pest."

"Well, he is!"

"He wants to marry me." This wasn't exactly true, for although Thomas had teased her about marriage, she knew his father would never permit it. It pleased Twyla to see Colin looking jealous.

He said stubbornly, "You don't love him."

Twyla laughed aloud, for she had learned to put up with Colin's persistent attempts to control her love life, such as it was. "Who made you an expert on love? Is your next book going to be on courtship and marriage, Colin?"

Colin was obviously irritated. "It bothers me that you *still* don't understand young men," he said stiffly. "I've told you a hundred times they aren't to be trusted!"

"I trust you utterly, Colin."

"Why, I didn't mean *me*! Of course you can trust me, but not that fellow Burke."

"Why can't I trust him?"

"He's got a look about him I don't like." Colin struggled to find the right words to say. "He looks like a sneak."

Twyla would have answered, but the outer door opened and the entire door frame was, it seemed, filled by the large figure of Adam. He looked troubled, but he brightened up when he saw

Twyla. "How are you today, my dear?" He reached out, took her hand, and kissed it. "You're looking especially well."

"Thank you, Adam. You look well too," Twyla answered with a shy smile.

"What's that I smell? Fresh bread? I'm starved to death!" Adam exclaimed.

"You two sit down. There's plenty of food. It was Kate's day off, so I did all the cooking, and I can cook better than she can anyway."

"You certainly can!" Adam exclaimed.

Twyla brought the food, and as the two men ate, she asked, "Are we really going to have a war with Spain?"

"Why, of course we are! No question about it! Walsingham's spies say the dons are building an armada with as many as two hundred ships. We don't even have forty! But we'll beat them! The queen's been prudent, but she knows she has to have a powerful navy. We can never beat Spain on the field, for we don't have the soldiers for it or the equipment. But they have to get here to put their army ashore, and that's how we'll stop them."

He leaned forward and his eyes gleamed. "The queen has had Sir John Hawkings working on a new design for a ship. The old galleons only did one thing: they put themselves next to an enemy ship and tried to board. All the time the cannons were blowing the sides of both ships apart. That's not what our new ships will do."

"What will they do?" Twyla asked.

"They're built to stand out of range of the enemy's cannon. We'll have specially made cannons called demi-culverins. They can throw a shot ten times farther than the Spanish cannons."

"Do you really think it'll work?" Colin asked doubtfully. "People are calling it *The Invincible Armada*."

"That's what the Spaniards are calling it, but they'll find out differently soon enough."

Adam stayed for a while and talked about the coming war, his eyes sparkling with excitement. Finally he arose and said, "I've got to go and see the admiral, and I know we'll be sailing soon. Would it be all right if Heather stayed on with you?" Heather had gone back to Adam's house after a long visit, but Adam said, "She's cut off from all the news living in our house in the country, so it would be nice if she could be with you until I get back."

"Of course." Colin hesitated and seemed embarrassed. "We have plenty of room, don't we, Twyla?"

"Certainly," Twyla said at once, but something in her began to grow cold. "She'll be welcome," she forced herself to say.

"I knew I could depend on you two! Now, I must go."

Colin stopped him. "Wait, Adam, I've been doing some experimenting. You know the popular treatment for a wound."

"Yes, pour boiling oil in it."

"That's right, but I've discovered that that treatment doesn't do any good. As a matter of a fact, it does harm."

"But that's what we've always done."

"You sound like the doctors at the college! All they can say is: 'We've always done it this way, so we must keep on doing it this way.'"

Adam stared at his brother. "What would you want us to do for wounded men?"

"It's very simple, Adam. After the last battle, I had to treat eleven badly wounded men. Dr. Teague and I treated half with boiling oil and the other with nothing. The ones with boiling oil almost died, but the others did much better. Stop and think about it, Adam. How would you feel if I took boiling oil and poured it over your arm, even with no wound?"

Adam flinched at the thought. "Not pleasant."

"Please talk to the admiral and tell him what I've said."

"I think you'd better tell him yourself," Adam said quickly.

"I'll be glad to do that. You'll be leaving right away, will you?"

"I think so. I'll bring Heather over." Adam came over and kissed Twyla on the cheek. "I knew I could count on you, as always." This put the smile back on her face, then Adam left to go see the admiral.

"I worry about him, Colin. It's so dangerous—all that fighting!"

"So do I," Colin soberly agreed. "We'll have to take care of his wife. At least we can do that much for him."

After Heather came, Twyla continued to work with Colin on the additions to the new book. She was aware that Heather often drew Colin away from the practice, which was unusual for him, for he'd always been diligent in his care of patients. Now Heather always seemed to find something for him to do, and Colin often neglected his work.

Twyla saw more and more evidence that Heather had no love for her husband. Until Adam set sail he stayed with them, but as soon as he was called away on one of Drake's raids, there was a change in Heather. She grew secretive, and quite by accident Twyla heard one of the maids whispering to another, "That Lady Heather, she's got a man."

"A man? You don't mean it?"

"Right in this very house. I've seen him myself. He comes late at night and goes to her room."

That was all Twyla heard of the conversation, but that was enough. She was determined to find out the truth, thinking, *I don't want to judge her unjustly.*

For two nights she sat up late waiting, but nothing happened. On the third night she was sitting quietly in a small room off the main hall. She heard someone coming down the steps and got up to peer down the darkened corridor. She saw at once that it was Heather and watched as she went to the front door and unlocked it. A man came in, and even in the dim light, Twyla recognized Sir George Beddington. She watched the two as they went up the stairs, Heather clinging to him. Twyla went to her own room, and doubt filled her. *What can I do? Colin is so besotted with Heather he'll never believe anything like this!*

For four days Twyla carried her guilty secret around, but finally she knew that she couldn't remain silent any longer. Adam had been gone for several weeks now, and early in the morning Twyla caught Colin as he was leaving to go to the hospital. "I—I have to talk to you, Colin. I've—got something bad to tell you."

"You're not feeling ill again, are you?"

"No. It's nothing like that. It's about—about Heather."

"What about her?" Colin's expression grew tense, exactly as Twyla had feared.

She dreaded speaking the truth, but she strongly felt that Colin needed to know. She faltered, then said, "She's having an affair with George Beddington."

"I don't believe it!" Colin said, but doubt showed in his eyes. "How do you know? Who told you this?"

"I've seen him myself several times, coming to the house."

"There's nothing wrong with a visit."

"Colin, he comes sneaking in after midnight! Heather lets him in and takes him into her room. I've seen him, and the servants know about it."

"I don't believe a word of it!" Colin said loudly.

"I saw them, I tell you!"

"You're just jealous of her! You always have been."

Anger flared up in Twyla. Colin was impossible. She saw clearly that he was still infatuated with this woman. "You won't ever be free of her! I'm leaving this house!" she cried.

"What do you mean, *leaving*? How will you live?"

"I've got enough money from the books and the illustrations. I've told you the truth, and you think I'm a liar. I refuse to stay in a house with a man who thinks I lie." She wanted to hurt him at that instant and said loudly, "I'm going to marry Thomas!" She whirled and left the room, confused and angry.

The next day Twyla packed some of her things and started to leave the house, but Colin was waiting for her. He obviously had not slept and said at once, "I know I hurt your feelings, Twyla, and I'm sorry. But I just can't believe what you said."

"That's because you're a fool, Colin. The Book of Proverbs talks about men who follow after strange women. It says her steps lead down to hell."

"Where will you live?"

"There's a little house for rent over by the church. I heard the pastor talking about it. I'll live there. Good-bye, Colin."

Colin saw the coldness in her eyes and said desperately, "Don't leave, Twyla, please! We can work this out!"

"You'll *never* work it out, Colin! You're blind about this woman. You always have been and you always will be!" She turned and left, ignoring his voice as he called after her.

April passed, then May, but Twyla saw Colin only at those times when she drew illustrations for his book. She saw that he was unhappy, and she also was aware that he was alone now with Heather. Twyla's suspicions grew dark, and she hated herself for it.

Late one afternoon, she was sitting by herself in front of the fire. She had adopted a cat she named Chester. He was a large, sleek gray cat with many scars from battles. He did love affection, though, and finally allowed Twyla to hold him in her lap. She was stroking him when the knock came at the door. She put the cat on the floor and got up to open the door. She was surprised to see Colin.

"I'm sorry to bother you," Colin said stiffly.

Twyla could see that his face was pale and troubled.

"What's wrong?" she asked.

"Adam is back. They had a battle with a ship of war, and he

was terribly wounded. I need help to care for him. Will you come?"

Instantly Twyla said, "Of course. Let me get a few things."

"Thank you, Twyla. I was sure you'd help," he said. "I'm not sure he'll even live."

"Don't say that! Let me get my things."

Ten minutes later they were in the carriage, and Twyla asked for details about Adam's injury. "I'm worried sick, Twyla! A shell went off and put some metal in his side, but we were able to take that out. He hasn't spoken, or ever regained consciousness."

"What does Dr. Teague say?"

"Just like me, he doesn't know what to say. I can tell he doesn't think Adam will live."

"But he will live! He's got to!" Twyla said in a confident tone.

"My parents are coming." Colin turned to her, and she saw that his lips were trembling. She had never seen him distressed like this before! Impulsively she reached out and took his hand. At that moment she forgot all the problems they'd had, and all the anger she'd felt toward him. "It'll be all right, Colin, God won't let him die." She felt his hands close on hers. "You'll see, Colin! God will give you wisdom and skill, just as He did when I was sick. You'll see, really you will!"

21

November 12, 1587

Although Philip II of Spain was the most powerful ruler in all of Europe, a certain timidity in his character was revealed in his nervous mannerisms. The execution of Mary, Queen of Scots, had forced Philip to move ahead with a plan that others in his court had been urging for years—the conquest of England.

Philip now had little choice, for his advisors had assured him that the execution of Mary had brought all of the Catholic monarchs in Europe together against England. Philip realized that he had to take action. Late one night he sat in an oversized chair, his eyes blinking rapidly, evidence of his unsettled mind. He looked at the man who sat opposite him and had a moment's doubt, but he quickly buried it. "My dear Santa Cruz, I've called you here because you are obviously the commander who must lead in the matter of England. You're our foremost soldier, and I trust you completely."

Don Álvaro de Bazán, Marquis of Santa Cruz, was an able soldier, the best in Spain. His record was impressive, but now there was a flicker of doubt in his eyes. "It will be a difficult undertaking, Your Majesty." His voice was coarse, as was his bodily presence, but there was no questioning his ability as a leader or as a soldier.

Philip leaned forward. "I've come up with a plan, and I think it is God who has given it to me."

"Indeed, I'm most anxious to hear it." Santa Cruz himself was a nominal Catholic. This was required of any soldier who served under Spanish colors. He wasn't confident in Philip's ability to lead in a military manner, nor in "visions" that supposedly came from God.

"This is what we'll do," Philip said eagerly, and his eyes brightened as he spoke, for he had thought much about this. "You will command the largest battle fleet ever gathered on the sea. It will be called *The Invincible Armada*. Now, my dear Santa Cruz, we're very aware that our forces can easily defeat the English in any battle on land. Getting our forces to England, that's the problem."

"It is indeed, Your Majesty. The Seahawks, as Elizabeth calls her admirals, may be heretics and ungodly men, but they are fine sailors! They also have new ships that are designed for the defense of the English coast."

"It can be done," Philip urged. "Here's my plan. You will sail in the Armada and you will meet with Alexander of Parma. You're well aware that he is one of the ablest soldiers on the continent, and he has promised to lead his large, well-equipped army against the English. You'll transport him and his army to the shores of England, and once they are landed, the English army will fall before our swords."

Santa Cruz was silent for a moment, then nodded and said grimly, "It can be done, Your Majesty. We'll begin at once gathering an army to be transported and planning the sailing of the Invincible Armada. God will smile upon us!"

While Philip II was planning the battle that would destroy England, Queen Elizabeth wasn't idle. She'd called together those men in the navy she trusted most, those she called her Seahawks. She glanced around the room and studied them carefully. Sir Francis Drake, the best of her fighting admirals, pleased Elizabeth well. She studied his tapered face with the tidy beard. He had glistening eyes, and Elizabeth knew that if she gave Drake his way, he would attack Spain immediately.

Elizabeth looked next at Lord Howard of Effingham, who would be admiral over the English fleet. He was an efficient man, though not the fighter that Drake was. Still, he was better organized and did not lack courage.

Elizabeth's glance moved on to John Hawkings and Martin Frobesher, two fine and experienced sailors, and she thought, *If any men alive can destroy the Armada, these four are the ones!*

Lord Burghley, as usual, sat beside Walsingham. Now he said sharply, "We all know that the Spanish are engaged in ship building. There can be little doubt of this project."

"Indeed, Your Majesty." Drake leaned forward and his eyes seemed to burn into Elizabeth. "The Spanish have but one goal: to send a fleet and land an army on our shores. They must be stopped! If you permit me, I'll take a fleet now and destroy them in their own harbors."

"That wouldn't be wise." Effingham shook his head. He was a cautious man, far more so than Drake. "We must prepare."

John Hawkings, the second best sailor after Drake, agreed. "We must have the ships and guns, and the men must be ready."

"Tell me more about this Spanish navy that is being built, Walsingham," Elizabeth said.

Walsingham shrugged. "It's almost impossible to get accurate information. My agents have tried, but the Spanish have grown wiser. Any man they suspect of being a spy is taken before the Inquisition and ordered to be burned at the stake. It's become extremely difficult to get a spy into place."

"You must do more, Walsingham!" Elizabeth said sharply. "What about the ships that we'll need, Sir Francis?"

"We must build a different kind of navy," Drake said eagerly. He clasped his hands together, and the fighting spirit in him seemed to glow. "Always before, the fighting ships have been large, uncontrollable things. The only way to win was to put the ship right next to the enemy. Both ships would fire their cannons until one ship was destroyed. Sometimes both ships would sink. That will not do!"

"What sort of ship are you proposing?" Elizabeth asked.

"They must be small, fast ships. Most important of all, they must be armed with culverins. The old cannons didn't have to fire more than a few yards because the ships were locked rail to rail. Our new ships must be fast and agile. They must be able to stand off away from the Spanish guns. They must be able to shatter them from a distance."

Elizabeth listened carefully as Drake went on speaking. Finally, she nodded. "Let it be done, then. I don't know where the money will come from, but money will do us no good if the Spanish conquer us. Go to it, gentlemen." She turned and looked at the men. "Don't forget, Walsingham, we must know all we can about *The Invincible Armada*, as they call it."

"It will be done, Your Majesty."

The Duke of Medina Sidonia was not an impressive man. He was of less than middle height, small boned, and neatly made. He had a thoughtful mouth, an intellectual forehead, and brooding eyes. The duke had a sensitive face, but it was entirely unheroic. Now as he sat across from Philip, he wondered why Philip would send for him. He wasn't left in the dark long.

"You're aware, my duke, that Santa Cruz died?"

"Yes, it was a tragedy for our cause. I don't know who will replace him."

Philip smiled. He leaned closer to the other and said, "*You* are his replacement, sir!"

Medina Sidonia couldn't have been more shocked if an emperor had commanded him to fly to the moon. That seemed at least as possible as for him to gain a victory over the English!

"But Your Majesty, I'm not in good health. And I'm not the soldier needed for this war."

"God has told me that you are."

"But my illness, Your Majesty! This enterprise requires a strong man."

"Then we'll get you healthy and strong." Determination was in the king's eyes. "We'll get the best doctors to be had."

Medina Sidonia shook his head. "My cousin Juan De Rosa had the same illness that has been troubling me. He came very close to dying."

"I remember your cousin. Is he still ill?"

"No, he was in England when he was stricken. Many English doctors failed him, as did our own Spanish physicians. But there was finally a young English doctor who treated him, and he recovered. It was like a miracle."

"You cannot go to England, but we will send for this doctor. Is he politically involved?"

"No. All his interest is in medicine."

"What's his name?"

"His name is Sir Colin Winslow."

"I'll send for him at once. If he's not political he will surely answer a medical emergency. Until your young doctor arrives, start all proceedings for assembling the Invincible Armada!"

Colin had been taken aback by the interview with the Spanish nobleman who gave his name as Basilio Lopez. Señor Lopez had appeared out of nowhere, it seemed. He had said immediately, "Dr. Winslow, you remember treating Señor Juan De Rosa?"

"Yes, he was very fortunate."

"I've been sent by his cousin, who is afflicted with the same ailment. I've been instructed to ask you to take on his case."

"I'll be happy to, sir. Just bring him in."

"I'm afraid that won't be possible. I'm speaking now of the Duke of Medina Sidonia."

Instantly alarms went off in Colin's head, for he had heard rumors that Sidonia had been selected by Philip to lead the Armada after the death of Santa Cruz. He said quickly, "I'm not sure that would be possible, sir."

"You must understand that money is of no object. You may name your own fee. And as a physician, I am certain that you want to heal the sick."

"Of course, that is what a physician does."

"Not all of them, Doctor." Lopez smiled grimly. "My master has tried everything. We beg you to come."

"Give me a day to think it over. It would involve finding someone to take over my patients."

"Certainly, I can wait a day. Not much longer, however, for the duke is very ill."

"Please call tomorrow about this same time, Señor."

"I'll pray that God will lay it on your heart to help this sick man."

As soon as Lopez was gone, Colin left the house. After some difficulty, he found Walsingham at the Nonesuch Palace, where he was admitted at once.

"Well, Doctor, what can I do for you?" Walsingham said. "I'm very busy, as you see."

Colin said immediately, "You need to hear this, Sir Francis." He related what had happened, and he saw Walsingham's eyes darken with deep thought. Colin somehow felt that Walsingham could read his mind.

"What an opportunity!" Walsingham exclaimed. "It's fallen in our lap! It almost makes me believe that God is interested in small things. But of course this isn't a small thing!"

"I can't go, Sir Francis. I have my patients."

"Your colleagues can take care of them. You *must* go."

"But my brother, Adam—you know how ill he is. I think he's dying."

"Your brother loves this country. If he were able to go, he wouldn't hesitate, but he cannot go. Therefore, you must!"

Colin argued desperately, but realizing it was a losing battle, he gave in.

Walsingham said, "Dr. Teague will take care of your brother and your patients. They will all be proud of you, Doctor. You must go." Walsingham leaned closer to Colin, saying, "That phenomenal memory of yours will be our secret weapon, Colin. Don't write anything down. The duke will be busy building the Armada, and you must make it your business to stay close beside him. We need to know how many ships they have, what sort of guns, how many soldiers, everything! Most important, listen to what is said. When you come home, we'll have what we need to meet this so-called Invincible Armada!"

"You mustn't go to Spain! It's too dangerous!" Twyla was shocked to hear Colin's news and said, "It's dangerous for any Englishman to be in that country. They can arrest you and send you to the Inquisition."

"That won't happen, Twyla."

"You can't know that!" Twyla twisted her hands together nervously. "You need to be here with Adam."

"I've already gone through that with Sir Francis Walsingham. He insists that Dr. Teague will be with Adam constantly. And of course, you'll be here, and my family. I have to do this, and you must not mention anything about this mission."

"You know I wouldn't do that."

Colin paused, then reached out and put his hand on Twyla's cheek. "I'm trusting you, Twyla. You're better for Adam than any doctor."

"Oh, Colin, that isn't true!"

"I think it is." He leaned forward and kissed her on the cheek. "Keep me in your prayers," he whispered. She didn't speak but she smiled, and her features were suddenly, for Colin, full of beauty and grace. He had thought of her as a child for a long time, but now he saw that she was rich in all the ways a woman should be. She caught his glance and held it, and he wanted to touch her, for her nearness brought forth all his hungers in a way he'd never known. Without consciously willing it, he drew her close and kissed her. She was there for him, waiting for him, with a wild sweetness in her lips. He whispered, "I never knew you were so lovely, Twyla!"

He turned and was gone, but Twyla sat down because she found herself trembling. It was the first time Colin had ever seen her as a woman, and she knew he would not forget the kiss, any more than she herself would. She began to pray, "God, please keep him safe. Don't let him come to an evil end in that place!"

22

December 1587

Colin stepped off the gangplank and was met by a large, burly man with blunt features and muddy brown eyes. "Dr. Winslow?"

"Yes, I'm Colin Winslow."

"My name is Gaspar Chavez. I'm the chief physician of the court."

Colin bowed slightly. "I'm happy to meet you, Dr. Chavez."

"And I you." Chavez seemed to be suspicious, which was natural enough, Colin thought. "I'm told you had success treating the duke's cousin."

"That is true. It was difficult to diagnose his case, but in the end he was completely cured."

"I'm sure you're anxious to see your patient. If you're ready, we'll go at once to meet the duke."

Colin agreed, and the two got into the carriage that was waiting. All during the brief journey, Chavez fired questions at him. When the carriage stopped and Chavez turned to face Colin, he stated gravely, "The duke must be cured. All depends on him." He hesitated for a moment. "Dr. Winslow, are you aware of the difficulties between your country and mine?"

"I've heard some things, yes. But I'm not political."

"I'm surprised to hear that."

"My brother is in the English Navy. He keeps me informed, but I see him rarely. I've given my life to healing. That's the only thing I'm interested in now. Of course, I hope there will be peace between our two countries."

"Good." Chavez nodded emphatically. "Come, I'll take you to the duke."

The two stepped out of the carriage and Colin followed Chavez. He was aware of frantic activities going on everywhere. The building they entered was clearly the center of the direction of military affairs. The place was swarming with sailors and soldiers of all sorts. He said nothing, but followed Chavez down a long corridor. The two soldiers guarding the door, upon seeing Chavez, stepped aside. Chavez opened the door, stepped inside, and motioned for Colin to enter.

Colin went into the room, and the man seated at the desk rose at once. "Your Excellency," Chavez said, "may I present Dr. Winslow? Dr. Winslow, the Duke of Sidonia."

"I welcome you to Spain, Dr. Winslow."

"I was very happy to come. I was quite fond of your cousin, Your Grace."

"He speaks most highly of you, Doctor. When I wrote to him to tell him you were coming, he was most enthusiastic. You made quite a favorable impression on him."

"I pray that I'll be of as much help to you, Your Grace."

"I trust that will be the case, for time is of the essence. Would you like to begin the treatment right now?"

"Yes, I would. Let me give you a brief physical examination. I'm sure Dr. Chavez has done so already and he can fill me in with the details."

"Of course, Doctor," Chavez nodded. He moved to stand with his back against the wall, obviously with no intention of leaving. Colin understood that he would be watched carefully, for Walsingham had warned him that this would be the case. He did a perfunctory exam, but almost at once he had made a diagnosis of sorts. *His problem isn't physical. His hands are shaking and he seems unsteady, and there's a nervous tic in his eye. Something disturbing is going on in his mind or in his spirit.* "I would like to follow the same procedure that I followed with your cousin, Your Grace. The treatment involves a series of medicines that will need to be administered faithfully, and I will need to observe you constantly. Would it be imprudent of me to ask to stay by your side during your waking hours?"

"That might be very difficult," the duke shrugged, then said, "but I have no objections. Do you, Dr. Chavez?"

"Whatever Dr. Winslow says, we should follow."

"Very well," Colin said. "I have brought a store of medicines that was helpful in curing your cousin. It's imperative that we begin treatment at once."

"Thank you, Dr. Winslow. You have our gratitude for coming."

As soon as the two doctors left, the duke sat down and began to write a letter to Philip.

> *My health is not equal to such a task, Your Majesty. I know from experience that I'm always seasick and always catch cold. Since I've had little experience of the sea or war, I cannot feel that I should command such an important post as this. The Adelantado Major of Castille is much more fit for this post than I. He is a man of much experience of naval and military matters. He is also a good Catholic. I beg you to reconsider your choice for the leader of this great enterprise.*

He sat looking at the letter he had written and noted that his hands were unsteady. He felt a heaviness in his chest that he couldn't ignore. As he sealed the letter and rose to give it to an aide, he prayed fervently, "God, let the emperor see that I'm no man to lead this enterprise!"

A single candle burned, but it gave enough feeble light that Colin was aware of the tiny mouse that crept out of a hole in the wall. Two weeks had passed, and Colin was all alone, one of the few times he had experienced solitude. Every day he had stayed constantly beside the duke, and it had been a busy time indeed. Now, as he watched the mouse, he smiled, got to his feet, and rummaged through a cloth bag until he came up with a bit of cheese. He broke off a morsel and held it out, and the mouse came to his hand. "You've become quite tame," Colin whispered and put down the morsel. The tiny creature came closer at once and picked up the cheese, then reared up, holding it in her front paws. "Ah, you're a nursing mother, I see. Where are your little ones?"

Colin continued to feed the mouse as he thought over what he could report to Walsingham when they met again. *I know now all the ships that are being prepared for the Armada. I know the number of soldiers that will be on board, and I also know the weaknesses of the Armada. Food is spoiling in the casks, and by the time the Armada sets to sea, most of it will be inedible—just as the water will be rank. I've heard the duke raging because ammunition for the guns is lacking, and when it does come, is often put on the wrong ship. It has become obvious to all—except to Philip—that the duke is the wrong man for this task.*

The mouse paused to wash her tiny paws and stared up at Colin with bright eyes. "All right, here. Take that to your little ones." Colin gave her the last fragment of cheese and thought over his efforts toward healing the duke. *Well, the duke does indeed have the same problem his cousin had when I treated him in England. It became obvious that the patient's problems weren't physical, but I never told them that. He had a case of depression, very serious, but nothing physical. Fortunately for him, I had a solution. There is a Peruvian bush that produces leaves called Erythroxylon coca. I'd learned some time ago that these leaves possess great virtues in cases of melancholia or morbid depression of spirits. Whether it be* rational or irrational, almost always a restless uneasiness of mind accompanies these conditions, and the drug brings about a euphoria, a sense of well-being, and makes the patient more lucid. The euphoria is far superior in every way to that produced by opium. The leaves produce this without causing the addiction we're all so well acquainted with. These coca leaves, which do nothing physically for the duke, do seem to calm his nerves. Everyone has commented on how well he is doing since I started the treatment.

The mouse finished her cheese, then scampered back into the hole in the wall.

The king himself had come down to the dock, along with the duke, to bid Colin good-bye. "I must give you some tangible evidence of my gratitude," he said and handed Colin a heavy bag. When Colin tried to protest, Philip shook his head. "No, you've done a marvelous piece of work."

"Indeed, you have, Dr. Winslow," the duke said. "I sleep like a child, and the burdens of my duties seem light as a feather."

"I'm so happy that you're doing well. But I must urge you to continue taking all your medicines. I've given all your prescriptions to Dr. Chavez, and he has promised to faithfully give you the same treatment. It's a combination of all the medicines together that has cured you."

Philip stepped forward and embraced Colin with an unexpected fervor. "You've done Spain a service that I can only say is from the hand of God."

"Our prayers do go with you, Doctor," the duke said warmly while holding Colin's hands in his.

Colin took their thanks, accepted the heavy bag of coins, then boarded the ship. Soon the ship began to move away from the dock, and as it pulled out, Colin noticed that a military officer had brought a band of scarlet-cloaked soldiers. They were all cheering his name at the command of their officer. Colin smiled and waved to them but thought, *I'm a hero to Spain. I wonder if that makes me a traitor to England.* He turned and went to stand at the bow. As the ship cleared the harbor, Colin felt a great long-ing for England—and for those there he loved. He watched the gulls for a time, but then found something sad in their raucous cries. Finally he turned and began to pace the deck, thinking of how he had deceived the duke, but found that he could bear such thoughts. *I did it for England!* was the thought that came most strongly to him, and he took comfort in that.

23

January 1588

Walsingham leaned across his desk, his dark eyes burning. "You were able to observe all of this, Doctor, and they never suspected you?"

Colin smiled broadly. He'd come directly to Walsingham after arriving in England, and for the past hour had given him all the information he'd gleaned. A secretary had taken down everything he said. "It was the easiest thing in the world, sir. They were so worried about the duke they would've believed anything I said."

Walsingham laughed aloud—a rare thing indeed for the director of the secret service! He picked up one of the sheets of paper and ran his eyes down it. "They didn't notice you paying attention to their ships?"

"No, not after the first day. They became so accustomed to me they didn't pay any attention to me at all. The duke went down to the harbor almost every day to confer with the different captains. I believe I could name the captains of seventy-five percent of the ships—and I can give you the kind of cannon on each ship."

"You're certain about the supplies being in such terrible shape?"

"Oh, yes. The duke was frantic. No matter what he did, it seemed things went wrong."

Walsingham got up and walked around the desk. Colin rose also, and Walsingham, in an unusual gesture of affection, put his hand on Colin's shoulder. "I'm very proud of you, Doctor! With this information, we'll be able to meet this so-called 'Invincible Armada.' You've done your country a great service."

"I'm glad to be of some help, sir. I'm equally glad to be back. I'm hoping for better news of my brother."

Walsingham's face clouded. "I receive word each day from Dr. Teague. I grieve to say that he's not doing at all well."

"I must go to him at once."

"Go, Doctor! Go and take the gratitude of your queen with you. As soon as I tell her you are back, she will want to see you."

As Twyla helped the elderly patient off the table, he grinned at her toothlessly, and she asked, "Do you feel better now?"

"Much better! Much better!"

"You just do what the doctor says, and you will be well in no time." She helped him to his feet and walked with him to the door.

When she came back, she found that Teague had entered the room. "Well," he said wearily, "I'm worn out from seeing patients. I'll be bound you are too, Twyla."

"I don't mind, Dr. Teague."

"You're a pearl of great price." Teague had grown very fond of Twyla. Even more so recently, since the two had been forced to carry the load that Colin usually managed. He glanced at her, then said, "You need to get some rest."

"I'll go, but really I need to spend time with Adam. His mother spends as much time with him as she can, and the servants have been a great help. But I don't want to leave him alone yet."

Teague asked sharply, "What about that wife of his? Is she a help?"

Twyla said faintly, "She's not too interested in sick people."

"But this is her husband! Surely that should make a difference!"

"I know that, but she doesn't seem to."

"Why, Twyla, I've never heard you speak unkindly about anyone." Teague knew that Heather was not a good wife but was surprised to hear Twyla speak so plainly of her.

Twyla had managed to bottle up her feelings about Heather, not saying anything to anyone since Colin had left for Spain. "I don't understand that woman. This is her husband, and he's dying, while she's going about—" Twyla didn't finish her sentence, but Teague had an idea of what she was going to say. Twyla was determined to change the conversation. "Dr. Teague, what are Adam's chances for recovery?"

"Not good, I'm afraid." Teague sighed. "I wish Colin were here."

Twyla bid him good night. She made her way back to the house and hurried to see Adam. His mother sat beside him. Twyla saw at once that his color was bad and his breathing was erratic. "How is he, Lady Eden?"

"No better, I'm afraid." Eden's face was worn and tired, for she sat long hours with Adam. She sighed deeply, adding, "I'm so afraid for him, Twyla."

"We'll just have to trust the Lord, ma'am."

"I do, of course, but it's hard to have faith when every day he seems to grow worse. I'm sure when Colin gets back, he'll be able to help."

"I know he will."

Eden looked at Twyla, then said, "You've worn yourself out working for Dr. Teague, then all the hours you spend here with Adam. You aren't sleeping or eating enough."

"I'm fine, ma'am." She walked over and laid her hand on Adam's forehead. "He still has that fever. It seems like he has had it for weeks now."

"Dr. Teague won't say much to me, but I know he's discouraged."

"We all are, ma'am, but we can keep praying for answers."

Eden lifted her head and looked at Twyla for a moment, then said gently, "I've been meaning to ask you something, Twyla."

"What is it, Lady?"

"How do you feel about my son?"

Twyla looked confused. "About Adam?"

"No, about Colin."

Twyla had kept her feelings for Colin concealed as well as she could, but now she flushed and couldn't control the nervousness that came to her. "I—I admire him greatly."

"It's more than that, isn't it?"

"What do you mean?"

"You love him, don't you, Twyla?"

Twyla looked down at the floor, unable to speak. Her throat seemed to close up, and she felt tears gathering in her eyes. Finally she looked up and whispered, "Yes, Lady Eden, I love him. I have for a long time."

"What does he feel for you?"

"For a long time he saw me as a child, and now he sees me as a servant." Her voice had pain in it as she spoke. Tears came into her eyes and she whispered, "He kissed me before he left. It was the first time he saw me as a woman."

"I'm sure that isn't true. He's told me so many times how he admires and respects you. You've come so far, my dear! I remember when you first came to live with the doctors—but just look at you now! Colin is very proud of you, and so are my husband and I."

Eden came over and put her arm around the girl. "You mustn't give up. If it's meant to be, it will all work out." The two women stood in a fond embrace. When Eden noticed the tears in Twyla's eyes, she gave her a kiss on the cheek. "I couldn't think of a finer wife for my son than you."

"He's always cared for someone else."

"You mean Heather? Why, there is nothing to that."

"But there *is*, my lady! He's never gotten over her."

"Twyla, she's married to Adam!"

"I know that, but Colin can't see what she is."

The two women stood there for a moment, then Twyla said, "Why don't you go get some rest? I'll sit here with Adam."

"Get one of the servants to stay, and you go rest yourself."

"No, I'll stay. You go on to bed." Finally, Eden agreed and went to her room. Twyla sat down beside Adam, weary to the bone. She had not been fond of Adam, but in his pitiful condition she had come to feel a great deal of compassion for him. The time passed slowly. Then the door opened, and Twyla stood as Heather entered the room.

"I thought you were at the hospital," Heather said coldly.

"No," Twyla said. "I've finished my work with Dr. Teague."

"Where is Lady Eden?"

"She's exhausted. I sent her to bed."

Heather came over and glared at Twyla, saying, "You may as well go home."

"I think I should stay here."

"You don't think I'm capable of caring for my husband?" Heather's voice grew shrill. "It's time for you to go from this place. You take care of Dr. Teague and his patients. I'll take care of my husband."

Twyla had no answer for that. She knew that Heather had no real love for Adam, but there was nothing she could do about that. She got up and left the room, and Heather glared after her.

Heather went over and looked at Adam. There was something inscrutable in her eyes. She stayed only for a short time, then ordered one of the servants to come and sit with her husband.

Twyla looked up and saw Colin. She thought of how she'd felt when he had kissed her before he left and wondered if he had thought of her. He came to her with a smile and took her hands in his. "I'm so glad to see you, Twyla! I missed you more than I thought I could miss anyone!"

"Colin! When did you get here?"

"Just this morning. I've been with Walsingham." He studied her face and said, "You look exhausted, Twyla. Are you not getting enough sleep?"

"I'm fine. How did your mission go?"

"Sit down and I'll tell you." They sat down in the two chairs in her room, and she smiled as he explained how successful the mission had been.

"I'm so glad. And the queen will be most happy."

"Yes, I suppose so. But I'm worried about Adam. He's no better?"

"I think he's worse."

The two sat talking for a moment. Then he said, "Come with me. I need to see him."

Twyla walked him down the hallway that led to the room where Adam was lying. Colin went to him at once and put his hand on Adam's wrist to feel his pulse, then leaned down and listened to his heart. "He looks bad. I can't understand why he's still not regained consciousness, nor can Dr. Teague, but I can see—"

Heather entered the room at that moment and said warmly, "Colin, I'm glad you're back."

"Good to see you again, Heather, but Adam looks worse."

"He *is* worse. It's frightening how he's going downhill." She turned and said, "Twyla, I told you you can go to bed. I can take care of Adam."

At once Colin said, "No, I want her to stay." Heather gave a startled look at Colin, then shrugged, saying stiffly, "It's your house." She cast a hard look at Twyla, then turned and left the room.

"She hates me," Twyla said.

"Oh, surely not."

"Yes, she does."

He didn't argue, but said, "You must stay. I—I need you."

Twyla dropped her head. "You'll never see me as anything but a servant."

"That's not true! I never thought of you like that."

"You're blind to what Heather is."

Colin suddenly had difficulty answering. "She's not as bad as you think."

"You're blind, Colin! I'm leaving!" She left the room, her eyes full of hot tears, and bit her lips to hold back the sobs.

Eden had arrived earlier and greeted Colin joyfully. Now she came in to find him slumped in a chair beside Adam's bed. She said at once, "You shouldn't have let Twyla go. We need her here."

"Heather is upset with Twyla. I don't know why."

"I could tell you, but you wouldn't listen."

"Of course I'll listen! I've always listened to you."

"That young woman is finer than you know. You've never appreciated her the way she deserves."

"I have always admired her. Her work is—"

"I'm not talking about her *work*, Colin. I'm talking about Twyla as a woman." She saw that Colin was confused. "I'm going to beg her to come back, Colin, but really you should do it."

"You're right, Mother. I'll go myself."

"Very good, but go now!"

Colin was shocked at his mother's insistence. "All right, but first let me tell you what I think about Adam."

"He's worse. I can see that."

"All the way back on the ship, even before that, I was praying for God to show us what is wrong with him. We simply don't know. He had wounds, but they seem to be healing.

Unless we find out what the problem is, we can't do anything for him. Will you pray with me, Mother, that God will give us the answer?"

"Of course I will!"

The two prayed. Colin's eyes clouded with concern as he left his mother watching over Adam.

"Twyla, I want you to come back. I need you desperately."

Twyla had been surprised when Colin had come to her house. He had asked her right away to return, and there was such an insistence in him, something so profound in his request, that she couldn't find it in her heart to say no. "Heather won't like it," she warned.

"Everyone else will. Mother and I have been praying that we will find a diagnosis. We have to find out what's wrong with Adam or he'll die."

"I'll pray with you, Colin."

"Good! God won't let us down."

The room was dark when Colin awoke, and he realized that it was the middle of the night. He had been awakened as abruptly as if someone had shaken him. Now he sat bolt upright and swung his feet off the bed. The floor was freezing, but he paid no attention. He put on his heavy socks, dressed quickly, then went down the hallway to the room where Adam lay. Twyla was there, and she stood at once. "What are you doing up this time of night, Colin?"

There was a hint of wonder in Colin's voice, though his words sounded unsteady: "I—I think God has answered a prayer."

"What prayer, Colin?"

"The prayer that we'd find out what's wrong with Adam."

"You mean God spoke to you?"

"Not with a physical voice. I was half asleep, going over and over again all of Adam's symptoms. We checked every one of them—except one."

Twyla had excitement in her voice as she asked, "Which one was that?"

"I must look at the wound in his head." Colin moved over to where Adam lay on the bed. He leaned over and parted Adam's thick hair, then exclaimed, "Here!" There was excitement in his voice. "Look at this, Twyla!" He waited until she leaned over, then said, "You see? There's an indentation in here. Very slight, but it's there. Here, feel it."

Twyla reached out and ran her hand over Adam's skull. "It does sink in, doesn't it? What does that mean?"

"It means that it's something I should've thought of before. He had several severe wounds in his side and chest, and we were looking at them, making sure they didn't get infected. When Teague and I examined him, the other wounds were so severe, we missed it."

"I still don't understand. What does it mean?"

"I think Adam's skull has been broken. If he has bone splinters penetrating the brain, those could be causing his coma. If we can get the splinters out, he could be as good as new."

"Oh, Colin, that would be wonderful!" Twyla exclaimed. "When can you do it?"

"Right away. I'll send for Teague, and the two of us can operate immediately. Adam's failing fast, so it's a fight against time. I'll send for him at once!" He hesitated, then said, "I'll go tell Heather we're going to do surgery on Adam."

He found Heather and said, "We've got to operate on Adam." He explained why it was necessary, and she merely stared at him and said, "I don't think he'll live."

"I'm praying he will." He turned and left, not seeing the coldness of her face.

"This is a job for steadier hands than mine," Teague said. "I've done this surgery twice, and both times the patient died."

"This one won't," Colin said at once. They were standing over the still form of Adam, and the morning sunlight was streaming in, offering plenty of illumination. Twyla was standing back, her eyes wide with wonder.

"His color is worse, and his breathing is shallower than it's ever been," Teague said.

"It'll be better once we remove the pressure. Here, I have several plates." He held up several shiny disks. Teague studied them and Colin said, "I had the blacksmith hammer out silver coins."

"He did a good job of it."

"What are they for?" Twyla asked.

Colin turned and said, "We have to cut into the skin to expose the skull, then remove the splinters. Afterward we have to protect the brain where the injury occurred, so we will put one of these over the skull and sew up the scalp over it. It'll be a weak spot. He mustn't ever take a blow there. But I'm confident it will work."

Once more Colin and Teague went over their preparations for surgery. They had fastened Adam firmly to the table, especially his head.

"Why do you have to tie his head down like that?" Twyla asked.

"Because it'll be a very delicate surgery. He mustn't move at all. In a way he is fortunate that he's in a coma," Teague said. "He won't feel anything."

"Let's do it quickly," Colin said. He moved to the head of the table. With a scalpel, he cut the scalp and laid it down flat. "Look, Teague, it's as we thought. See, the skull was shattered, and there are tiny pieces of it pressing into the brain. We have to get it all out."

"You'd better hurry," Teague said.

With tweezers Colin began pulling tiny fragments of bone out, dropping them onto the dish that Twyla had placed on the table. The tension in the room was almost physical as Colin worked as quickly and carefully as he could. Teague stood by to blot away the blood. Twyla watched silently. Finally she heard Colin say, "I think that's all of them. Do you see any more, Teague?"

"It looks clean."

"I'll put in the plate. Then will you do the sutures?"

"No, you finish up, Colin. You're doing a wonderful job."

Colin took a curved needle threaded with gut and began to sew the flap. He moved painstakingly, taking tiny stitches. When he tied the last knot he looked up. "There, it's done." Twyla moved closer to where she could see his face, but she didn't say a word.

"That's the finest surgery I've ever seen!" Teague exclaimed. "Look, I think his color is better already."

"We have to watch him closely," Colin said, "but I think he'll be fine."

"I'll stay," Twyla said at once.

"All right, but I'll stay with you. We must keep on praying. Adam's life is in God's hands now."

24

January 15, 1588

"Oh God—help my brother! Save him, O Lord, for there is no other help but you!"

Colin was standing over the still figure of Adam, his face twisted with agony. It had been three days since the surgery, and both he and Teague had expected their patient to regain consciousness quickly. He had not done so; in fact he showed no significant improvement. Colin feared the surgery had done nothing to stop Adam's imminent death.

Leaning over, Colin picked up Adam's hand, holding it in both of his. Anguish filled him, and he hadn't realized how much he loved his brother until this crisis had come. For three days he had fasted and prayed, but God had been silent. At times Colin felt that there was a brass cloud over him, and his prayers couldn't get through that barricade to touch God. Colin had never felt so frustrated or helpless. It was true enough that he'd struggled with diagnoses before, but these days of crisis had been a time of pain beyond anything he'd ever imagined. In addition to Adam's crisis, Colin's heart seemed to break as he remembered how Adara had died and he had been unable to do anything.

His body ached and his mouth was dry, so when he prayed

aloud, his voice was raspy and his words seemed to get caught in his throat. "I—I can't find the words, Lord! I don't know how to speak to you. I know you love my brother, and I know that you've promised to answer prayers, so I ask you, Lord, to heal him! Don't end his life!"

The door opened a few minutes later and Giles, a servant to the doctors, stepped inside. He said, "Dr. Winslow, there is a woman who wants to see you."

Colin shook his head and muttered wearily, "If she needs to see a physician, tell her to go see Dr. Teague."

"Yes, sir, I'll tell her." The servant left, and Colin put her out of his mind. Patients often came to the house instead of the hospital, many of them because they had no money and they needed free treatment. Others came because they had reached the point of no return with a sickness. Colin was usually ready to receive them, but not now. A streak of irritability ran through him as the door opened again. Giles stepped in and shook his head. "She won't go away, Doctor! She says you're the one who's sick and God has sent her here to help you."

Colin snapped angrily, "She needs to be in Bedlam! Throw her out if you have to, Giles."

"Aye, sir, I'll do that." The door closed and Colin tried again to pray. He'd used up all the words he knew, and all he could do was cling to Adam's hand with his spirit in anguish. Then he heard angry voices in the hall, and suddenly the door burst open. Colin was astonished to see Meg Caradoc with a gleaming knife in her hand, the tip of it pointed at Giles, whose face was pale. "I couldn't stop her, sir! She threatened to cut my gizzard out!"

"Get out of here, you oaf!" Meg spat out. She made a sweeping motion with the knife, and Giles backed up at once.

"Let her come in, Giles. It's all right," Colin said. He waited until Giles had fled, shutting the door behind him. Releasing Adam's hand, he turned to face the woman. Meg shook her head, saying with disgust, "He isn't much of a servant, is he? Can't keep an old woman from bothering you!" She put the knife away in her voluminous clothing and came over to look at Adam. She was silent for a moment, then said, "He's dying, isn't he?"

"He's very ill, Meg. I'd do anything to save him, but nothing seems to work."

Meg was looking down into Adam's face. She was silent for a moment, then turned and fixed her dark eyes on Colin. It seemed to him that she was searching his very heart. She finally said, "It's your fault he's dying, Colin Winslow."

Colin looked stricken. "You don't know what you're talking about! I've done everything—used all the medicines, performed surgery—but nothing seems to work!"

"It's your fault! God has told me so."

"That's impossible!" Colin said angrily. "I've been praying to God day and night. But I've not heard a word from him."

"Not a word will you hear from him, Colin, until you fix the sickness in yourself."

Colin shook his head. He was so tired that none of Meg's words made sense. "I don't know what you're talking about, Meg. I know who I am."

"God spoke to me about you. It came in the form of a dream. You remember in the old Bible when Joshua was leading the people of Israel into the Promised Land? They fought a battle against the army of Ai, and they were overwhelmed with a terrible defeat. Their men were slaughtered, and they fled from their enemies."

"Of course I remember that. What about it?"

"I seemed to see all of that in my dream. I saw Joshua after the defeat as the Bible said. He tore his clothes, put ashes on his head, and cried out to God. That's the same thing you've been doing, isn't it, Colin? Well, God didn't answer Joshua; at least he didn't solve Joshua's problems."

"I don't know what you mean."

"Do you remember what happened in that story?"

"Of course I do. God told Joshua that there was sin in the camp. He warned him that Israel would be defeated until that sin was cleaned out."

"Did they find the sin?"

"Certainly! Joshua went before the people and found out that a man called Achan had sinned against God."

"That's right. I wonder, boy, if you remember what God said to Joshua before he did something about the problem."

"I don't remember."

"He said, 'Wherefore liest thou upon thy face?' In other words he said, 'Get up! It's time to stop praying and do something!' And he did, as you remember. Achan was found guilty and executed. After that, the problem was solved and Israel won the victory."

"That's just a story in the Bible, Meg."

"No, it's more than that! God spoke to me and said, 'Unless Colin Winslow confesses and repents of his sin, his brother will die.'"

"You heard the voice of God?"

"No, not a literal voice, but it was like a whispering deep in my heart. Now, do you believe this is from God?"

"I don't know, Meg."

"You'd better believe it! You need to find out what the problem is, and I can tell you it's something buried deep in your heart. If you don't get rid of it, your brother will die, and maybe you too. I've watched you since you were a boy, Colin. You had a good, pure heart when you were young, but something has darkened it. Find out what it is, or face a God who will in no way clear the guilty. I'll pray that you'll rid yourself of this sin." She turned without another word and left, slamming the door behind her.

Colin desperately attempted to put his thoughts together. He looked down at Adam, then at the door through which Meg had left. *She's a good woman, and she does know God. But what have I done, God? What have I done? Don't let my brother die because of my sin! Show me my faults!*

For a long time Colin cried out to God. Still there was nothing in his heart but a dead weight. He prayed in every way he could think of, and he confessed every sin he could think of. Finally, he slumped down in a chair beside Adam with his eyes closed. He fell into a fitful sleep.

"Colin! Wake up!"

Colin's eyes opened slowly, and he sat up in the chair. His neck was stiff, so he rubbed it. He looked up at Heather, who was standing over him, and got to his feet painfully.

"He's no better, is he?" she asked.

"No, he's not."

Heather was wearing a silk dressing gown that revealed the contours of her figure. She came closer to him; there was something strange in her eyes. As groggy as Colin was, he could see that she was deeply stirred. "What is it, Heather? What's the matter?"

"Have you ever thought, Colin, how hard it would be for me and for you if Adam lives? He'll probably be a helpless invalid, and I'll be his wife. We could never have each other."

"You mustn't talk like that."

"I have no faith. Before you operated you said he would be cured."

"I thought he would be, but he's not." He thought for a moment of telling her of Meg's message but knew that it wouldn't be received well. "I've got to sleep a little. Could you sit beside him, Heather?"

"I can't! I can't stand to look at him! I can't live with an invalid, Colin. You know I can't!"

Colin's eyes opened and anger touched his spirit. "He's your husband! You promised to love him for better or for worse! Well, this is the worst!"

Heather suddenly put her arms around Colin's neck. She pressed herself against him and whispered, "I've never loved Adam, Colin. I've always loved you."

"That is not fit talk!"

"It's honest talk. We've always loved each other. You love me too. I know it."

Colin reached up to remove her hands, but she clung to him. The words that came from her lips shocked him. "Let him die, Colin . . . !"

"Why, you don't mean that, Heather!"

"Yes, I do, because it's the only way. If he lives he'll be a cripple, but if he dies you'll have the title. We can marry. We'll have each other as we once did."

At that moment Colin had an epiphany. *This is the sin that's been in my heart—it's my unholy lust for my brother's wife!*

Colin couldn't move for a moment, for he was sickened by shame and he knew that God had touched him with a truth that he'd refused to face. He thought back to the affair he'd had with Heather and cried out aloud, "God, forgive me for this terrible sin!"

Heather clung to him, insisting, "Let him die, Colin! He's going to die anyway. You know ways to do things like that. We've got to have each other."

Suddenly a strange sense of anger mixed with grief became a strong force within Colin. He reached out and shoved Heather away, filled with disgust. He said slowly and distinctly, "I would never do such a thing, Heather. I love my brother! I could never sin against him and against God in this way."

"You love me! You've always loved me! This is our one chance for happiness, Colin."

"There's no happiness in the sin you're asking me to commit, Heather. Yes, I had impure desires for you, an awful lust from the time we met. Even after you married Adam, I couldn't put you out of my mind. But I know now that if I don't judge myself for this terrible sin, God will judge me for it."

"Don't be a fool! We can have it all if Adam dies!"

Her words seemed to hang in the air, and the silence of the room was almost palpable. Suddenly, a third voice spoke. It was a weak voice and unsteady—and came from the lips of Adam Winslow! "Sorry to—disappoint you, my dear wife—but I'm going to live."

Colin straightened up and whirled around to see Adam's eyes opened. "Adam! You're conscious!"

"Yes, just in time it seems." Adam turned his head to look at Heather. Something in that brief look seemed to strike her with the force of a bullet. Her eyes flew open, and she began to whimper, "I didn't mean it, Adam! I didn't know what I was saying!"

"Heather, we both know you meant every word of it." Adam's voice seemed to grow stronger. "You won't be my wife, but then it seems you never were. I'll see that you're provided for, but I never want to see your face again."

Heather began to cry, but she took one look at Adam's face, then whirled around and ran out of the room.

Colin bent over and took one of Adam's hands in his again. His brother had a strange look on his face, and tears came to Colin's eyes. "Well, you've heard my confession. I've confessed it to God, and I've confessed it to you."

Adam still had the strange look on his face. There was some strength in his hand, so he squeezed Colin's. "Brother, I've always thought that I was the strong one and that you were the weak member of the Winslow family, but I was wrong. You're the one who should have the title."

"No, Adam, I never wanted it."

"It's a miracle that you refused to listen to the hellish proposal of that woman who was my wife." His grip on Colin's hand tightened and he smiled at him. "You could never harm me, could you, Colin?"

"No, I've always loved you, Adam."

A sadness seemed to fall over Adam's face. "I thought I knew what love was, but I was a fool." He squeezed Colin's hand, and a smile turned the corners of his lips up slightly. "But I'm willing to learn if you'll help me, brother!"

There had been no joy in Twyla's life since the surgery. She had not heard from Colin. All she could think about was the love she had for him and how it was not returned. She had loved him for so long that she couldn't tell at what point it changed from the affection of a child to the passionate love of a woman. She only knew it was there, and as she sat in the semidarkness of the room, she was unaware of anything except the grief in her heart. She had lost track of time, and nothing seemed to be right in the world.

A knock at the door startled her, and getting up wearily, she went to answer it. She opened the door. "Colin, what are you doing here?"

"I need to talk to you, Twyla."

Twyla didn't really want to speak to him, for he had never had words for her that pleased her as a woman. She started to turn away from him, but she saw something in his face and asked, "What is it?"

"Can I come in?"

"Yes." He entered, and Twyla turned up the lamp. "What is it? Is Adam worse?"

"No." Colin came and took her forearms, holding them tightly. "He's awake! God is healing him."

"Oh, that's wonderful! It's a miracle!"

"Yes, it is, but I have to tell you all of it, Twyla."

Colin told her the whole story of Meg's visit and the dream she'd had. Then he told her how Heather had come and made a terrible proposal. "I've been the world's biggest fool, Twyla. I've let that woman dominate my life." Tears came to Colin's eyes, and he continued, "It was all true, that dream of Meg's. I've had sin in my heart, and I didn't even recognize it. Maybe I just didn't want to, but I recognize it now and I've asked God to forgive me. Of course he has. I've asked Adam for forgiveness, too, and we're closer than we ever were. He's going to live and be a well man."

Twyla said, "I've seen this in you for a long time, Colin. I've been sick with fear that you would give in to your love for Heather."

"No, Twyla, I never had love for her. It was a worldly lust, and only the grace of God and your prayers kept me from disaster." He suddenly moved his hands from her forearms and wrapped them around her waist and whispered, "I've got you to keep me now. You're my good angel, Twyla."

Twyla waited, for she had so longed to hear him say words of love—words that a man would say to the woman he loves. But all he said was, "I've got to go back and tell my parents. I need to see to Adam, too. God bless you, sweetheart! It was a good day for me when I found you!" He turned and left, and tears began to flow down Twyla's cheeks.

He didn't say a word about—about love or marriage. He doesn't care for me! I'm just a waif he took in, a servant. That's all I'll ever be to him!

25

July 28, 1588

Twyla had been listless and dull for the past few months—actually, ever since Adam had recovered. She had hoped when Colin told her he had overcome the illicit passion he felt for Heather by the will of God that he would declare his love for her, but he had not said a word like that. Everyone had noticed that Twyla smiled only very infrequently and that she went about her work in a listless fashion.

Colin hasn't said a word to me, not what I want to hear, anyway. Now as she sat sewing a dress, she suddenly realized that she had no need for pretty dresses. She threw it to one side and rose from her chair. She would have left the room, but through the window she saw Colin ride up, dismount, and head for the front door. She didn't want to see him, for he brought her only pain and grief. He came in quickly, however, and caught her as she was heading down the long hallway that led to the stairs. "Twyla, I need to talk to you."

"What is it?" Her voice was short.

"Is there something wrong?" Colin asked.

"No, of course not."

"The Spanish fleet is on the way. Walsingham's agents tell us they'll be here very soon."

"We knew that was going to happen."

"I've been thinking about something, Twyla. I wasn't going to say anything, but now I must. It's about something I must do. I know you won't like it, but I feel it's proper."

"Just tell me what it is, Colin."

Adam had divorced Heather and had gained rapidly in health, so he was able to report to Drake that he was capable of serving on the fleet as the English were preparing to meet the Invincible Armada. Adam was back at his ship, ready to fight.

"I've decided to serve on Adam's ship as a physician. Men will be wounded, and they'll need someone to care for them."

"Colin, you're not a fighting man!"

"No, but I can take care of those who do fight. Suppose I had a son one day, and he asked me what I did to keep England free when the Spanish came. All I could say to him is, 'I stayed home while other men fought for England.'"

"Many men can fire a gun, but none can save lives like you do. You mustn't do it, Colin!"

"I knew you'd take it badly." Colin dropped his head for a moment, then lifted it and reached out to take her hands. "I know you're worried, but just think of this: there are women all over England who are sending their men off to fight. I know it's hard, but that's the way war is. I don't want you to be so concerned."

"How can you say that? You think concern is something you can turn on and off? Don't you know how much—" Twyla almost finished the sentence with *I love you*, but said, "—how much I owe to you? You've made my life what it is. I don't know what would happen to me if you got hurt in battle. I don't even want to think about it."

"Let's go into the sitting room. We will talk about this."

The two moved into the sitting room and sat down on an oversized sofa. Twyla listened with a sense of dread as Colin tried to explain his actions. She knew he was a man of honor, but to her it made no sense that with his talent he should risk everything.

"I don't want to listen to you anymore."

She got up to leave the room, but Colin caught her hand and said, "Twyla, please don't act this way! I knew it would hurt you, but this is something I have to do." Suddenly Twyla felt his arms go around her, and he pulled her close. She looked up, startled. She knew that this man she had grown to love had little idea of how much she cared for him. As a last desperate measure, she reached up and put her hands around his neck, pulled his head down, and kissed him. Colin was shocked, and Twyla felt a sudden tremor in his body. She held to him, and his lips were firm on hers. At first they were just passive, but then they grew demanding. Twyla held him close. Finally when he lifted his head, she whispered, "Don't you see how I feel, Colin? Please don't go!"

Colin looked shocked. He didn't speak for a moment but finally said, "I'd like to say things to you, Twyla, but I don't know what lies ahead of me. I can't make any promises, because I may not live. This is going to be a difficult battle, but I'll try to come back to you."

"Please don't go, Colin!"

He shook his head and freed himself from her embrace. For a moment he held her hands, then lifted them to his heart. "Pray for me," he said. "When I come back, we'll have time to talk." He turned and left quickly.

Twyla just stood there helpless. Her only enemy now was a war that threatened to destroy the finest and best of England's young men with a terrible blow!

Sir Francis Drake was always a man for sport, so when the word was out that the Spanish would soon be in sight, he was playing a game of bowls on Plymouth Hole. A messenger named Flemming came running up so out of breath he could barely speak.

He did manage to gasp, "Sir, the Armada has been sighted at the Scilly Isles!"

Drake turned and winked at Adam, then grinned and said in his West Country drawl, "Well, we'll have time enough to finish the game and beat the Spaniards too."

They did finish the game; then Drake seemed to be electrified with energy. "Come, my brave fellows, it's time to singe the beard of the king of Spain! Better yet, to roast him hoof, hide, and toenails!"

The sailors followed Drake down to the harbor. When they arrived, Drake suddenly turned and spoke to Adam. "I don't feel right about this, Winslow. You were badly wounded, and you're not fully healed even now."

"I'm completely able, Sir Francis. I can't be left behind."

Drake studied Adam for a long moment, then turned to face Colin. "What about you, Dr. Winslow? This will be a little bit different from administering a pill in a quiet hospital or sickroom."

"I hope I can be of service, Sir Francis."

"I wish every ship could have a qualified doctor on it. Some poor fellows die for lack of good medical care. You understand that a Spanish musket ball has no brains? It won't stop because you hold the title of physician."

"I want to do my duty, Sir Francis. That's why I've come."

"Stout fellow! Well, let's get to it!"

Despite all the efforts of her council, Queen Elizabeth was determined not to stay at home while her country was under attack. Elizabeth may have been easy to upset, but she was impossible to frighten! She led a marshal procession of barges down the river and landed at Tilbury Fort. It was here the Duke of Parma would land—unless the Seahawks were able to hold him and his army away.

Elizabeth was met by her general, the Earl of Leicester, and on the morning of August 14 she rode on a beautiful horse to address her troops. There was a review, and all the captains of her army came to stand before her. The soldiers were lined up crowding around her, and Elizabeth's voice was strong as she spoke.

My loving people, you've been persuaded by some that are careful for our safety to take heed how we commit ourselves to armed multitudes, for fear of treachery. But I assure you, I do not desire to live to distrust my faithful and loving people. Let tyrants fear! I have always so behaved myself that, under God, I have placed my chiefest strength and safeguard in a loyal heart and the goodwill of my subjects; therefore I am come amongst you as you see, at this time, not for my recreation and disport, but being resolved, in the midst of the battle, to live or die amongst you all and to lay down for my God and for my kingdom and for my people my honor and my blood, even in the dust. I know I have the body of a weak and feeble woman, but I have the heart and stomach of a king and of a king of England, too, and think foul scorn that Parma or any prince of Europe should dare invade the borders of my realm; to which rather than any dishonor shall grow by me, I myself will take up arms, I myself will be your general, judge, and rewarder of every one of your virtues in the field. I know already for your forwardness you deserve rewards and crowns, and we do assure you, the word of a prince, they shall be duly paid you.

The troops broke into wild cheering—Elizabeth of England knew that this was her finest hour!

All of the Seahawks opposed hand-to-hand fighting in sea battles. They advocated battering the enemy from a distance with new long-range guns. The fact was that only thirty-four of the queen's ships could be put to sea to meet the enormous Armada of Spain. The British, by superior skill, gained the weather gauge, which meant that they would have the choice of when and where to attack. Drake, followed by Admiral Howard, swept into the main body of the enemy. Howard reported, "The Spaniards are forced to give way and flock together like sheep." Indeed, the waters in the Channel were difficult for the Spaniards. The guns of the English ships raked the decks of the galleons, killing crews and demoralizing soldiers, with much less damage done to the English.

Throughout the battle, Colin felt himself to be more of a hindrance than a help. The ship commanded by his brother had stayed at long range, so that no cannon or musket fire could reach them. With their long-range guns they had decimated the Spanish ships. As far as Colin could see, the battle had been won. All the English had to do was stand off at long distance and blow the Spanish out of the water.

Suddenly, he saw a messenger coming in a small craft. He watched as the message was passed to Adam. He advanced at once, asking, "What's happening, Adam?"

"Our ships are almost out of ammunition, blast it! If we had enough balls and powder we could finish them off, but there's not enough."

"What can be done then? Will they be allowed to escape?"

"No, leave it to Drake to think of something! We're going to attack with fire ships."

"What is that?" Colin had to yell over the gunfire.

"We take ships and load them with flammable materials. We use old ships usually. Put skeleton crews aboard them, and aim them toward where the Spanish ships are gathered. Just before they strike, the crews set the ships afire. The crews escape on small boats, and the fire ships go in the midst of the Spanish ships."

"Do you think it will work?"

"The worst danger to a fleet of wooden sailing ships is fire. Everything can go up—their sails, their sun-dried decks and spars. There is only one problem, Colin. We've been assigned to take charge of one of the fire ships. That means we'll be forced to get in close, so there'll be some cannonballs coming our way. I want you to go down below at once."

"No, I'll stay here. If there is danger to the men I want to be able to help them."

"We can bring them below. Now, get off the deck!"

Colin had never disobeyed his brother's word, but now he did so. "I won't do it, Adam! If you put me down there you'll have to tie me, because I'm staying where I can help!"

Suddenly Adam laughed, and the light of battle was in his eyes. He reached down and hugged Colin. "All right, Brother, try to dodge all the musket balls you can."

"You do the same, Captain!"

Adam left then to bring the ship closer to the action. They found the fire ship they were in charge of, and Colin saw Adam consign a small crew to raise sails and guide the ship into the Spanish. Ten minutes later he well understood what Adam had feared of. They were close now to the Spanish ships that were packed tightly together. Colin looked up and saw a small army of musket men along the rails of the galleons aiming at them. The natural tendency of a man caught in a target like this was to duck or to run away, but Colin did neither. Men would be hit, and he stood ready to help them.

Then the fire ship seemed to ignite, and the crew steered it directly toward the center of the massed line of Spanish ships.

Colin turned and stared at a line of muskets only a hundred feet away, and they all seemed to be pointed at him! At that moment he knew that when the volley came, he would be killed. Colin had always heard that if a man was caught in a situation like this, his whole life would flash before him. This didn't happen to Colin Winslow. Thoughts of Twyla were swirling in his mind when suddenly one of the officers, a thickset lieutenant, came running up. He stood in front of Colin, waving his sword and cursing the Spanish. Just as he did so the volley sounded. The lieutenant was driven back, hit by dozens of bullets it seemed. He crashed into Colin, who fell to the deck under his weight. Colin pushed the soldier off and saw that he had, indeed, been struck by many musket balls. *If he hadn't been in front of me, I would be dead!* Others were down, but Adam had turned the ship away. Colin watched as the fire ships struck all up and down the line until the Spanish ships were blazing.

"A beautiful sight, isn't it, Colin?" Colin turned to see Adam's face lit up with a smile. "Are you all right?"

Colin looked over at the burning Spanish ships and smiled too. "Yes, Adam, for the first time in my life I think I am."

The rest of the battle was determined by a fierce windstorm that scattered the Spanish fleet, destroying many of their galleons. Queen Elizabeth smiled and said, "This is the wind of God!" And so it came to be a proverb: "The enemy came, but God blew on them. The Wind of God saved England!"

Twyla was walking the floor, though it was dark now, well past midnight. The news had come that the Spanish had been driven away. The ships that hadn't caught fire had fled down the coast, pursued by the Seahawks. Now as Twyla tried to block out the terrible thoughts that came, she knew there was nothing she could do but pray. Praying was all she seemed to do lately.

She heard the clock strike three. The house was dark, for she had snuffed all the candles except one in the sitting room. She sat down; her hands trembled as she covered her face. How long she sat there she didn't know, but she continued to pray fervently. She finally heard a faint sound.

Someone's trying to break in! The sound wasn't at a door, but at a window. She rose and went at once to the side room and saw a dark form struggling to open the shutters from the outside. Twyla had been warned that there would be looters, and she looked around frantically for a weapon. She had no pistol, so she picked up a huge thunder mug used for toilet purposes. She stood holding it over her head, and as the shutters opened, a dark form climbed inside. Instantly, Twyla brought the thunder mug down on the intruder's head, and the man cried out and fell to the floor. The shock of the blow drove the mug from Twyla's hands. She suddenly felt hands grabbing her, dragging her down, and terror came to her then, for she knew what a woman could expect from a man who would break into a house!

"Twyla, is that you?"

"Colin!"

"Yes, it's me! Please don't hit me again, sweetheart."

Sitting on the floor, Colin drew her to him. She felt the strength of his body with his arms around her. "I'm back," he whispered, holding her tightly.

Twyla put her arms around his neck. "I was so afraid, Colin!"

"What in the world did you hit me with?"

"A thunder mug."

Colin laughed and held her tightly. "Not a very dignified weapon! Why did you hit me with that?"

"I thought you were a robber. Why didn't you come in by the door?"

"I lost my key! Twyla, I've got something to tell you." A smile was forming across his lips.

"What is it?"

"I was on the deck of Adam's ship, and I was looking across at the line of the Spanish ships. The decks were lined with musket men. They held up their muskets, and I was looking down the barrel of a dozen guns. They were getting ready to fire, and I knew I was about to die."

He got to his feet then and pulled her up with him. He held onto her tightly. "You know what I thought of when my time on earth was ending?"

"What, Colin?"

"I thought of you, Twyla. I've been such a fool! You've been right under my eyes all this time, and I've never seen you as you are. Like a stupid man who has a diamond and treats it like coal or a muddy stone!"

"How did you live in all that fire?"

"A lieutenant happened to stand in front of me. He died right there, poor fellow!"

Twyla felt his hands moving over her hair.

He pulled her closer and said, "I love you, Twyla! I know now I love you more than any man ever loved a woman!"

"Truly, Colin?"

"The day I die is the day I'll stop loving you, my love!"

As Twyla heard these words, she knew that life for her was just beginning. She surrendered to his embrace and, clinging to him tightly, whispered, "Never let me go, Colin!"

EPILOGUE

January 1600

A dam Winslow entered the room holding the hand of Colin's ten-year-old son, Edward. Beside Adam was his wife, Abigail, an attractive woman in her mid-thirties.

"We have come to see the new arrival, Colin. Is he presentable?"

Colin smiled as he greeted Abigail and Adam. "I appreciate your taking care of our boy. Come and see the new baby."

Colin led them into a room where Twyla was in bed cuddling a baby. It was January, and the weather was cold, but a warm fire blossomed in the fireplace. Twyla smiled and said, "Come, Brother and Abigail—and you, too, Edward. See what God has blessed us with."

"Let me see that fine fellow!" Adam moved forward, and Edward crowded close to see the baby. Adam then took the bundle in his arms and smiled down at the red face. "He's as fine a boy as I've ever seen! And look at that hair! It's going to be chestnut-colored, like yours, Colin."

"He's a fine boy," Abigail said. "I pray that Adam and I have one just as fine."

Colin was pleased. He and Twyla had been thrilled when their first son was born, and now they had another boy. "What will you call him, Colin?"

"Gilbert."

"Gilbert Winslow. A fine name for a fine boy! You know I'm no prophet, but I have a feeling that this one will be the best of all the House of Winslow."

Colin moved closer to Adam and Gilbert and put his hand on the baby's dark hair. He reached over and picked up Edward. "Be kind to your brother, Son," he smiled.

"I will, Father."

Colin took the baby in his arms and looked down. "Gilbert Winslow. I like the sound of that. My son, may God make you a noble member of the House of Winslow!"

AS
the
SPARKS FLY
UPWARD

$\mathscr{GILBERT\ MORRIS}$

Reading Group Guide

ABOUT THIS GUIDE

The following reading group guide is intended to help you find interesting and rewarding approaches to your reading of *As the Sparks Fly Upward*. We hope this enhances your enjoyment and appreciation of the book.

1. In this novel, much of the material deals with marriage. In the first chapter, we see Eden and Brandon alone, and much is made of the happiness of their marriage. Do you think their fine relationship is possible, that is, is it realistic? Is too much space in the novel devoted to this theme?

2. In the first chapter we see Adam Winslow, age eight, taking advantage of his brother, Colin, age six. Does the scene foreshadow the characters of the two men well? Is, for instance, Adam painted as evil and Colin as good?

3. Queen Elizabeth has been the heroine of a plethora of novels. Is the queen (as we see her in this novel) (a) kind, (b) cruel, (c) heartless, (d) selfish? How closely does the character in this novel reflect the historical Queen Elizabeth?

4. Colin Winslow is not normal in the eyes of his parents. He does not fit into the usual pattern that most young men follow. This disturbs his parents greatly. What is to be done with a child who cannot seem to "fit in" with his world? Should parents force him into the pattern of others? What is the danger of doing this—and what is the danger of ignoring such a problem?

5. Even minor characters should bear part of the weight of the plot and theme of a novel. What is the significance of Meg Caradoc in this novel? Does she in any way give direction to Colin's life?

6. How does Sir Francis Walsingham influence Colin's life? Does he help him to a better way—or a worse way?

7. Colin's experience at Oxford does not make him happy. He is a gullible young man, and some students play a cruel trick on him. Is this sort of behavior prevalent among young people even today? Would it be better to shield a son or daughter by keeping him or her in a more protected environment?

8. Phineas Teague becomes a powerful influence on young Colin. What happens when a young person is not fortunate enough to have someone to guide him or her? What happens if he or she falls into the wrong hands?

9. Colin aids Teague in breaking the law when they steal a body. Does this show weakness in Colin's character? He loves Teague, but should he have refused to take part in the incident?

10. Colin is forced to fight the establishment in order to fulfill his dream of being a physician. Is he right to challenge the College of Physicians? How is one to decide when it's the right thing to go against the powers of society?

11. Colin is seduced by an older woman. How can this happen to a young man of high moral standards? What can he do when this mars his life?

12. What prompts Colin to take in Twyla Hayden, a poor, homeless girl? Is he wise—and is it wise for us to do something of this nature?

13. How large a part should coincidence play in a novel? Is it too unrealistic that Twyla should prove to have exactly the gift that Colin needs in order to do his work? Some would argue that this is not realistic, but have you ever encountered a seemingly accidental circumstance that you attributed to God?

14. Is it believable that Adam would stand in for Colin in a duel? How does this make you feel about Adam?

15. When Colin becomes, in effect, a spy for Sir Francis Walsingham, does this give him problems? Is it ever right to do a wrong thing in order to bring about a good end?

16. How would you sum up Colin's experience with God? Are there other admirable believers in this novel?

17. Queen Elizabeth said that England's victory over the Spanish Armada was the work of God. Does God take sides in wars? Can you give some examples?

LOOK FOR THE WINSLOW BREED SERIES BY

GILBERT MORRIS

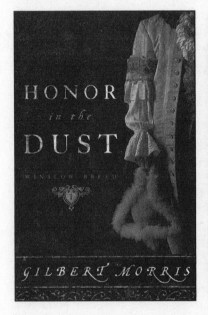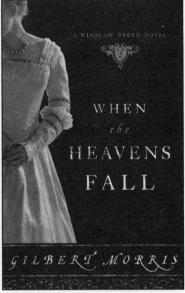

Available wherever books are sold or at www.simonandschuster.com